Earth had been h...
the body

"That is not good," Garin said as he sidled up beside Annja and looked over the scene. "You think it's the dig supervisor you wanted to talk to?"

"Someone looking for me?"

They turned in unison—Garin with pistol extended and ready to fire—to find Jonathon Crockett holding an AK-47.

"I believe my Kalashnikov trumps your Glock," Crockett said.

Annja felt Garin's elbow twitch against her arm. He was the last man Crockett—any man—should issue a challenge like that to.

"You think so?" Garin held the pistol barrel skyward with his finger off the trigger to show he meant to surrender. Annja knew that wasn't going to happen.

Reaching into the otherwhere for her sword, she clasped the grip and swept the blade across Crockett's wrist, taking him by surprise. The machine gun dropped to the dusty ground. In an agile move, Garin bent to claim it, as Annja released the sword back to where it had come from.

"Nice," Garin said. He hooked the Kalashnikov under his arm and held both guns on the whimpering professor. "She's my backup."

Titles in this series:

ROGUE ANGEL

Alex Archer

THE MATADOR'S CROWN

A GOLD EAGLE BOOK FROM

WORLDWIDE®

TORONTO • NEW YORK • LONDON
AMSTERDAM • PARIS • SYDNEY • HAMBURG
STOCKHOLM • ATHENS • TOKYO • MILAN
MADRID • WARSAW • BUDAPEST • AUCKLAND

Recycling programs
for this product may
not exist in your area.

First edition September 2012

ISBN-13: 978-0-373-62158-3

THE MATADOR'S CROWN

Special thanks and acknowledgment to
Michele Hauf for her contribution to this work.

The
LEGEND

...THE ENGLISH COMMANDER TOOK
JOAN'S SWORD AND RAISED IT HIGH.

The broadsword, plain and unadorned,
gleamed in the firelight. He put the tip against
the ground and his foot at the center of the blade.
The broadsword shattered, fragments falling
into the mud. The crowd surged forward,
peasant and soldier, and snatched the shards
from the trampled mud. The commander tossed
the hilt deep into the crowd.
Smoke almost obscured Joan, but she continued
praying till the end, until finally the flames climbed
her body and she sagged against the restraints.

Joan of Arc died that fateful day in France,
but her legend and sword are reborn....

PROLOGUE

The woman walking thirty strides ahead of him moved like a flamenco dancer. Powerful, forceful, yet graceful. She reminded him of Ava, the dancer in the club where he played guitar.

Ava barely acknowledged his existence and frequently complained he did not keep proper *compas,* marking the beat, which spoiled her dance and made her look bad in front of the audience. As a guitarist, he was attuned to the dancer and singer, but his concentration tended to waver around Ava.

He'd thought her just another dancer when he'd taken the job at the Gato Negra club. But there was a shadow inside Ava and he felt its presence every time she took the stage. Darkness emerged in her footwork, in the aggressive expressions that contorted her face and the fierce control with which she captured the audience nightly.

So he did not hurry his pace to catch up with this other woman. Best to admire from afar.

With the guitar he'd made from German spruce and

Spanish cypress strapped across his back, Diego Montera carried the cumbersome wooden crate at stomach level. He had to deliver it at midnight. In a cotton bag tied to his belt loop, he had a change of clothing and enough euros to cover a meal. He also carried the small bronze artifact he had to deliver the following morning. He had seen that much—that it was bronze—as his employer had wrapped it and handed it to him. What was in the crate, he didn't know. It wasn't much heavier than his guitar.

His employer had rented him a room in the Hotel Blanca tonight for the first delivery. It was not as if he could complete the transaction on the street, in the open. Or at his home where Diego's mother would question a stranger's visit. The buyer preferred a private meeting, valued his privacy.

Diego was excited about tonight. That his employer had trusted him with two jobs within a day of each other meant he was moving up, earning respect. If both exchanges went well, perhaps he'd earn a position as a regular liaison. A guitarist's wages were nothing to write home about, and he still lived with his mother, who complained when he didn't help clean around the house. A guitarist shouldn't do manual labor such as fixing the plumbing! Diego wanted his own apartment so he could entertain friends and bring home women without the curse of his mother's condemning eye.

Even though he had no information about who would arrive to pick up the wooden crate and its contents tonight, Diego felt confident the meeting would go well. The money would be transferred electronically through a secure service. Then Diego got paid in cash. He knew to go online and verify that his employer had received the transfer before handing over the item. He had one of those fancy cell phones with the internet browser in his jeans pocket. The device, a hand-me-down, had received a pounding from one of Diego's brothers and was on its last legs.

Tomorrow morning's handoff would be at a public place—a city fountain—not far from the Museum of Cádiz. What he did when he was not playing in the club wasn't legal, but it paid too well to pass up. He hadn't learned the name of the outfit he worked for, but it probably didn't have one. Most of the deals, if not all, were made under the table.

His mother would never look him in the eye again if she knew who he was involved with. But if Diego wanted to finally attract the eye of Ava, the beautiful flamenco dancer, he had to have money.

Hours earlier, the sun had set in fiery amber ripples on the horizon over the sea. A sharp slice of moonlight glimmered on the waters close to shore. The streets were busy at all hours in Cádiz. The city offered so much to experience in food, music and festivity. And with the bullfights on the mainland in Jerez, Cádiz celebrated with all-night dancing in the streets.

Diego turned a corner into an empty street. Though he'd been a Cádiz resident all his life, the sudden street-to-street changes from festive to silent startled him. He was tired, but the coffee he'd slammed down before leaving the club after tonight's performance had given him a jolt.

Exiting the momentary solace, he crossed a main street peopled with tourists in jeans, sandals and baseball caps, and entered the Hotel Blanca's whitewashed stucco facade. Diego smiled at the squat matron behind the front desk who wore black edged with touches of white lace. She was someone's grandma, surely, and her jet eyes brightened at the sight of him. Yet as he approached, she blew him a kiss that seemed more flirtatious than motherly.

He was always startled to notice a woman's reaction to his appearance. His mother had called him *ma bonita,* "my pretty," but his three brothers had pounded him regularly because of his looks…and possibly because of their mother's affection for him. And because he had no inclinations toward the bullfight. In a family of toreros dating back three generations, Diego had opted to study music.

His hotel room was on the second floor, overlooking the Atlantic Ocean, several blocks from the avenue Compo del Sur that fronted the beach. Setting the crate on the small, wobbly table near the bed and untying the cotton bag, he let it slide down to his feet and land on the floor. Sitting on the narrow bed, he pulled the guitar around from his back. Quickly, he loosened the E, A and D strings, and drew them out from the wooden tuning pegs so they sprang like whiskers from the bridge. He slipped his hand inside the guitar's sound hole.

The small statue had fallen out of the cloth bag and felt cold against his palm as he carefully eased it, and the duct tape he'd used to secure it, from inside the guitar. He shouldn't have taken it out until morning, but he couldn't play with it inside the instrument, so he set the shiny piece aside next to the wooden crate. Maybe it wasn't bronze. Maybe it was gold. He was no expert on metals.

He considered what he could buy if he kept the statue for himself. A lot. But if he didn't deliver it tomorrow morning, he knew he wouldn't see tomorrow evening.

Now all he had to do was wait for the first meeting—at midnight. An appropriately menacing time to meet a stranger.

Diego passed the hours strumming his guitar.

As MIDNIGHT TOLLED, the door to Diego's hotel room creaked open. Diego abruptly stood as a tall stranger in a long black leather coat stepped in. He wore sunglasses and a dark fedora, the crown of it circled with a red ribbon. The brim was tipped low over his eyes. Cordoba leather shoes caught Diego's eye. Very expensive. His father had once owned a pair.

He flexed his fingers. He couldn't recall leaving the door open, but he hadn't locked it.

"You Diego Montera?" the stranger asked in a low tone.

A dreadful chill froze Diego at the end of the bed, his guitar held ready as if it was a weapon.

"Yes. Are you the liaison for—"

"Yes, the liaison. You have it?"

"Yes. Ah! I need to check a message first." He eyed the corner of the battered cell phone on the floor, which lay half out of the cotton bag. "Verify the transaction before we do this."

The other man tipped his sunglasses down and looked over the rim at Diego. "You've not done this before, have you, Señor Montera?"

Diego rubbed his sweating palms down the sides of his jeans. He didn't like that his employer had given his full name to the client. "What makes you think that?"

The thin man smirked as he approached the crate. "Do what you must. All my accounts are in order. Is it in here?"

"Yes." Diego opened up the cell phone and turned it on. The thing was four years old, taped across the cover and slower than an adagio. He waited for the screen to boot up.

The liaison didn't seem to notice him. He paused to look at the statue of the bull in bronze…or gold… before pushing aside the top of the crate.

"This was nailed down originally. With more rivets?"

"Hmm?" Diego looked down at what he was doing, studying the cell phone in his lap. "Uh, not sure. That's exactly the way it was when I received it."

The cell-phone screen flashed and the icon that indicated it was searching for service blinked.

"So…" The stranger exhaled in a heavy sigh. He tapped a rough wood slat of the crate. "You've touched what's inside?"

"Damn." The battery warning flashed red and the screen flashed to black. Diego scampered to the other side of the bed trying to find an outlet to recharge the device. "Touched it? Oh, well… Yes, the cover came off easily, so I did look at it. I didn't take it out." An outlet. Excellent. He plugged in the phone.

"That's unfortunate."

Diego straightened and immediately had to take a step backward because the man suddenly stood before him. His brain registered the swing of an arm, a fist soaring in an arc to deliver a punch, but the man moved so rapidly, Diego had no time to duck.

Knuckles bruised the side of his jaw, and his head snapped back sharply. A loud crack could have been the man's knuckles or Diego's teeth. His equilibrium faltered, but he managed to stay on his feet.

The liaison emitted a guttural grunt, similar to a workman lifting a bale of hay. His thin, leather-clad body rose before Diego. He propelled himself into the air by stepping onto the bed, knocking the guitar onto the tiled floor.

Not his guitar!

Who was this man?

Searing pain pierced Diego's spine at the base of his

neck. He cried out, but only a gurgling mumble came out of his throat.

He tasted more blood and swallowed it back. He started to choke. He couldn't catch his breath. Blood bubbled up into his throat. His spine felt numb, but his heart pounded rapidly. His neck and face were on fire.

Grasping for the man who had removed his sunglasses and stood calmly before him, Diego dropped to his knees. Grasping at his chest, he closed his eyes. He choked to death on his own blood.

1

Annja Creed dragged herself out of the narrow, lumpy bed mumbling, "Must find a new place to stay."

Her regular morning routine found her rising, showering and fitting in a jog before the first glint of sunshine hit the rooftops. But today? Six o'clock was absolutely torturous after spending the night at a hostel populated with more partying teenagers than she could shake a fist at.

But after nearly two months straight of traveling, she teetered close to an edge no one wanted to see her step over. She powered up her laptop and located a hotel by the sea. She was financing this trip to Andalusia herself, so had initially thought to go cheap. She'd been invited by James Harlow, the head of acquisitions and curations at the Museum of Cádiz, to view their recently acquired collection of Greek coins featuring Hercules's twelve labors, found in Egypt. He must've discovered that she was writing an article on coins depicting mythological heroes. She'd jumped at the opportunity. The collection was pristine, and she'd taken some excellent pictures yesterday. Today, she planned to take notes and make pencil rubbings of both the obverse and reverse of each coin.

Two days previously she'd been in Puerto Real, across the Bay of Cádiz, squatting alongside Professor Jonathan Crockett on a small dig she'd learned about while researching the area for hotels. The bay area was made up of tiny villages dotted with small white houses and was rich with Moorish and Roman remains. So she'd planned a few extra days to dig in the dirt. Frankly, it had been months since she'd participated in a dig. She'd been unable to resist.

The Cádiz website featured a list of recommended hotels, most bordering the Atlantic Ocean. Annja made a reservation, hoping for less of a party atmosphere. A touristy hotel was fine with her.

She swept her chestnut hair into a ponytail, stuffed her few articles of clothing and essential tools into her backpack—laptop, flash drives, camera, trowel and dental pick, latex gloves, passports and SPF 30 sunscreen—and headed out to find the Hotel Blanca.

On the sidewalk outside of the hotel, she splashed through a puddle, evidence of an early-morning rain shower. Her sure strides scattered a clowder of feral cats sprawled around the furry remains of what must have been a rat.

Set by the sea, Cádiz was a cosmopolitan Spanish city. Yet being one of the oldest cities in Europe, it clung to its heritage, steeped as it was in Gypsy culture and the art of flamenco dance and music. Farther inland, the province was covered with national parks and mountains. She'd once backpacked through Moorish villages to study an ancient fortress believed to have been Ferdinand II's stronghold.

Founded by the Phoenicians in or around 1100 BC, Cádiz was interesting to Annja in that no archaeological strata on the site could be dated earlier than the ninth century BC. Historians decided Cádiz, or Gadir as the Spaniards called it, had once been a shipping stop instead of an actual port, which may be reason for the lacking pre-ninth-century archaeological finds.

Nothing of major importance had been found at the dig site until yesterday when she'd turned up a bronze bull statue. Possibly an effigy to Baal, the bull god, she had decided. Baal was associated with thunder and rain, and had been killed annually by Mot, the god of summer heat. Killing Baal stopped the summer rains so Mot could scorch the earth. Baal's sister, Anath, brought him back in the fall, and he renewed plant life and allowed the earth to once again be plowed.

Annja figured Mot had worked his alchemy this week. The thermometer was rising, and out on the dig, the earth had been hard, which made for easy brushing, but challenging trowel work.

She'd taken photos of the bronze statue in situ and then again after digging it out and placing it on the finds table. After being cataloged, it would be sent to a local university. She'd shown James Harlow at the Cádiz museum the photos, and he'd been fascinated.

Annja dodged as a toddler, chasing a red rubber ball, with no mind for obstacles, zoomed toward her. His parents, exasperated tourists, apologized as they ran past her calling out in what she recognized as German.

A beam of sun glinted in her eye, magnified by the silver waves ridging the sea to her left. The water was clear and the sand on the beach bright and clean-looking. After a few hours at the museum, she intended to walk down to the shore. A perfect way to end the trip before her flight back home.

Much as she enjoyed travel, she was looking forward to returning to her apartment in Brooklyn and stealing some writing time. Annja had collected notes from digs in Austria and Turkey and wanted to translate them onto the computer and see if she could wrangle a worthy story in the mix. She loved writing, and had published a few books on archaeology, but found writing time spare because, more than pounding away at the keyboard, she loved actual digs, searching for new discoveries. Generally being outdoors. Adventure ran through her veins.

The Hotel Blanca's white-tiled lobby was filled with potted palm trees, and the overhead latticework created crisscross patterns of sunlight. The elderly receptionist wore a severely tight bun of salt-and-pepper hair and gave Annja a rote welcome to the beautiful city of Cádiz. She looked Annja up and down—taking in the hiking boots sorely in need of new laces, her khaki cargo pants sorely in need of an iron and her T-shirt that featured a fading Women for Women logo—then took her credit-card information and handed her a key.

Annja thanked the receptionist and took the concrete stairs featuring brightly colored paintings along the risers two at a time. Not authentic Spanish design, but the entire city couldn't be authentic, she figured.

She had always been curious about Spanish culture and artifacts—okay, artifacts from *any* culture and time period. She'd spent two summers interning on digs in Granada during her college years and had fallen in love with this country. The Andalusians were proud of their history, which began with the Phoenicians, and over the centuries incorporated influences from the Visigoths to the Islamic empire. They were most famous for Christopher Columbus's journeys and Ferdinand and Isabella's rule. Not to mention their monopoly of the sea trade in the eighteenth century.

Annja found her room, and as she slid the key card through the lock, she noticed the door next to hers at the end of a hallway move inside a few inches, creaking.

With little more than a bend forward, she peered inside and noted the edge of a neatly made bed, and then two booted feet, facing down, hanging off the side.

"Must have partied over at the hostel," she muttered. "Hello?" she called softly and moved to pull the door shut to give the guy some privacy.

But the sight of an acoustic guitar facedown on the floor instead prompted her to push the door open.

A stale, meaty odor assaulted her senses.

Clenching her fists, Annja stepped around the guitar and looked over the man sprawled on the bed. Blood stained the back of his blue shirt and had soaked the shirt through and puddled on the faded yellow bedspread.

Clasping her hands together to keep from inadvertently touching anything, Annja looked back to the door she'd left open.

"What went on here?" she wondered as she again studied the body of what appeared to be a young man. Long, dark hair covered his face. There were no signs of drug paraphernalia, no needles or spoons.

"Drugs usually don't result in bleeding out," she whispered. "He's been attacked."

The largest bloodstain was over the left side of his back, directly over his heart. He could have been shot in the back or stabbed. She'd call the reception desk to alert the police immediately.

Just as she was about to leave to do that, her gaze fell onto the bronze statue on the table next to a wooden crate that spilled out brown paper packing strips. A very familiar bronze statue in the shape of a bull, about the size of her fist. She knew that because she had held the statue not a day earlier.

Annja dodged around the dead man's feet and tugged

a pair of latex gloves out of her backpack. She put them on before picking up the bull statue.

"I just dug this out of the ground yesterday."

It had been coupled with a bent silver platter she and Jonathan Crockett had assumed had been part of thieves' booty. Probably nineteenth century, to judge from the strata layers where it had been found. Yet the actual statue and platter could possibly date to the eleventh century. That was her guess.

She turned it over now, noting bits of dirt were still embedded in the creases that outlined the bull's head. It had to be the same statue. Wasn't every day a person stumbled on something like this, though it certainly wasn't remarkable. The bull was a symbol and totem used throughout the ages. Baal, the bull god? Maybe. Or perhaps a simple study of a bull.

No matter what it was, she knew without doubt this was the same piece she'd dug up yesterday. How had this gotten into a small seaside hotel in the hands of a dead man in less than twenty-four hours?

The impressions in the paper packing strands of the crate indicated a round object had been inside, about three times the size of the statue, perhaps a ring like a halo. Something else could have been in the crate. Maybe the bull had been set in the center with something bigger around it.

No, it didn't look as though the packing paper had been disturbed in the center.

Had the man on the bed been transporting stolen

artifacts? It made sickening sense. Port-side cities like Cádiz were rife with small operations that trafficked in stolen and looted artifacts. Annja wanted to string them all up and force them to understand they were robbing an entire culture.

"Who was here before me?" she asked the dead man. "And what did he take from the crate?"

She was no forensics expert but could make an educated guess how long the man had been dead. His skin was pink at the bottom of his hands, which were flat on the bed, indicating the blood had settled. That meant six hours after death. He must have been murdered around midnight. It was a guess, though.

Slipping a hand inside her backpack, she drew out a digital camera and took a picture of the statue, flipping it over and getting edge shots of it as well as inner shots, trying to match the previous shots she'd taken while at the dig site. She and Harlow had uploaded those photos to their laptops. Then she snapped shots of the empty wood crate from all angles.

She wouldn't take a picture of the dead body, but she did take another look at the man's back to note the exact position of the wound. Set at the base of the neck and to the left of the spinal column, it looked too messy and wide for a bullet, but an exit wound could tear the flesh if the rifle had been high caliber. She adjusted her guess to a knife with a narrow blade.

She had the urge to search the dead man's pockets for a wallet and identification except that she heard footsteps down the hallway. The door, which she hadn't pushed closed, crept inside an inch.

Stepping out into the hallway, she spied a maid and grabbed her by the arm and said in her most theatric Spanish, "He's dead! I was going into my room, and his door was open. Send for the police!"

2

Annja had waited until a pair of officers had arrived at the hotel, and answered their brief questions. They'd asked her to come along to the Cádiz city police station.

She relayed all the information she could to a Maria Alonzo—a female officer Annja decided wasn't in a high position. She merely nodded and jotted things down and didn't prompt with leading questions. The officer then said she'd return with Annja's belongings in a few minutes and left the room.

Having been escorted to an interrogation room upon arrival at the police station hadn't bothered Annja. Of course they would be thorough. And, having been on the scene, she could understand how she might be construed a suspect. But she wasn't going to sit patiently for long.

She still had one more day at the museum planned, working alongside James Harlow. The murder mystery she would leave in the capable hands of the Cádiz police. But the question of what had been inside the wooden crate tread on her turf. And whatever it was had been worth murder to someone.

It wasn't related to the bronze statue, she suspected. Or else wouldn't the murderer have pocketed that, as well? There was a possibility whatever had been stolen wasn't even an artifact. But the crate and the packing materials screamed archaeological interest.

She got up from the uncomfortable metal folding chair and stretched her arms over her head. Despite its seaside location, the heat index could rise to blistering before noon and the room didn't have air-conditioning. She had waited an hour alone in this room before an officer had arrived to get the details from her. She was hungry, yet her system buzzed with nervous adrenaline.

"Señorita Creed?"

A second officer strolled in, favoring his left leg with a slight limp. He set her heavy canvas backpack on the table. He stood back, thumbs hooked into the front pockets of his brown, creased slacks. He wore the force's green flak jacket with the gold *policia* emblem emblazoned across the back over a yellow-and-blue-striped shirt. Visible under his left arm, a holstered pistol. The big silver buckle of his belt was either a black enameled bucking horse or a bull. Annja couldn't be sure and didn't want to look too closely.

"César Soto," he offered, but didn't offer his hand. "Chief Inspector, Cádiz PNP."

He wore a nonissue beige cowboy hat low over his

brow, which emphasized his dull, black eyes. He needed a shave, and sweat slicked his cheeks and nose.

"Am I free to leave?" she asked, fingering the backpack strap. "I answered all the other officer's questions."

"Just a few more minutes, if you don't mind, Señorita Creed." He spoke English well, with only a hint of a Spanish accent. "My assistant is typing up her report, but I wanted to go over a few key points with you that I don't quite understand."

He pulled a credit-card-size digital camera out of his jacket pocket and set it on the table. It was her camera. Annja picked it up and turned it on.

"We uploaded and then erased the contents," Soto said before she could verify that for herself. "Tell me why a woman who happens upon a murder scene moments after renting a room in a hotel takes pictures of the incident."

"I didn't photograph the victim." She winced. As if that made her amateur-photography expedition sound more virtuous. "I'm an archaeologist, Officer Soto. I explained to your assistant, when I arrived at my room the door next to mine was open, and I am, by nature, curious."

"And apparently quite brave to walk in on a dead man?"

"I'm also accustomed to dead bodies."

"Is that so? How often do you come across a fresh kill?"

More often than she was willing to reveal.

"Not often," she offered carefully. "I've learned to view the scene with an unemotional eye for detail. I hadn't expected to see an item on the man's dresser that I had touched less than twenty-four hours earlier."

"The bronze bull we've taken into evidence?"

"Yes. It's possibly a statue of Baal, the bull god of thunder and rain. A fertility god."

"And you dug that up at a dig site near Jerez?"

"Puerto Real, yes. Professor Jonathan Crockett's dig. I've given the officer this information. So, yes, at the time, it felt natural to photograph the evidence."

"You Americans are a strange breed." Soto shifted his jaw and a bulge pushed out his cheek. Annja figured he had chewing tobacco and now noticed the leathery scent that surrounded him like a rancid perfume. "You ever work forensics?"

"No. But I've worked alongside professionals from the field. I know it sounds odd, but trust me, it was an innate reaction to take out my camera."

"With a dead body lying feet away. Yes, I'd mark that as odd, for sure. If not suspicious."

"He was dead before I arrived, Officer Soto. Even without a forensics background I could determine that, as I'm sure your investigating officers also did."

"You didn't take any pictures of what had been in the crate?"

"There wasn't anything in the crate when I arrived."

"You could have removed evidence."

"I didn't take anything. I give you my word."

His forehead lifted in a dark chevron beneath the hat brim. He didn't know her from a tourist. Or a thief, for that matter.

"Who was the man, if I can ask?"

Soto studied her with slow calculation. "He was a guitar player from a local club."

"His name?"

"That's not public information."

She nodded. It had been worth a shot.

"Although, you'll learn soon enough. It has already leaked to the press." He eyed her as if she'd just spat at him. The tobacco bulge shifted from one cheek to the other. "I hate the press and all forms of media."

"They have a job to do. I'm sure they can't all be bad."

He winced and again shifted the tobacco to the other cheek. "You some kind of movie star?"

The thought process that had generated such a question baffled her. She hadn't mentioned her work with *Chasing History's Monsters* to the other officer. Even so, hosting the cable television show hardly qualified her as a movie star. "Why do you ask?"

"I did a search for you on the internet. Something about a monster chaser came up."

Good old Google.

"It's a cable television show that explores the facts behind monsters, legends and other myths throughout history," she explained. "I am one of the hosts. As an archaeologist, I offer a unique perspective. But I am far from what you'd consider a movie star. What does the television show have to do with this case?"

"Just wondering what sort of publicity is going to develop if you start opening your mouth."

"I—" That had been a clear threat. She could feel his condemning stare penetrate her skull. "I've no intention of speaking about this to anyone. I'm hardly in a position to be doling out details on a murder case. In fact, I'm headed out of town soon. I've been working with the city museum, looking over a recent acquisition of Greek coins found in Egypt. In another day I'll have all the notes I need for my project, and then I'll hop a flight back to New York City."

"Then I wish you a good journey." He tipped his hat to her. "Thank you for the information, señorita. Please give your contact phone number and the location you'll be staying at after leaving Cádiz with my secretary. You are witness to a crime scene, you understand."

"Of course." She slung the backpack over her shoulder and offered her hand to Soto, which this time he shook. "Luck with the case."

After speaking with the secretary and signing the report of the information she'd given, Annja pulled out her cell phone and dialed Roux. It was a spur-of-the-moment decision. The man had connections worldwide. She recalled listening to him and Garin wax over their visits to Spain in the 1950s and how they'd loved the country and the bullfighting. As well, the man was interested in art and antiquities, so she figured he might have some connections.

His phone rang over to an answering machine, which surprised her. Usually the former soldier—fifteenth-century soldier, to be accurate—had a cell phone on him. She had no idea where in the world he could be right now. But if he was at his Paris château, they were in the same time zone.

She tucked her phone away and decided to try back later.

Foregoing a return to her hotel room—surely the police would still have the dead man's room marked off—she headed toward the Cádiz city museum on the Plaza de Mina. But a block away from the museum, James Harlow waved her down on the sidewalk and redirected her to a nearby tapas bar.

James Harlow was a slender man in his fifties who walked with a cane, due to an injury to his hip he'd never explained to Annja. He dressed in Oxford plaids and bespoke leather shoes, and had a habit of checking his watch with a tap to the crystal face.

Inside the cool bar, with walls painted blue and wicker ceiling fans, Annja ordered lemon water from the waitress. Harlow followed that up by ordering lunch for the two of them. The *tortitas de camarones* sounded delicious.

Harlow hooked the cherrywood cane on the edge of the table and leaned on his elbows toward her. "You're getting a late start this morning, too, I see."

"Not by choice. I spent the morning at the police station."

"The police station? I've heard the hostels tend to have some wild parties, but, Annja, what were you up to?"

She liked that he joked with her so easily. No professional rivalries between the two of them.

"I decided sleep was more valuable than partying, so this morning I checked into a place I thought would prove more restful. But in the room next to mine I found a man who had been stabbed to death."

"Are you serious?" He sat back in his seat and stared at her. "What are the odds of that? You do have a manner of sniffing out intrigue wherever you go."

He'd confessed to following her adventures on *Chasing History's Monsters,* but that show was just the tip of the iceberg with Annja Creed. The man couldn't possibly be aware of all the adventures that had demanded she wield a sword to save innocent lives.

"Must be the young man I heard about on the radio twenty minutes ago," he said. "A guitar player?"

"Yes. Did they mention his name?"

"Uh, Diego someone. Montera? That could be it. I noted it because I think there's a family of toreros by that name. It's also what they call the hat a matador wears in the ring, a *montera.* So, someone didn't like his music?"

"Well, there was a stab wound in his back, but I won't make a judgment call on his talent."

Harlow choked on his beer. He set the mug down on the napkin and, face tight, smoothed the napkin out neatly to each corner before tapping his watch. "I'm so sorry, Annja. Finding a dead body is certainly not the best way to start the day. What the hell happened?"

"Someone killed him for an artifact."

"Is that so? How do you know?"

"Listen, this is privileged information and the police are handling the case, but…"

"A mystery? Tell me."

"There was a wooden crate in the room, and whatever had been inside it was gone. I suspect the murderer stole it. I also suspect it was an artifact, though I can't be sure. I took pictures, but the police erased them from my camera."

"Bold. On both your parts."

"You've still got the pictures you transferred from my cell phone, right?"

"Of the bronze statue."

"Great." She paused. "There was another artifact that wasn't stolen. One I actually unearthed a day ago."

"What? You don't mean…"

She nodded. "The bronze bull statue."

"But how? You just discovered that on Crockett's dig." The man wiped a hand over his face and shook his head. "Damned looters."

"That has to be the case. Someone looted Crockett's site and made a quick turnaround, hoping to sell it. But apparently Diego Montera was carrying something of even more interest and value if his killer left the statue behind."

"Which would give one reason to assume what was stolen was more valuable," Harlow deduced. "Where's the Baal statue now?"

"In the police evidence locker room, I'm sure. I handled it, with gloves on, and took pictures, but—"

"You should have slipped it into a pocket, Annja. That piece was an awesome little find."

She hadn't thought it so remarkable, but then remembered his interest in bull artifacts.

"It'll run through the system eventually. You'll get your hands on it sooner or later, I'm sure."

"Don't bet the farm on that one. Police evidence tends to find its way to the University of Cádiz on the mainland. Damned Edmond Rogers, head of acquisitions, will have his hands all over the thing before I will. That they get first dibs at police seizures is such a bloody crock. They don't even have an archaeological department. Their focus is marine studies."

"Well, you've still got the picture I took on-site."

He nodded and looked aside, wincing. Disappointed, surely. But what could either of them do? Annja didn't make it a habit to steal police evidence. Not that she hadn't done so before; she just wouldn't call it a habitual thing.

"I'm going to look into it," she said. "If the site was looted, and the artifacts were turned around in less than a day, that tells me there's an illicit antiquities operation in town."

"There are likely many operations in town. This *is* a seaport."

"True. I've got to call Jonathan Crockett. Or rather, I think I'm going to head out there after we've eaten."

"You've more work at the museum. You think you have time to do that?"

Annja tilted her head at the man. "Professor, I'm surprised. This reeks of everything I thought you abhorred. I thought the museum took a hard stance against acquiring items without provenance?"

"Damn it," he said softly. Clasping the mug, he stared out the window at passing tourists. After a few moments, he swung a look at her. "Annja, forgive me. I'm being absolutely rude. You must be in a state to have found a body. Are you okay?"

"Sure. Nothing I haven't—" She cleared her throat and took a long swig of the cool lemon water. "I'm fine."

"I'm sure you've seen things," he said. "But as archaeologists we usually find the bodies long after death, and that involves little blood or gore." He reached across the table and laid a hand over hers. "If you need to talk, I can take the rest of the afternoon off."

She appreciated his kindness. His reputation as being a hardnose had never been apparent to her. "Thank you, James. But I really am fine. And I am going to drive out to Crockett's site, so I won't be at the museum this afternoon. Is it all right if I stop in tomorrow to finish my work with the coins?"

"Of course." He rubbed a hand along his thigh, the wounded leg, she assumed. He'd mentioned he felt constant pain, yet was able to bypass painkillers by using visual relaxation. "Yes, you're right. Spain's cultural heritage is not a renewable resource. If illicit trade is going on in the city, it's our responsibility to put a stop to it. Now that I think on it…perhaps you'll want to take a closer look at Jonathan Crockett. He's a retired college professor who can't find funding for a big-time dig so he's taken what he can to keep his fingers in the dirt. A man like that…you never know what he'd do for cash."

Annja didn't know Crockett well, but the few days she had worked alongside him, she hadn't gotten the murderer vibe from him. Or the I-will-sell-potsherds-for-cash vibe, either. But she wouldn't assume anything right now.

"You worked with him?"

"It's been over a decade, but we headed a dig together in Egypt along the Nile valley. I had to keep an eye on him. Finds went missing that I couldn't prove."

"Thanks, I'll keep that in mind."

The waitress arrived with two steaming-hot plates. Annja dug into the thin omelet stuffed with onions and tiny prawns.

The professor studied her intense enjoyment for a few moments, smiling before diving in himself. So she was a hearty eater. It was always wise to eat her fill whenever she was around food, because there were long times when she wasn't able to eat. Either because of her work schedule, travel or, more often, because of mysterious dealings that involved her stowing away in a ship's hull or battling gunrunners or falling into a pit in the middle of the Sahara Desert.

After they'd eaten, with a promise to stay in contact with Harlow regarding details of the case, Annja stepped out of the tapas bar into the searing summer sun, courtesy of the god Mot. Glancing to the left, she spied the sea and a beautiful white-sand beach littered with bikini-clad women and children. Out on the water a windsurfer cut through the silver waves.

And then she saw the tall, broad-shouldered man leaning against a metal street pole pasted with posters for flamenco dance concerts. Arms crossed high over his broad chest, and a smirk softening his square face from its usual steel to the lesser iron, his presence wasn't as much of a surprise as it should've been.

"Garin Braden," she muttered, not in an altogether welcoming tone. She'd decide soon enough if she was pleased, indifferent or just plain offended to see the man.

3

"Surprised?" Garin asked in Spanish, waiting for her to approach, which Annja did with forced disinterest. He looked abnormally vacationy in his pale cream linen suit and straw fedora. Garin presented her with a different side of himself each time she ran into him.

Annja replied, using the local dialect, "I'm never surprised that you always seem to know exactly where I am at any given time. It's your innate Annja radar, right?"

"Something like that." His dark eyes, shaded by the hat, held hers. Annja didn't flinch. "Also not a surprise to learn you were in a building of authority earlier."

"That would be what most people call a police station."

Likely, it wasn't innate radar but rather GPS coordinates Roux had gotten from her earlier call. And he'd already let Garin know about it? Interesting. The two men didn't work together unless there was something in it for both of them.

"Is that so? And here I thought my Spanish was so good." He switched to English. "So what adventures have you been up to? Slaying bad guys? Leaping tall buildings in a single bound? Chasing after dusty old pots?"

She walked along the stretch of stucco and brick buildings fronting the beach and he paralleled her. "I have a feeling I don't need to answer that one. You already know why I'm in Cádiz. Actually, I'd be disappointed if you didn't."

"I confess I do know the reason you were at the police station. That sort of information just comes to me, you understand. My people keep a keen eye out for threats, danger and—"

"I'm a threat?"

"No, you fall squarely in the Persons of Interest category."

"Of course." He did, too. Sort of like an ancient Grecian urn was interesting to her. "So Roux is one of your people?"

"When it serves me."

The sidewalk narrowed and the big man's arm brushed hers as they walked. He was a good head higher than her five foot ten inches—probably pushing six-four—and his shoulders were as broad as the *toro bravo* they bred for the bullfight here in Spain. Annja mused that he even possessed all the qualities matadors looked for in a bull: aggression, strength, stamina and intelligence. He was also several centuries old, which made him irresistible to her. And that offended her moral need to remain aloof toward the man.

"Headed anywhere in particular?" he asked.

"Off this sandspit to Puerto Real, to a little dig tucked on the edge of town."

"Ferdinand and Isabella's town," he commented.

Annja searched historical dates in her head. Puerto Real had been founded by King Ferdinand II of Aragon and Isabella I of Castile near the end of the fifteenth century. Garin had been walking this earth since the early fifteenth century.

Okay, she'd give him that one.

"The town has been around since before the Romans," she said. "Ferdinand made it a royal port to lure trade from North Africa his way."

"He was not a stupid king. And his wife was hot." He gestured to the black Jeep parked ahead. "I'll give you a ride. It'll give us an opportunity to catch up."

Blinking into the sun, Annja agreed she did want to catch up—and learn what Braden knew about her latest adventure. Even if she didn't trust the man as far as she could toss him. And with his bulk, that was more like a drop down her body before she sprained a wrist.

Sliding into the Jeep's passenger seat, she buckled up and tossed her backpack into the open truck bed. She hadn't missed the dried mud on the wheel rims and quarter panels. "You doing some off-roading in the area?"

"Rained yesterday."

"Sure. And that pitiful sprinkle managed to splatter your rearview mirror with mud."

"You got it."

Garin probably fancied himself an international man of mystery—which he was—but Annja knew he used the persona around her only when he wanted to tease her. On the other hand, he had secrets. Lots of them. And sometimes it was better to let things slide than to question them.

Garin eased into traffic and headed toward the ancient defensive walls that had circled the city since Roman times. Gadir, the name the Phoenicians had given the original outpost, meant "walled stronghold."

They didn't speak as Annja took in the scenery. Two massive electricity pylons hugged either side of the Bay of Cádiz as they neared La Pepa, the bridge that accessed the mainland. It was one of the longest cable-span bridges in the country. On the pylons, steel framework supported electric power cables. She wondered with amusement how long before Wi-Fi and satellites obliterated the need for such things.

"So tell me what you know," she said, her attention following the construction crew working on the bridge with pneumatic hammers and drills. "You always know something."

"I know you stumbled onto a body this morning."

"Word travels fast. And you rushed to Cádiz to console me?"

He chuckled as he drove off the bridge. "I've been in Cádiz a few days. Roux knew that and sent me to see if you needed any assistance."

"Awful swell of the guy." Of the two of them, she would have preferred Roux's assistance. The old man was more like a father to her and she never felt overly threatened by his presence. "Yes, a dead body, placed most conveniently next to the room I had rented."

"And it's related to some kind of artifact?"

She wouldn't question the man's knowledge. Garin Braden had access to intel that would make the CIA blush. "A bronze totem in the form of a bull, possibly representing Baal. Ceremonial, I assume, or it could have been a commemoration piece. Who knows, it could have been a tourist tchotchke. Did you hear about the other artifact?"

"Just the one. What was the other?"

"I don't know. It was missing."

He flicked her a questioning glance. "Stolen?"

"From the dead man. The dead musician."

"Ah. I sense an adventure coming on."

"In fact, we're headed to the first stop right now." The stretch of road around Puerto Real quickly segued from pavement to gravel. "Turn left. It's only a few kilometers ahead. So, do you also have information on the dead man? I was given his name, but not by the police."

"What did you tell the police?"

"I was first on the scene, but I could only tell them what I knew. Which was very little."

"A little is more than nothing. You hungry?"

"Just ate. We can stop if you are."

"I'll do for a bit." The Jeep navigated the increasingly

rough road like a dream. "Looks like you're taking us into the boonies, your favorite kind of place."

"Don't worry, we're not heading into mountainous terrain."

"The tires are off-road all-terrain."

"Yes. Glad you've already tested them when it sprinkled yesterday."

"It was a damn good downpour."

"Sure, if you say so." Changing the subject, Annja said, "I'd held that very bronze statue a day ago."

"Is that so? Now I'm intrigued."

"It takes a lot to get your interest."

He lifted one dark eyebrow, which was more a come-on than castigation. She ignored the flirtation.

"I unearthed it on the dig we're heading to right now. It had been waiting for cataloging to be sent back to the University of Cádiz. I believe it was Spanish. It had a decorative Moorish arabesque circling the bull's neck. But beyond that, I hadn't the time to do further research."

"Spanish artifacts are to be expected when one digs on Spanish soil."

"Not always. Pieces of history travel all over the world and can be found thousands of miles from their original country of provenance. At the time I found it, we thought it was part of thieves' booty."

"So it had once been stolen. You unearthed it. Then it was stolen again? Or do you suspect someone from the dig of handing it over to the dead man?"

"I don't know. The dig supervisor, Jonathan Crockett, seemed on the up-and-up. I'm a pretty good judge of character. But I have no clue regarding Diego Montera. The dead man," she added when Garin raised a questioning eyebrow. "He may have been some guy on the dig crew who was handed a valuable artifact and wanted to get some fast cash for it."

Garin stared at her. "A musician on a dig?"

She shrugged. "Maybe he stole it, but if that was the case, I suspect it wasn't planned. Although, if he wasn't crew, someone had to have smuggled the bull off-site. I don't know. Its value is questionable. It was small, a simple piece."

"Sounds like a delicious mystery. Too bad you're not a homicide detective."

"No, I'm not. Doesn't mean I don't have an interest."

"In the objects a dead man was carrying?"

"Archaeology is all about deciphering the objects people carried, wore, used, lived in. I'm an object detective."

This area of Spain had been gone over by archaeologists many times in the past century, but a recent chunk of mountain had been dislodged and had changed the landscape, prompting new discoveries.

The dig supervisor, Jonathan Crockett, was a laid-back Englishman who had never aspired to anything but squatting in the sun all day, his hands in the dirt. And he had a trust fund to make it happen. He was a hardcore archaeologist. Quiet, he never bragged about his finds or elaborated overmuch. He measured his words, and Annja had been fine with that. The sun had toasted his skin nicely and enhanced the distinguished lines at the corners of his eyes and temples. His sun-streaked brown hair never did stay in the ponytail he tied at the back of his head, and as dirty as he got, his clothing always looked freshly pressed. A well-seasoned man, he was movie-star fodder, without the ego or need for fame.

That James Harlow had suspected him of underhanded dealings didn't feel right, but Annja would reserve judgment until after she'd talked to him.

Garin pulled the Jeep outside the main—and only—tent, dirt billowing up from the tires in a cloud. The soil was a fertile mix of gravel, sand and silt in the southern areas of Spain, ideal for viticulture.

Annja jumped out into the dirt cloud. "You stay here," she told Garin.

"Don't think so." He patted the linen jacket over his heart. The man, who now made his home Germany, tended to favor semiautomatic pistols manufactured there or in Austria. "I'll be your backup."

"Don't go all alpha on me, now. The villagers are not going to attack with trowels and buckets."

"If someone here is selling artifacts to people who apparently kill to obtain them, you want to be safe."

"I don't know Crockett is selling artifacts. I highly doubt he is. Ambition is not one of his finer points."

"Don't worry. I'll be inconspicuous."

Garin got out and stood beside the Jeep. With his

height, broad shoulders and chiseled square jawline, he looked the medieval warrior trying to masquerade as a regular Joe. The man would never achieve subtlety.

"Inconspicuous. Bang-up job." Annja stabbed him with a look, then strode toward the tent, leaving the misplaced warrior to guard the battlements.

The dig area was quiet. The excavation unit marked off with stakes and string before she'd arrived days earlier looked like the pit to hell, blackened by the shadows. It was only four feet deep. Crockett had gotten a lot done with the few college students who had occasion to drop in for a day at a time. No one except Crockett stayed on-site overnight, so either they had all taken a day off or had decided to start late. Really late. It was after noon.

She called out, but no one replied. Crockett's tent door was untied and flapping in the breeze. She peered inside. Empty, except for two tables used to sort out artifacts, and bag and catalog them in a field notebook. Toward the back stood an old army-issue cot and dressing table with water canisters, basin and towels, and a hand-crank radio.

Wandering around the south side of the tent, she caught sight of Garin's bulky figure out of the corner of her eye. He leaned against the Jeep's hood, ankles crossed, head tilted back to take in the sun.

"Some backup."

Not that she expected anyone to jump out from behind a rocky outcrop with guns blazing. On the other hand, experience had taught her to never presume any situation was safe.

Where had Crockett gone? He wouldn't abandon the site without leaving an assistant to watch over the supplies and finds.

Her instincts suddenly flared. Tensing, she slowly tracked along the side of the tent. The smell of dirt-dusted canvas material was like perfume to Annja's soul, but the buzz of flies nearby made her suspicious. Odd. Crockett kept a tidy site.

A rancid odor grew as she turned the back corner of the tent and stepped into a pool of congealed blood. She quickly took in the blood spatter that had dried to brown across the tent canvas.

"Garin!"

She tracked the path of blood until she came to the edge of the pitoned-off dig square. A body had been rolled into the four-foot-deep area, which measured about sixteen by twenty feet. Earth had been hastily shoveled over it, but the booted feet, hands and the back of a dark-haired head showed.

"That is not good," Garin said as he sidled up to her and looked over the scene. "You think it's the dig supervisor you wanted to talk to?"

"Someone looking for me?"

They turned in unison, Garin with pistol extended, to find Jonathan Crockett standing behind them. Holding an AK-47.

4

"I believe my Kalashnikov trumps your Glock," Crockett said to Garin.

Annja felt Garin's elbow twitch against her arm. He was the last man Crockett—any man—should issue a challenge like that to.

"You think so?" Garin held the pistol barrel skyward and finger off the trigger.

Crockett gestured with the machine gun for Garin to toss the pistol aside. Annja knew that wasn't going to happen.

Before Garin could react, Annja reached into the otherwhere, felt the sword's power tingle in her fingers and clasped the grip. She swung out, sweeping the blade across Crockett's wrist and taking him by surprise. The man yelped. The machine gun dropped to the dusty ground. In an agile move, Garin bent to claim it.

Crockett clutched his bleeding wrist. Sweat beaded on his forehead and he winced with the pain. He looked to Annja, but she'd released Joan of Arc's sword back to where she'd found it.

"Nice," Garin said. He hooked the Kalashnikov under his arm and held both guns on the whimpering professor. "She's my backup," he said with a nod toward her. "Who would have thought I'd need her in such an innocuous place? Pothunters shouldn't play with guns."

"*Pothunter* is a derogatory term," Annja corrected him. Had Crockett turned into a merciless pothunter? Had he killed the man in the pit for his own gain?

James Harlow had intimated he didn't trust Crockett, yet she'd brushed if off as all-too-common collegiate rivalry.

"I was trying to protect myself." Crockett sank to his knees, clutching his wrist against his chest. Blood soaked into his white shirt. "They came so quickly. Yesterday evening. Hours after you left, Annja." He gasped. "Took everything. When I heard the vehicle drive up just now I thought they'd returned to finish me off, so I hid in the gorse."

"You didn't kill this man," Annja stated.

Crockett shook his head. "No, they did. Yesterday."

And the body was still lying out in the open? Annja winced. Why hadn't Crockett contacted the authorities? And for that matter, why was he still here?

"Who are *they?*" Garin demanded. "Did they take your field phone with them, too?"

"Let's move him inside the tent for some first aid. We need to bandage your wrist before you lose too much blood," she said to Crockett, then with a glance in the direction they had come from, added, "We should take him to the hospital."

She met Garin's fierce stare, leaving her in no doubt that he thought her suggestion a bad one. Cleaning up the mess by taking out the professor with a bullet to his heart would probably be his suggestion. Joan of Arc wasn't into vigilante justice. Neither was she.

"No hospitals," Crockett said as Annja led him into the tent.

"Why? You got something against hospitals?"

"My sister died five years ago when she caught an infection following surgery."

"I'm sorry. But we do need to alert the authorities to the dead man. He's been lying in the pit since yesterday?"

"No police, either," Crockett pleaded as she helped him settle onto the cot, and then grabbed the water flask and a towel. She had cut him on the side of his wrist and hadn't severed an artery, so the injury shouldn't prove life-threatening. "I think I've done a very bad thing."

"Murder is a bad thing," Garin commented matter-of-factly, tilting back a swig of whiskey from the bottle on the professor's bedside table. "But it is sometimes necessary."

Crockett screwed up his face in disbelief at that comment, but then he winced again, leaning forward over his arm. "You think I killed that man out there? I didn't. I swear it to you. Who *are* you?"

"A friend of mine," Annja quickly said. "Trust-

worthy." For the moment. "Did the man out there attack you?" she asked while inspecting Crockett's wrist.
The battle sword had cut neatly to the bone, but she
was able to close the flesh with liquid bandage and
figured it shouldn't get infected thanks to the whiskey.
She wrapped a tight bandage around it. It would serve
until he could get medical attention.

"Attack me?" Crockett was starting to hyperventi-
late and sweat beaded on his forehead. "Didn't you see
who that was?"

"His face was covered with dirt. Who dragged him
into the pit?"

"I panicked. I didn't know what else to do."

"Call the authorities?"

"I…" The professor tugged away from Annja's hold.
"I didn't kill Simon."

Annja stilled. "That's Simon Klosky out there?"

He'd arrived on the morning of her last day at the
dig. Annja had only worked with him half the day before leaving for Cádiz to meet James Harlow. Nice guy.
Young. But either the Spanish sun or—her strongest
suspicion—extracurricular drugs had made Simon a
little loopy and gregarious. He'd had a habit of singing
random lines from gospel songs.

"Who did kill him? And why are you still alive, Jonathan? Has this to do with the stolen artifacts?"

Crockett wiped the sweat from his eyes and studied
her. "You know about the theft?"

"I saw the very same bronze bull statue I unearthed yesterday in a dead man's room this morning."

His jaw dropped. "Dead?"

"Do you know Diego Montera, Jonathan?"

His unwounded hand shook badly, but from the bits and pieces Annja was cobbling together, maybe he had been defending himself against robbers. Maybe. If there had been robbers.

"I haven't heard the name," Crockett offered. "He had the bull? I didn't have a chance to research it, but was beginning to think it was newer than we'd suspected. Maybe medieval or even seventeenth century. Whoever stole our artifacts certainly circulated them quickly. But you took pictures, right?"

"Yes." Which had all been erased from her camera, except for the ones she had transferred to her laptop. "So you were robbed?"

"Of course! Why else do you think I'd come after you with a bloody machine gun? I thought you were *them*."

"Why are you alive?" Garin asked carefully. Pacing the small tent, he still held the Kalashnikov ready to fire. "Makes no sense. Surely the top man in charge of the dig would be considered a target. Criminals don't generally leave a man behind to tell tales of their notorious escapades."

Crockett gaped, apparently aghast to have his fate detailed for him so coldly. "I—I hid when they first came to the camp. I was back in the gorse just now, like I said…hiding. Simon was the only other person here. They shot him, then took off with all the artifacts in the tent."

"Why didn't you report this to the police, Professor Crockett?"

He caught his forehead in a palm and rubbed roughly along his cheek. "There's a body outside my tent, rotting, and I just…don't know. I haven't been the most upstanding citizen over the past few years. Since leaving the university, my life has taken a decidedly negative turn. I can't get legit jobs. I suspect someone has it in for me. I want to be on a flight out of the country before the authorities arrive. I've already begun to pack up the site, but every time I walk past the body I get physically sick. I know it's wrong. Simon has a family. I will report this, but not directly to the police. I can't do that."

He must have done something pretty awful to be so afraid of contact with the police. Annja couldn't imagine what. She didn't want to know.

"They'll find you for questioning," she said. "And they'll be very curious to learn why you felt it necessary to bury a body that you had no hand in killing."

"Will you vouch for my innocence?"

She couldn't do that because she hadn't witnessed the crime.

"Exactly," Crockett said in response to her silence. "I wouldn't ask you to, either, Annja. Why are you here?" he posited. Regaining his usually cool exterior, his eyes searched hers, then Garin's.

"By having worked with you, and being the one who

found the stolen statue in a dead man's possession, I am indirectly involved. If someone is trafficking in antiquities I want it to stop. I wasn't sure the police would follow this lead so…"

"So, I'm not telling you, or your henchman, anything else. You've got no authority. I'll ask you to leave."

"Fine. We'll call in the dead body," the henchman remarked.

Annja met Garin's steely gaze. Who was he kidding? The man kept his distance from any form of authority. He'd sooner dig the grave outside this tent than have his name typed in permanent ink on a police report.

"Very well," Crockett conceded angrily. "But you won't need to. The authorities already know."

"How's that?" Annja asked.

Crockett sighed and gestured out to where the body lay. "Simon was killed by the Cádiz police."

5

Garin whistled and stepped outside the tent. "I'm out of here," he called. His boots tracked the dusty earth toward the Jeep. "Come on, Annja!"

She held Crockett's gaze, but there was no need for him to repeat what he'd said. According to him, the Cádiz police had murdered Simon Klosky and stolen the artifacts. The cops were dirty? Always a possibility.

On the other hand, it could be a lie from a man who'd never had to face the kind of guilt murder could induce.

"You didn't hand the bull statue over to one individual? Sell it on the antiquities market?"

He shook his head miserably, but didn't meet her eyes.

"So it was stolen from here, along with the rest of the worthless potsherds we found."

"There was the platter and I did unearth a few drachms after you left."

"Was there anything you'd packed into a wood crate, about this size?" She held her hands out.

The professor shook his head again. "It wasn't packaged up yet, as you know. I had no intention of sorting through anything until this weekend. You see now why I can't report this?"

She nodded. If the police were involved that could make things touchy for Crockett. If.

"It would be wise if you left town," he said. "That is, if you'd prefer to keep a low profile. You're not involved, but the police are thorough and they have eyes everywhere."

"I'm already involved. And I'm not about to stand back and allow this kind of blatant robbery and antiquities trade to continue."

Crockett nodded, clutching his wounded wrist to his chest. "You're skilled with the dagger. I didn't even see you move before I felt the pain. I'd heard you were talented before you arrived for the dig. But I thought your talent lay in archaeology, not the martial arts. I have to ask. Why this particular dig? It was nothing remarkable. Nothing newsworthy. And yet, the theft occurred only after you arrived."

"You're not seriously accusing me, Crockett."

He bowed his head and shook his head slowly. "No, that was unkind of me. Sorry. Just…out of sorts, you understand."

The Jeep's horn honked. Garin was showing a surprisingly impatient side of himself.

"You should head directly to the airport," Crockett warned her.

She nodded. "How long do you think it'll take you to pack up the site?"

"Another few hours."

Annja nodded a third time, then stood up from the cot. "I'll hold off calling the authorities until after Garin and I to return to Cádiz. They're going to love hearing from me again."

GARIN DROVE BACK to the city proper, offering little in the way of conversation. He'd wiped the AK-47 clean of his prints before leaving it with Crockett at the camp. It wasn't a gun he needed, and it was never wise to claim an unidentified weapon from a man he knew next to nothing about. Besides that, he didn't want to draw police attention to him, especially in Cádiz. He liked it here and didn't want to give the local authorities any reason to force him to leave.

Leave it to Annja Creed to involve him in a questionable situation.

He chuckled at that thought, and she looked over at him from the passenger seat.

"Just thinking how you always get me in trouble," he offered.

"Me? You've done your share of being a bad influence in my life."

"That I have done, and I'm not ashamed to admit it. Extra sunglasses in the glove compartment."

"Thanks." She put on the Armani shades and, sighing heavily, flipped her ponytail around to fall over her shoulder. "I can't believe he let that body sit out there all day."

"Puts him on top of the suspicious-persons list, if you ask me."

"I'm not sure."

He couldn't help but frown. "I'll never figure you out, Annja. That's probably a good thing."

"You don't believe Crockett about the police being involved?"

"It's possible. In any town, in any country, there are always bad seeds who hold a position of authority. But like I said, I'm taking myself off this list. I like the city too much to lose the privilege of visiting."

"I understand, and I wouldn't ask you to participate in anything that challenges your tender moral position."

"Annja."

"Couldn't resist."

He'd show her what a tender moral position looked like. Just keep it up with the digs at his character.

Annja Creed was a breed of woman like no other, and that made her so appealing he sometimes felt humbled near her. But that feeling only lasted as long as it took to remember she could best him in a fistfight if he let his guard down.

"I appreciate the ride and the backup," she said.

"So, you up for a little afternoon entertainment?"

"What did you have in mind?"

"Bullfight's in a few hours."

"Seriously? I...don't know."

Her mind was back at the dig site, working all the angles and plotting her next move. But for him this visit was strictly vacation.

"Come, Annja, I can't be seen at the corrida without a woman by my side."

"You fresh out of the pretty ones so you're slumming with me?"

"After a shower and something nicer to wear, you'll look fine. I'll drop you at your hotel to change and be back in an hour for you, okay?"

She disguised her humph by turning away from him. Garin pulled the Jeep to a stop before the Hotel Blanca. She gave him the look. The look that said she wasn't stunned he knew where she was staying. He had his ways, and he'd never divulge his methods to her. Made it more intriguing that way.

"One hour!" he called after her retreating back.

CLOSING THE HOTEL room door behind her, Annja shucked off her boots and patted off her dusty cargo pants before starting up the coffee machine on the bathroom counter. A bullfight? There were less interesting ways to spend an afternoon. But she couldn't enjoy anything until she got a little research done and made the call about the body at the dig site.

She dialed the police station, asked for Officer Soto and was put through to a machine. Fine with her. Made telling him about the body, but forgetting to mention whether or not she had seen Crockett, easier. She left her cell number because she predicted Soto would have real smoke coming out of his ears once he got her message. Unless he already knew about Simon Klosky's death... because he'd been there when the guy was killed.

If the police had stolen artifacts and were reselling them on the black market, they were likely involved in looting other digs in the area. Annja immediately got online and searched for digs in progress. The closest was in Granada. Two hundred and fifty kilometers away. Depending on the illicit operation's size, it could be local or international.

The museums, along with dealers and collectors, often inadvertently supported the illegal antiquities trade, and sometimes made the unconvincing argument that looters put history into the hands of the people. History yanked from its origins and placed without provenance or context before the unaware but appreciative public. Right. She was glad James Harlow was one museum employee *not* on that list. Much as he'd wanted to get his hands on the bull statue, he was as concerned about the illegal buying and selling of antiquities as was she.

Archaeologists and the source nations would continue to fight the underground trade, but it was getting more difficult every day as war, and pillaging of the spoils, saw major museums looted and priceless artifacts damaged or lost.

Sipping the passable coffee, she paced before the open seaside window, breathing in the ocean breeze.

Professor Crockett's suggestion the Cádiz police were accomplices in the looting still didn't place a name to Diego's murderer. If the police were involved they would cover it up. Had likely already marked the file Unsolved.

She hated knowing Diego's death would be swept under the carpet like so much trash. She didn't know the guitarist, but everyone deserved justice.

Flipping open her cell phone, she dialed James Harlow, who answered on the first ring.

"I've just returned from Crockett's dig site."

"So what have you learned?"

"I spoke to Jonathan Crockett while he held an AK-47 on me."

"I knew it. The bastard," Harlow said on a hiss. "He's implicated himself. He's probably behind the young musician's murder, as well."

One thing was clear, James Harlow really wanted to pin this on Crockett. Annja made a mental note to find out if the two men had a rivalry. She wasn't about to judge anyone until she got all the facts. And what did she really know about Harlow?

"Crockett's site was raided, he claims, by the Cádiz police."

"What? Really? That doesn't make sense. The authorities have always proved helpful to me." She heard the familiar sound of a fingernail tapping a watch crystal. "Don't you suspect it was a lie? The man is shifty."

"Not sure. The dead body in the dig pit makes me

wonder. Crockett said the police killed Simon Klosky, his assistant. Did you know Simon?"

"No, sorry. Another dead man?" The pause on the line was disturbingly long. She had second thoughts about revealing this information to Harlow, but his knowledge of the city and the local archaeological digs and personnel could help her. He finally asked, "Where's Crockett now?"

"Said he's going to pack up and get out."

"Did you call the police?"

"I left a message about finding the dead man. This links me to the two deaths. I worked on the dig for two days. I handled the bull statue before it was stolen."

"Right. I didn't think of that. You could also be im-plicated. But still…you had to call in a report."

"It's my duty."

"So the product circulates in a close range," Harlow said. "Interesting. Though it could be a starting point for something larger. I can't pinpoint a source. I sus-pect they must be operating close to shore, for ship-ping, perhaps. I haven't gone so far as to cruise the area, mind you. Skulduggery is not my strong suit. Besides, I imagine there are countless illegal operations in the area. Always seem to be in rich archaeological geog-raphy."

"Can you run some kind of background check on all of Crockett's other digs?" she asked. "See if there have been other robberies?"

"Sure, gladly. In fact, I've been looking into Crockett since you brought him up yesterday. I've got records for most of his work in the area, but I haven't been able to come up with anything for the past year. He hasn't turned in any field reports or catalogs. Hence, the reason I suspect him in dirty dealings. Will you be coming to the museum tomorrow?"

"That's my intention. I still have some final notes to make on the coins. Thanks, James. I'll talk to you soon."

When she should have felt relieved to have discussed the details with someone else who could relate, Annja was now uncertain if James Harlow was the man to share that information. He hadn't sounded gung ho about tracking the looters. Maybe he wasn't as on board with the idea of refusing artifacts without provenance as she had assumed?

Or maybe it really was a rivalry between the two men, and he was more focused on slandering Crockett's name than the real issue.

Clicking over to the Photos file on her laptop, Annja opened the six shots of the bronze bull she'd taken onsite and studied the few details in the Moorish carvings around the neck.

Online, she turned to archaeology.net and uploaded the photos of the Baal statue. She was calling it a Baal statue, but really, it could have been made to represent anything, not necessarily the mythic Canaanite god of fertility. She usually got a few replies to her queries, and some often led her to the truth about the particular item she had posted.

"Let's hope the bull can be traced."

6

Much as she was ambivalent about the corrida—she was neither for nor against bullfighting—Annja had to admit the atmosphere of the bullring satisfied her love of competitive sporting events. She wasn't convinced, though, that the corrida was competitive, unless that competition was between the matadors.

Sea scented the air, combined with sweat and women's perfume. Cádiz didn't have a stadium for bullfighting so they had driven back to the mainland to Jerez de la Frontera, where the summer festival featured two weeks of fights.

The audience was colorful, peopled with stalwart aficionados sporting cigars, straw hats and beers who had probably never missed a fight in decades, alongside tourists toting seat cushions emblazoned with the stadium's logo. And local women wearing the flamenco-style dress, which ruffled in many layers from the knee down to the ankle. Odd. They must be dressing for the tourists.

Flamenco guitar music played over the loudspeaker,

and down in the *barrera*—the outer row of seats that circled the ring—an impromptu set of dancers stomped out a beat, arms twisting above their heads. The people in the grandstands around them clapped *compas* and cheered them on with shouts of "Olé!"

This was a medium-size bullring, probably seating around ten thousand. Garin led her to what he'd said was his usual seat on the shady side of the ring. The most expensive and exclusive seats were in the shade, and in the *contrabarrera,* which was the second circle of seats around the ring. Close to the action, it was the place to sit for the best view of the matadors, who stood behind the barriers while eyeing up their competition, the bull. Just before the *contrabarrera* was the circular *barrera,* where Annja believed Hemingway used to be photographed sitting with cigar in hand.

The first matador had left the ring minutes earlier, and as Annja had learned from the advertisement outside the stadium, there were only two fighters today. Normally there were three, sometimes as many as six. Manuel Bravo would walk onto the grounds soon. Right now they were dragging out the dead bull from the previous fight, harnessed to two mules, accompanied by the orchestra, which played a lively paso doble. A cleanup crew followed with rakes to sweep sand over the blood so as not to spook the next bull.

Annja knew Spaniards were zealous about their national pastime. More than a pastime, it was a sport highly revered throughout the ages. Though the sides for and against bullfighting were equally passionate. She'd watched a few bullfights on YouTube and found she could relate to the art of the fight, yet she couldn't help but want to look away when it came time for the kill.

Garin tipped his cigar to her before the next fight. The man possessed a wicked charisma. Yet with his twisted morals, he wore the costume of a villain as easily as the hero.

Annja winced. *Hero* was too powerful a label to give the man. It was also a label used too often and easily by the media. Real heroes never expected to be recognized for a brave act. At his best, Garin Braden tended toward helpful citizen. At his worst? She did not want to be in his vicinity.

The man was an enigma. He'd lived for more than five hundred years thanks to the sword she controlled. He was connected to the battle sword, having been there when Joan of Arc had been burned at the stake. He'd witnessed the British soldier break her sword and scatter the pieces among the crowd who had damned Joan and made her a martyr through their own ignorance.

For some reason Garin and his friend Roux, whom Garin had been apprentice to at the time of Joan of Arc's burning, had both obtained immortality that fateful day. And a lifelong connection to the ineffable sword.

The two men had tracked the pieces over the centuries, and when finally the last piece had been placed, Annja had touched the sword—and as it had become whole, it had also become a part of her. She had not asked for possession of such an object, nor had she anticipated anything of the sort. But now that she did wield the sword, she did so as if it had always been meant for her. It was, in fact, her destiny. Only she could bring it forth from the otherwhere, and as soon as she released it, it was made intangible once again, unless she allowed another to hold it. Then the battle sword would maintain its solid state until she decided it should not. She couldn't explain the innate process even if a gang of terrorists held AK-47s to her heart. That was just how it worked.

Garin wanted the sword—hell, she'd let him hold it for a few moments of wonder—but she hadn't decided if it was because he believed keeping it whole would render him mortal or if breaking it would ensure his continued immortality.

Either way, she never let down her guard around Garin Braden.

She accepted the beer he offered her, which had been delivered to his hands moments after they sat down. Obviously, he held some status here. Then again, the man could make things happen no matter where he was. That wasn't incomprehensible magic, but rather confident command honed over centuries.

She hadn't taken time to shower after he'd dropped her at the hotel, she'd been so involved in research. She still wore the ponytail she'd hastily tied back this morning after her escape from the hostel, which had dried tightly and was probably looking pretty scrappy right now. Add to that her dark, loose camo pants, standard wear for Annja Creed, adventurer and archaeologist, and a T-shirt. Garin was just lucky she hadn't dug her boonie hat out of the backpack. But from where they sat the sun promised to stay out of her eyes.

"So how is it you always manage to stumble upon dead bodies, Annja? That's, what? Two in one day." He tilted his beer bottle to her in salute, then swallowed down half.

"I think I have a kind of dead-body radar, actually. It does kick in more often than not. I'm never to blame, of course."

"Course not. Not my sword-wielding adventuress. How is the sword, by the by?"

"True, straight and always there when I need it."

"They say the man in the hotel room was killed by a sword."

"Really? Why didn't you mention that on the drive out of town?"

"You didn't ask about it."

She gaped at him.

With a shrug, he added, "I suspect the authorities decided to keep the details from you in case you could be goaded to cough up said details."

"And how do *you* have the details?"

"I heard it on the radio."

Officer Soto had mentioned a media leak. Was there a mole on the force? Interesting. Perhaps there was a dirty cop who had an interest in artifacts?

She watched as the parade of banderilleros and picadors preceded the next matador into the ring. "Can you get more information for me?"

"Why? Who was Diego Montera to you?"

"I didn't know him. But this hit close. As I've said, I had only recently unearthed the bull statue."

"Alas. I so had hopes for your descent into nefarious deeds."

"We can't all be unscrupulous like you, Garin."

"Of course not."

"I took pictures."

"Ah, there's my girl."

"The Cádiz police erased them from my camera."

He gave her a look that said "did you expect anything less?"

"The murder isn't my concern," she said. "But it could aid my investigation into the stolen artifacts. I know you have connections. I wouldn't ask if I couldn't get answers some other way."

He nodded, but didn't say he would look into it for her. Annja marked her request off as Ignored. It was a lot to ask. But generally he didn't mind helping her, so his silence gave her concern.

Garin leaned forward, resting his elbows on his pale linen pants. His attire was de rigueur for hot Spanish summers. He wore the look well, but then he always seemed to blend into any situation or country. Despite his size and sometimes menacing presence, he had that everyman look.

Cheers erupted around them, and Annja turned her attention to the ring. The matadors spilled out onto the sand ring in suits of black and blue and violet. The man she pinpointed as the principal matador wore a brilliant gold *traje de luces* or "suit of lights," along with a black felt *montera* hat, fuchsia stockings and the classic black flat shoes that reminded her of ballet slippers.

"That's Manuel Bravo, simply called El Bravo. Fearless. He is this generation's greatest bullfighter from Cádiz," Garin explained. "He completed one hundred corridas last year and is on schedule to do the same this season. The man's a marvel."

One hundred fights in one season was a marker the pro matadors worked toward. It was an elusive goal, but those who made it were honored and guaranteed a full fight schedule the following season. A great matador could earn up to twenty-five thousand for one fight, so a hundred fights in a season added up nicely.

Annja couldn't share the excitement the surrounding crowd displayed as they cheered and waved white handkerchiefs and colorful scarves at the matador.

"Though I'm not willing to get out a flag and protest," she said, "I'm not sure how I feel about the blood sport."

"It is not a sport, Annja," Garin reprimanded her. He tilted his beer bottle toward the ring. "Bullfighting is an art, a spectacle. But never a sport."

"Okay. I defer to your expertise to explain it to me."

Crossing her arms and leaning back in the chair, she braced herself to be convinced.

"I will do my best, but you must know there are over thirty different ways to describe the placement of the torero's sword according to depth, position and entry point. Tauromachy is an elaborate art. I think we'll just enjoy it today, okay?"

Right now it wasn't the matador who swung the cape before the hulking bull, but rather a banderillero dressed in a smart red costume detailed with jet beading. El Bravo stood off beside a portion of wood fence, a barrier the matadors could flee behind during a bull's attack. The matador was tall and slender. Regal in his suit of lights, he studied each move the bull made as his assistant goaded the animal with the magenta-and-yellow cape.

"Why doesn't El Bravo test the bull himself?" she asked.

"That's his assistant's job. El Bravo needs distance to take it all in. Looking for which horn the bull favors, and whether or not the beast charges straight and with its head down or high. This one is calm. A good bull."

"How would you know a bad bull?"

"Those cartoons that feature the snorting bull that paws the ground with a hoof? That is a bad bull. Too cocky and fearful. Easily riled and nervous. The matador desires a calm, brave animal to put him to the ultimate test."

"The bull being an herbivore," she mused, "it's surprising they charge a man at all."

"Rhinoceroses are herbivores. I wouldn't want to stand alone before one of those tanks."

"Point made." Annja noted the matador's keen eye on the bull as it lowered its head to charge the cape. "Do they know what they're getting before the bull comes to the ring?"

"Not usually. The bulls are selected before the fight in the *sorteo*. The matador never does the selection. He sends his second in command, who pays close attention to horn size, sharpness and shape. But it's difficult to determine the animal's mien in a small stockyard." Garin finished off the beer. His attention swerved to her. "I assume you're going to stick around and look into the murdered man's life?"

"Like I said, I'll leave that to the police. It's curious, if you ask me, that someone would leave behind a piece such as the bronze bull at the scene. Even if the murderer had no idea the value of the object, he—"

"Or she," Garin interjected.

"Or she, should have been able to take one look at it, known it was an artifact and pocketed it."

"Perhaps their morals for stealing were stronger than for taking another man's life?"

"That makes no sense."

"Why? I'm not much for theft myself. Yet if faced with a situation where I had to defend my life by taking another's life, I wouldn't question the choice."

"Are you suggesting whoever killed Diego did it in self-defense? A knife to the back is hardly a defensive wound."

"No. Just showing you there are many ways to reason a man's actions."

"Explain to me, then, a man's choice to watch another man murder an animal before a crowd?"

"Ah, but it's not a defenseless animal. Name one other situation where an animal raised for slaughter is allowed the opportunity to defend its life?"

Annja opened her mouth to reply, but said nothing. He had a point. A vague, far-reaching point.

"Besides, the man isn't safe from danger," he added. "The matador faces danger for us all. He offers us that risk we are unwilling to take for the thrill of near death."

"This coming from a man who I know takes risks daily."

"Well." Garin shrugged. "I'm speaking about the others."

The *common* people was the unspoken part he left out. So like Garin, and not at all offensive when delivered with his charming smirk.

The matador had stepped out from behind the fenced barrier and swirled the magenta-and-yellow cape to attract the bull's attention. The cape moves were called veronicas, named after the veil Veronica had used to wipe the sweat from Jesus as he marched to his doom.

"Left horn," Garin muttered. "He'll present the cape to that one because that's the dominant one."

The crowd cheered when the bull passed close to the matador, one deadly ebony horn brushing his hip. The matador didn't step back, but instead leaned in toward the bull, bringing man and beast together as one. The bravery required to maintain that stance and not step aside was incredible, at once brutal and graceful. Annja nodded, impressed.

"As I've said, bullfighting is an art," Garin said into her ear to be heard over the approving shouts of "Olé."

And yet the word *matador* translated to *killer*. Annja took another sip of her beer, avoiding comment.

"The crowd doesn't attend to witness a grisly murder," Garin continued, "but rather the art of man against beast as each offers his very life in a competition that pits grace and style against ferocity and danger."

She could buy into that. To a point. "Except when the picador enters, then the grace and style fades and the cheating begins."

Garin shook his head and popped open another beer that again seemed to have materialized out of nowhere. "Annja, I won't even try. I had expected you, of all people, to have an open mind about this event."

"I can look at it objectively." There was a certain art to bullfighting. "Just call me a nonpartisan observer."

She understood the first capework performed by the matador was designed to tire the bull, to seek out its weaknesses and exploit them. It was a mind game between man and beast. It was the moment when the bull showed its mettle, be it gentle and awkward when approaching the cape or determined and ferocious with each charge. It was also the first time the bull had ever seen a man on foot and not mounted on a horse.

But her carefully restrained judgment nudged loose as the picador rode in on his horse, wielding the long spear he would use to poke the bull in the shoulder muscle to further weaken it. Rumors held that often the horse was drugged to keep it docile and less skittish.

The horse the picador rode was shielded with a heavily padded mattresslike fabric and was turned to one side to give the bull a charging target, diverting its attention from the matador, who had successfully avoided all the bull's charges, giving the beast nothing to connect with. The picador provided the bull something to charge after so many false charges against the matador, to give it encouragement as the beast's instinct to charge the cape might fade.

With his eight-foot lance, the picador stabbed the bull in the *morillo,* the huge neck muscle, in an effort to make it swell and weaken the animal. Before the picador could maneuver the horse to move in for the second lance, the crowd hissed as the bull pinned the horse against the wood barrier surrounding the ring. The picador flew off over the side of the barrier and into the *contrabarrera,* leaving the horse alone with the bull. A horn penetrated the horse's unprotected chest and the dying whinny forced Annja's attention back to Garin.

The man wasn't watching. His gaze followed the matador, who'd retreated behind the protective barrier.

The matador was no fool. As much as Garin argued that bullfighting was an art, the horse was the most unsuspecting victim of it all.

"So what brings you to Cádiz?" she asked, unable to take in what was happening below. "You mentioned you were already here. What, were you following me?"

"I had no idea you were in the city until Roux's call." He nodded toward the ring. "Manuel is a good friend. He's invited me for the week. I'll introduce you to him following the match."

It would intrigue her to meet the man who currently caped the bull away from the dying horse. A man who stood arrogantly bold and waited for the bull to charge before swishing the cape behind him and redirecting the bull's aim.

To more rousing cheers of "Olé," the matador worked a crowd-pleasing performance and even picced the bull himself, placing the bright blue-and-pink-ribboned barbed darts—which looked to Annja like big cocktail sticks—at the hump of the bull's neck with a daring charge directly at the animal. The trick was to jump high and to the side to avoid the horns. Normally this act was performed by the banderilleros, but some matadors chose to do it themselves out of machismo and to further impress the crowd.

The second set of darts El Bravo held high to acknowledge the crowd's cheers before waving them before the bull. Taunting it. Then, with a nod and a curt bow of respect, the matador ran counterclockwise around the bull, highlighting the beast's sinuous ability to turn on a dime as it tracked its opponent. The matador stopped. As he backtracked the bull lowered its head to charge. And then he struck, jumping high to bring down the darts and land them directly on the hump.

Blood spilled down the bull's hide, and once again Annja decided to take in the crowd instead of the spectacle. Was Diego's murderer watching this display of savagery?

Where had Diego gotten the bronze bull?

Thinking about the few valuable items unearthed from the dig, Annja wouldn't consider any of them the correct size for the wood crate. If Professor Harlow suspected a local gang of selling artifacts, it was possible they had either obtained pieces from various locations through theft or could have received them from other countries through the shipping port.

Had it been the police who then passed the booty along to buyers? It would make sense a police officer, wishing to remain anonymous, would use a liaison to deliver the goods. And yet, would a public official wanting to keep his or her identity a secret involve a second party like Diego?

She needed to find someone who had known Diego. Garin had guessed correctly—she couldn't resist a good mystery when it involved an artifact.

The crowd had settled to a hush, bringing Annja's attention back to the ring. Garin sat forward in his seat, the empty beer bottle dangling from his fingers, between his knees. Anyone who glanced his way would guess he was a man in his late twenties to early thirties, not the five hundred years he had tucked under his belt.

In the ring, the matador stood before the bull, his posture defiant. The line of his body was erect and graceful with his shoulders thrust back and his hips forward. The bull stood squarely, its head slightly down and its tongue lolling over its lower jaw in proof of its exhaustion. They stood less than eight feet from each other. Staring each other down.

The matador held a smaller red cape now and he moved minutely to the left, the bull reacting by adjusting its front feet. This third part of the match was called the faena, the final act, in which El Bravo squared up his opponent for the kill.

Compelled to witness what Garin described as an art and a spectacle, Annja watched as the matador led the bull in a series of close passes along his body with elegant sweeps of the cape. When the bull stood, tongue lolling and weakened, the matador approached him, holding his stiff bolero jacket open in defiance of attack.

"Center of the ring," Garin commented. "A bold place to perform the kill."

The matador bowed grandly before the bull. Then he turned to the crowd, lifted his chin as if to ask permission—when, in fact, he was asking permission to make the kill from the *presidente,* who oversaw the fight—and with a renewed roar of cheering, he turned back to the bull.

Lunging, he leaped into the air and brought down the *estoque,* a special sword with a curved tip designed for the kill, piercing the bull's swollen and bloody *morillo* and shoving the blade up to the hilt. The blade delivered correctly would sever the aorta and bring death quickly. But rarely instantly.

In a renewed burst of energy, the beast charged. El Bravo slapped his palm to the bull's forehead, tracking it in a circle until it came to a thundering stop. The bull took two unsure steps and fell to its front knees. The matador again bowed before his opponent. The crowd offered uproarious approval.

His second in command, dressed in a dark blue suit of lights, rushed in for the coup de grâce, delivered with the *puntilla,* a stab never given by the matador.

And it was over.

Annja met Garin's eyes and was surprised to find that he seemed sad.

Did the immortal man lament the death he could never have?

7

As the audience swept the air in a storm of white hand-kerchiefs, the matador and his entourage made a victory lap around the ring and were granted the bull's ear by the *presidente*. El Bravo then threw it into the grandstand to renewed cheers. Their local hero had once again mastered death for them. As the bull was being dragged out of the stadium by a team of two mules, the crowd clapped in rhythm to acknowledge the beast's bravery.

Once out of the grandstand, Garin led Annja toward the inner workings of the stadium, and the crowd thinned as they went where only invited guests were allowed. Where the matadors and their crew packed the vans near the loading docks.

It had been an afternoon fight, so it was still early, around six in the evening. The open-air backstage area provided a view of the pink sky shot through with gold clouds. Women in colorful, ruffled skirts and elegant updos dotted with roses and peonies swarmed the vicinity where Annja suspected the matador stood. She was suddenly conscious of her sun-baked ponytail and casual attire meant for hiking, not an after-event celebration. A glamour girl she was not, but she did like to blend in.

Garin, as usual, worked the crowd with the practiced ease of a celebrity. He attracted the women's interest, which, Annja knew, pleased the self-professed playboy.

When offered sherry on a silver platter, he took two goblets and handed one to her. "The local sherry is sweet, but I think you'll like it. Let me introduce you to Manuel."

"He looks busy signing autographs. I'd hate to intrude."

"Annja, you need to exercise your social skills. Swordplay and dirt-flinging do not an appealing woman make."

"Is that so? And yet on certain occasions you seem to find some appeal in me."

He leaned in close. "I've seen many sides of you, and each one holds immense appeal. Perhaps you're right. Stick with the adventurous-archaeologist look. Keeps the other men away— Manuel!" Garin shook his friend's hand and kissed him on both cheeks. They shared some hearty man-speak with pats on the shoulders. "I'd like you to meet a friend of mine. She's an archaeologist."

Manuel Bravo dropped his interest in the women who flitted around him. "Can't be," he said, staring at Annja. "She must be a model or celebrity."

Now she really felt like an unpolished pebble among a scatter of gemstones. El Bravo's eyes were as black as his slicked-back hair, and his face was thin and chiseled to the bone as if by the harsh Spanish sun. The hint of a five-o'clock shadow gave him a brooding, dark look. If she hadn't seen him slaying a bull thirty minutes earlier, she'd never peg him as capable of such a brutal act.

Then again, it was his profession; he'd trained years to master the elegant moves, the unflinching postures, the seemingly innate bravery. He was a master, and certainly he didn't look upon what he did as murder.

And Annja was impressed.

He lifted her hand and kissed the back of it.

"Yours was the first bullfight I've seen live," she ventured.

"And your opinion?" His dark eyes glinted.

"You are indeed the maestro." She used the title those in his field would.

"Thank you. But had I known someone so beautiful was in the audience today, I would have dedicated the kill to you. Please accept my belated dedication to your beauty." Another kiss to the back of her hand, and Annja tugged away and clasped her hands behind her back.

She caught Garin's smirk, which only made her feel more like a fish out of water.

"Maestro!"

Manuel nodded to the man who gestured for him to follow. Before leaving, he said, "I hope the two of you will do me the pleasure of coming to my villa later?

We'll be celebrating tonight's success with a grand feast."

"Wouldn't miss it," Garin said.

"Garin is staying with me at the villa. Miss Creed, do you have a place to stay tonight?"

The twinkle in his eye made her briefly forget she did have a room. Quickly she shook her head and thanked him for the offer. "But I would love to see your home and celebrate with you tonight."

"With you in attendance it will be far more interesting than I'd hoped," Manuel said, then winked. "The two of you will ride along with me in the van, Braden?"

"Of course."

"Very good." Manuel turned to be sucked into the crowd of hungry-eyed women.

"He's quite the charmer," Annja noted.

"And he succeeded in luring you in with only a few words. Have you eyes for a man you consider a murderer, Annja?"

"He's not—" Perhaps Garin had been right. There were many ways to look at the reasons behind a man's actions. Bullfighting an art form?

Two killers had entered her life today. Now to determine if they were standing on equal—albeit shaky—moral ground or if one might be granted the excuse that art trumps blood.

THEY STEPPED OUT into the sultry evening under the glaring streetlights behind the van painted along the side with Manuel's moniker, El Bravo. A decal featured him posed before a bull, cape sweeping gloriously. A rock star's tour bus, Annja mused. Every culture had their idols. Spain happened to worship a man who slaughtered animals raised only for the one appearance in a ring, a fight that virtually always ended in the animal's death. It was the rare bull that was granted its life for bravery.

Maybe that's why she'd stepped a little closer toward the side of the bull and the line of protestors who stood behind a safety blockade wielding signs to Stop the Torture! She accepted that all cultures had their own beliefs, rituals and ceremonies. But that didn't mean she had to subscribe to those beliefs.

As Garin leaned close to say something to her, a flash out of the corner of her eye caught Annja's attention.

A woman in the crowd milling about the van cried out as a glass of sherry shattered on the ground. The metallic ricochet of a bullet hitting the van's back quarter, just above the decal of Manuel's eye, simultaneously drew Annja's and Garin's gazes like trained sentry dogs to scan the area for danger.

One of Manuel's assistants shoved his maestro into the van.

"Was he hit?" Annja called, but didn't wait for an answer.

Her heartbeat quickening, she reached for the sword hilt, but with so many around her, she stopped short of grasping it. She'd seen a flash, and turned to scan the row of brick buildings lining the opposite side of the street. The pink sky provided a contrasting background to the dark buildings.

A sniper? Possible. But a professional shooter wouldn't position himself too close to the stadium and risk being sighted. Another flash from a rooftop a quarter of a mile down, possibly from sun reflecting off the shooter's sunglasses, Annja decided. She said to Garin, "I'm going after him."

He palmed the pistol he always wore under his left arm. "Right behind you."

She took off down the street, pushing through the crowd that had become knit in a tangle of legs and arms as men and women attempted to see if their idol was safe. In Annja's wake, a chorus of approval from the protestors weakened their argument against cruelty.

"Was he hit?" Annja called back to Garin.

"The bullet was four feet off its mark. What did you see?"

"That building on the left side of the street. Three-story yellow brick with the curved windows along the top and Moorish tile work." The city was old and didn't boast many buildings over three stories high, so the skyscape was easy to pick out. "I'm going around this side. You take the north wall."

She dodged down a narrow, cobbled street where the streetlights didn't reach and, seeing Garin didn't follow, was surprised he'd taken orders without argument. He was a man who gave orders. And the only time he listened to a female was if she'd whispered a sweet nothing in his ear or dangled an HK P7 before him like a carrot.

Festive music close by kept Annja from picking out the sounds of footsteps, but the clang of metal against brick signaled someone had dismounted an iron stairway hugging the building. Turning right she spied a dark figure racing away from the scene, toward the music and glow of colored lights.

Annja had a revelation. If that was the shooter, he—or she—was dressed in the least likely attire.

Garin veered around the other side of the building, and she signaled with a slashing gesture the way the shooter had run.

"You get a look?" he called.

Dare she admit what she'd seen? It couldn't have been the shooter.

They converged in an alleyway littered with graffiti and headed toward the street where the live music was coming from. Arriving at the end of the street, Annja's heart sank. The crowd was thick, dressed in bright skirts and colors. When the bullfights were in town there was always a party.

"The shooter was wearing a skirt," she said as they paused in the passageway before entering the fray.

Garin quirked an eyebrow at her. She sensed he was holding off a snort of laughter.

"The shooter was female," she reiterated, confident in what she had seen.

"Let's hope so, because I'd hate to think it was a man. You sure? Maybe you saw a dancer from the crowd?"

"I saw what I saw. No rifle, but running like she had a reason to run. I think the skirt was red with polka dots, though with the shadows that's only a guess."

"Polka dots? A common fabric choice for the locals. Which will make finding the shooter virtually impossible."

They walked into the center of the festival. The street was packed wall to wall with tourists, children and dancers whirling near guitarists and singers.

"Let's scout the area," Annja said.

As they insinuated themselves into the crowd loitering beneath colorful swags of bright paper flags and lamps, skirts of many colors swirled about them. Everywhere flashes of red and white polka dots caught Annja's eye.

"They all have polka dots," she grumbled.

"Not all of them, just a healthy number of them," Garin assured her. "You want to refine your description? Any particular facial attributes that stood out?"

"I didn't see her face. She had dark hair." Annja winced. Dark hair was de rigueur here in Spain. "Probably best to circle back and take a look up on the roof, see if a weapon was left behind."

"That's best left to the authorities, Annja. You don't want to overstep the line here."

He was right about that. But she hadn't seen a patrolman on duty outside the stadium.

"I'm heading back to the stadium to check on Manuel. Come along, Annja."

"Why would someone want to kill a matador?" she wondered, dodging a spinning flamenco dancer's fringed shawl and ducking under low-hanging pendants that advertised Summertime Sangria.

"I don't know. But that's two murders and one attempted murder for you in one day. I think that's a record, eh?"

If he didn't count her run-ins with murderous pirates, ambushing guerrillas or Irish gunrunners. "I attract adventure."

"More like chaos."

They veered toward the stadium, but Annja paused and looked toward the celebration. Her instincts weren't ready to let this one go.

"Can I meet you back at the stadium? Or even at El Bravo's? I want to wander through the crowd a little longer."

"Call me on my cell for directions," Garin said and stalked off, his tall, bulky figure sticking out like the proverbial bull in the china shop as he navigated the festivities.

Annja swung around and eyed the alleyways and streets that turned off from the main road. The best place for a sniper to hide would be away from the crowd. Unless she was dressed as a dancer...

She passed a group of three dancers in polka-dot skirts in varying shades of red. They were all gray-haired and too well-rounded to have given Annja such good chase. A boy and girl she guessed were about ten danced with each other in a circle of clapping tourists.

Coming upon a dancer in a red-and-white polka-dot dress, Annja joined the crowd that stood around her. She held a regal pose, arms arced above her head and chin thrust down defiantly as she worked some fancy footwork on the cobblestones to no more than the clatter of the crowd's claps. *Palmas,* Annja knew the rhythmic clapping was called. It punctuated the dancer's moves, as did the occasional shouted "Olé!"

The woman's hair was pulled back into a loose ponytail. Not nearly as smoothly coifed or styled as the other dancers around her. A sheen of perspiration beaded her neck and chest.

Annja moved to the front of the crowd, clapping in unison and mastering the open-palmed echoing *palmas* after a few tries.

The dancer spun around, her ruffled skirts dusting the air and revealing her rapid footwork beneath. It was amazing the punishing motions she could perform so forcefully and yet gracefully. Must be hell on the Achilles tendons.

Annja's sight fell on the black mark on the woman's wrist. Looked like a tattoo, but her rapid movement wouldn't let Annja make out the design. Clutching her skirts at her hips, the dancer brought her dance to an end with a triumphant thrust of her hand to the sky.

The crowd cheered and some called for another performance, while the dancer's head tilted down and her eyes angled to Annja. Her steady, dark gaze did not falter as she read Annja's daring look. A smirk curled the corner of the dancer's mouth. She stepped back and performed a twirl, fitting herself between two men in the crowd with a flirtatious ease, and then—she dashed.

Who danced and dashed? Only someone with good reason.

Annja took chase after the dancer, knowing with certainty she had found the sniper.

She dodged a basket seeming to float in the air, until her shoulder slammed into the basket carrier's shoulder and the huge wicker conveyance wavered and toppled. Angry shouts followed in her wake.

The dancing and festivities stretched far ahead and down the street, seemingly endless. The partying would continue all night. Perhaps the hostel hadn't been so wild, after all.

The dancer dodged into the crowd, but Annja stayed close. A swirl of skirt frilled alongside her, and the tourists jostled her off balance. Gripping a street pole, Annja swung her body around and, using the momentum to lunge upward, almost managed to grasp the dancer by the arm.

She saw Annja, then shoved a heavyset man drinking from a pewter mug toward her. Splattered with tequila, Annja apologized and swiped the back of her hand across her cheek without stopping.

They passed a group of men smoking cigars who

whistled at the dancer as she swept by. In response, the woman flicked them the international symbol for "get out of my face." They jeered and made some comment about Annja chasing her girlfriend as she raced by.

The dancer's heels clicked madly as she picked up her pace. The nails in her shoes designed to make loud, exacting beats when flamenco dancing did not serve well for stealth. And Annja couldn't imagine they provided good traction.

The dancer turned right, and the alley was so narrow Annja had to turn sideways. The dancer was thirty feet ahead of her and veered left down another alleyway.

Noting the fallen garbage can ahead, Annja sped up and jumped over it, landing smoothly. She swung around the corner where the dancer stood, poised for her approach. Charging her, Annja took a punch to the shoulder, which threw her off balance and against the brick wall. A heel kicked her in the hip and she felt a nail head tear her skin.

"You are *loco!*" the dancer accused her. Body poised in a half crouch for another punch, she waited for Annja to shake off the blow, then followed with another swing.

Annja was able to avoid the second punch with a dodge of her head to the left. She wasn't dealing with a delicate dancer who liked to swing her skirts for a few coins, so she dropped all apprehension and swung her leg in a high kick, connecting with the dancer's ribs and knocking her against the brick wall.

Sensing a battle sword would be overkill in this

match, Annja didn't summon it. Instead, she employed some martial-arts moves. She'd taken as many classes as New York City's municipal gym offered to learn to protect herself. She used a muay thai elbow strike and followed that with a karate kick.

As she bent forward, the swing of her attacker's fist missed. Coming upright, she charged the woman, slamming her against the wall a second time.

"You were on the rooftop," Annja said in Spanish. "You shot at the matador."

"I've been dancing for my supper all night," the woman hissed.

The dancer lunged at her with both fists up. She swung, missing Annja's head, but veered back with a left hook that skimmed her shoulder.

Annja blocked the foot that swung for her calf. "I'm not with the police," she said. "I just want answers."

"I sighted you earlier. You are working for the murderer," the woman growled. Annja gripped her ponytail and shoved her cheek to the wall. She swore at her in vibrant Spanish.

"What murderer?" Annja demanded.

"El Bravo!"

Seriously?

"I don't work for Maestro Bravo. I am, however, curious why a tiny thing like you likes to target practice with a famous matador."

"His fame is bought with blood."

"Isn't that the point of bullfighting?"

Did the protesters go so far as to use real bullets? Enough of this. The woman matched her in skill and would go at her as long as Annja could manage. She needed backup.

Still bent in the position to regain her breath, Annja called the sword to her grip and swung up and across her torso. She charged the dancer, slamming her against the wall a final time with a fist to her shoulder. She fitted the blade up under her chin.

"Hey, now," the dancer said in perfect English. She tried to get a good look at the sword, but Annja held it firmly against her neck. "You're mighty intent on protecting a murderer, eh, *Americano?*"

"Protesters usually carry signs and shout angry epithets. I can't believe you'd go so far as to shoot the guy."

"You think I'm protesting the senseless killing of bulls?" Despite the deadly blade at her neck, the woman laughed in a deep, throaty tone. "Oh, señorita, you have got it very wrong."

Overhead, Annja heard giggles from a couple young boys who had stuck their heads out a second-story window to see what was going on. They held a huge paper airplane and made zooming noises.

"If I'm wrong, then correct me. Why did you take a shot at Manuel Bravo?"

"Because someone needed to."

"That's a poor excuse. Give me one good reason why I shouldn't make a citizen's arrest—"

Something poked her above the ear. The dancer

shoved Annja's shoulders and slipped out of her hold. The paper airplane slid down Annja's shoulder. The hard sole of the dancer's shoe connected with her kidney. Pain shocked through her system. Letting out a guttural moan, she stumbled, crushing the paper airplane underfoot.

The dancer's heels clicked away down the street.

8

They didn't speak until the van arrived at Manuel's villa on the beach in Cádiz. A crowd had already gathered, and they could see people out back on the veranda.

"Where is your beautiful American archaeologist?" Manuel Bravo asked as they got out of the vehicle.

Garin considered the question. If the man wasn't pursuing the bulls, it was women. Few other pursuits interested him. Not bad interests to have. Both, in their own manner, dances with death.

"She stayed in Jerez. Went after the shooter." He straightened his linen jacket.

"Is that so? Quite the adventurous woman. I like that. But unlike most other women I've seen on your arm. She is a challenge to you, yes?"

"You could say that. It doesn't bother you a little that someone took a shot at you after the fight?"

A woman in a tight red dress, which she discreetly tugged to cover her lushly rounded assets, winked at both of them as she passed them, heading toward the crowd. Bravo tried without success to keep a lascivious smile from his face. "A man has his enemies, both dangerous and seductive. You are a perfect example, Señor Braden. I have never seen you without that pistol under your arm. Who do you need to protect yourself from?"

"One never knows." And that was enough of this conversation. "Who is that woman over there?" Garin asked, nodding toward the blonde with the dangling earrings and—damn, but that dress would not stay up.

"Isabella. She prefers her men rough. Let me introduce you."

He followed the maestro, not giving Annja Creed another thought. The woman could take care of herself.

ANNJA GASPED IN a breath, her vision focusing on the empty alleyway. She tilted her head to home in as she followed the noisy footfalls of the dancer's retreat.

Jogging forward, she stretched her torso to defeat the pain that seized her rib cage. The muscles had been bruised, which caused the most pain. Working through it, she began to run. When she reached a T in the street where the dancer had turned right, the alleyway stood empty. Strings of laundry fluttered like festival flags in the night.

The rattling bark of a noisemaker directly behind her startled her to spin around. Bringing up her fist, Annja stopped before connecting with the face of a man pushing seventy. His stance wobbled and tequila wafted from his breath.

At sight of her clenched fist, he waved her off with

a dismissive gesture, muttered something about gringos and teetered down the alleyway in the opposite direction.

Annja stalked down the street, taking in all the shadows, recessed doorways and turns. Instinctively she knew she wouldn't find the sniper tonight.

She returned to the stadium, where the crowd had thinned. The protestors still remained, their chanting as determined as ever. They'd taken to shoving flyers in the windows of passing cars.

According to a passerby Annja questioned, Manuel's van had driven off ten minutes ago. Garin must have been in the van. Half a dozen police marked out the area, and Annja sighted César Soto's cowboy hat. Beneath the brim, he grimaced at the protestors. She could feel his frustration.

She wasn't aware the Cádiz police had jurisdiction on the mainland but Cádiz was a province, so possibly they did operate on all the surrounding towns.

At sight of her approach, he shook his head in disbelief. Hadn't expected to see her again so soon. And not looking too thrilled, either.

"Guess I shouldn't be surprised after your message earlier," he said as she came up to him. The body out at Crockett's dig.

"You're quite the character, Miss Creed. You joining the protesters?"

"You've pegged me wrong, Officer Soto. I followed

the shooter." She gestured over her shoulder in the direction she'd come from. "But lost her."

"You followed the— Her?"

Annja nodded, predicting another trip to the police station in her near future.

The officer eyed her warily. "Me and you? We need to talk."

"I'll give you her description and answer any questions you have."

"Yes, you will. And we've another dead body to discuss. Simon Klosky was brought into the morgue an hour ago."

"Like I said, I'll tell you all I know."

Without comment, he directed her to the passenger's side of a waiting patrol car. They drove across Le Pepa and back to the police station, which had a great view of the Atlantic Ocean from the dispatch area. Once again, Annja found herself seated on a hard metal folding chair in the interrogation room, giving details of the shooter's face to Officer Soto, while an artist in the corner sketched quietly.

Annja detailed how she had chased the woman after realizing she was more than a dancer, and that she had spoken briefly to her. She didn't mention Garin. It was always easier, if not wiser, to keep that man's name quiet.

"Are you often compelled to take the law into your own hands, Miss Creed?" Soto asked in a tight tone.

She had decided *tense* and *pissed off* were his two standard settings.

"There were no officials outside when the matador was shot at, so I followed her."

Soto tapped the table with the eraser end of the pencil he'd been clutching for the past half hour of questioning. "Twice in one day you've graced my humble office. That's a new one for me."

She felt no need to respond.

"You done, Sophia?"

"Yes." The artist set the sketch on the Formica table before Annja and she leaned forward to study it. She had come pretty close, but the dancer's face had been rounder on top and narrower on the bottom.

"May I?" Annja asked and gestured to the artist's pencil.

With reluctance, and a nod from Soto, Sophia handed over her pencil. Anna was used to sketching when she was out on a dig. She drew objects in situ by stretching out string to form a grid over the site to ensure accuracy and scale. And while she didn't fancy herself a portrait artist, she erased some of the lines and drew a narrower jaw, adding a long sweep of ponytail at the side of the head, until she was satisfied.

Placing the drawing on the table and turning it to Soto, she said, "That's her. Dark hair and eyes. Heart-shaped face."

"That's half the female population of Cádiz," Soto said, unimpressed. "More than half."

Annja studied the portrait again, then held it back as if she were looking at the face of a woman standing in the festival crowd. It was a common face, with no remarkable shape to it or odd scars or distinguishing hairstyle beyond the ponytail, which was odd for a dancer, but not for a tourist or local.

"Well, that's her," she said, sliding backward against the ungiving chair. Her body language had slid into defensive disinterest, but she was tired, and yes, her defenses were up. "She had a tattoo on her wrist but I wasn't able to get a good look at it. Left wrist, I'm sure."

He made a notation of that. "That could help. You two fought?"

Rubbing her hip where she'd taken a brutal kick, Annja nodded. "She wasn't a street scrapper. Definitely trained. But then if she's a sniper, I assume she received training somewhere."

"We try not to make assumptions here, Señorita Creed."

"Of course, that wouldn't be wise. When are you going to ask me about Simon Klosky?"

The artist shifted uncomfortably on her chair. Soto drew out a new file from beneath the one he'd been making notes in.

"Simon's death may be related to Diego Montera's murder," she said. "But I'll leave the police work to you."

Soto's mouth gaped open. "How do you know Simon Klosky, Señorita Creed?"

"I told your officer this morning that I had been working on a dig in Puerto Real alongside Professor Jonathan Crockett. Klosky was one of many college students who spent a day or two on the dig to get hands-on experience. No one was scheduled for a particular shift. It was very laid-back."

Soto drummed his fingers across the thick manila file on the table before him. She wondered how to bring up the possibility that the police were involved.

"I returned to the dig this morning to find Crockett in a state after he was robbed yesterday evening."

"Still in a state after a robbery that took place almost twenty-four hours ago? How come he didn't report it?"

"You'll have to ask him."

Soto pierced her with a hard gaze.

"Officer, the theft of minor artifacts from dig sites is so common, and it isn't often local police have the time or the consideration to look into it. I suspect Professor Crockett was still…in shock. One of his assistants was murdered during the robbery."

Soto sat up straight and gestured for the artist to leave the room. Then he clicked on the intercom attached to his lapel and requested another officer join him to take notes.

The same officer—Maria Alonzo—who had questioned her earlier this morning entered the interrogation room, took one look at Annja and her eyebrows rose under her shock of dark bangs. She was about to say something when Soto gestured for her to sit and start taking notes.

"I didn't know Simon well," she began. "Only met him and worked alongside him about six hours."

"And when was that?"

"Two days ago. I left the dig around three in the afternoon because I had an appointment at the museum with James Harlow, the head of the archaeological department. I've already explained that, too."

"And how did you discover the death of Simon Klosky?" Soto asked.

"I almost stepped on his body. He'd been thrown into the dig pit and covered with dirt, but not well. His hands and feet were visible."

"And you said Jonathan Crockett was still at the site today when you returned?"

She nodded.

"He wasn't there when we retrieved the body of Klosky." Soto said to the other officer, "Send a car to the dig for Jonathan Crockett. Get me a detailed profile. Do you know if he's still there?" he asked Annja.

"No idea. He said he had plans to pick up and leave."

"Without notifying the authorities of the murder?" Soto wiped a hand over his face and rapped the pencil angrily upon the manila file. "Two dead bodies in one day, Miss Creed. That's got to be some kind of record. Is it?"

She simply shrugged.

For the next twenty minutes she relayed all the details, the directions she'd taken to get to the site, the condition of the place when she had arrived days earlier as well as how it had appeared this morning. Crockett's demeanor and any other details she could recall. She neglected to mention the struggle with Crockett and nearly cutting off his hand or that Garin Braden had accompanied her. Surely they had found the AK-47, and if Crockett was smart he wouldn't have handled it after Garin had wiped it clean of prints.

Soto had almost rubbed his forehead raw by the time they finished. Incredible as it sounded, she knew he believed her and was doing a thorough job of police work, which she appreciated. But he could stop with the gibes about her attracting death at any time.

"Is there anything else you need from me, Officer Soto?"

His tension-laden sigh must've hurt his throat, he'd used it so often since sitting down across the table from her. "I don't believe so. We appreciate your efforts, Señorita Creed. Know that we will pursue this matter. Also know that you are not required to take chase should you witness yet another illegal occurrence during your stay in our city. Why I have to warn you about that baffles me, but something tells me it is necessary."

Again, a reply wasn't necessary.

The other officer excused herself, leaving them alone.

"As for stumbling upon dead bodies, I suggest you

avoid yet another by keeping to the well-populated tourist sections of town."

"I'll take that into consideration. There is one other thing."

"Which is?"

"I wanted to tell it directly to you because it may be sensitive information."

He turned to look at the closed door then shrugged. "Are you making another assumption, señorita?"

"I'm not sure. It's a detail Jonathan Crockett gave me. He said the gunmen who murdered Simon Klosky and looted the site were with the Cádiz police."

Soto clasped the pencil in a grip that should have snapped it in two.

"I thought you should know," she added.

He nodded. "I appreciate you giving me all the facts when I had asked for them."

Meaning, he probably still thought she was holding back information. "That's it. That's all I know."

That he hadn't protested the suspicion struck her, and now she worried she may have spilled the beans to someone who already had that information.

"Did you have plans to leave Cádiz soon?"

"Probably tomorrow afternoon," she said, though that would be if she could learn something about the stolen artifacts and pass the information along to James Harlow. She sensed Soto didn't like that answer. "I've a few details at the museum to settle tomorrow and then I'm off on a flight back to New York City."

"I know the museum staff works late hours. Take care of those details tonight. I've gone ahead and booked you a midnight flight." Soto dug inside his coat pocket and handed her a plane ticket. He gestured for her to pick up her backpack from the floor near the door. "I'll assign an officer to escort you to the museum and then on to the La Parra Airport in Jerez. Good evening, Señorita Creed. It's been nothing but a delight having you visit our city."

She snatched the ticket and shoved it in the backpack. "If it's been so delightful, then why are you so eager to get rid of me?"

"Rid of you? Not at all. I merely thought it a courtesy to offer the flight. Do you not appreciate that?"

She nodded. He was reading her, and she'd best keep up her defenses. "Yes, of course. Where am I headed?"

"London. You're on your own from there."

"You'll contact me if you need someone to look over the bronze artifact connected to the Diego Montera case?"

"We work with experts at the university and the museum, Señorita Creed."

"Of course."

So why did she sense those experts would never learn about the case? Could the police really be involved with the looting at Crockett's site? She hadn't given Soto James Harlow's name. She wasn't sure if that was a good thing or not.

With that, she was removed from the office. Annja

felt as though the police escort to the patrol car was a bit much. Clearly, they wanted her out of town.

Her hackles rose. Something was not right in Cádiz.

But now was no time to make a break. She slid into the back of the patrol car and closed her eyes while she was "escorted" to the museum. She made a big show of going inside, but couldn't find James Harlow. An assistant said he'd gone home an hour earlier. She had all her photos on the laptop. All she required now was a few notes on the coins, things the camera might not pick up. Which would take longer than the half hour the officer had allowed her.

Not a problem. She'd do that tomorrow.

Back in the patrol car, she was escorted to Jerez de la Frontera, a long, quiet drive Annja used to doze. After being dropped off outside the small airport, she waved to the officer behind the wheel, who nodded politely to her—then did not drive away.

She lingered inside the airport, certain she was being watched, and then decided to approach the counter and ask about exchanging the ticket she had for another a few days from now. By the time she turned back, the patrol car had left.

Annja dashed outside to hail a taxi.

9

Once back in Cádiz, Annja directed the cabdriver to pull around behind the back of the Hotel Blanca. She wasn't going to take the chance of being seen. She hadn't thought she'd been followed from the airport, but she had learned to always keep one eye over her shoulder.

Tipping the cabbie and thanking him for the ride, she entered through the hotel's kitchen door, which was propped open to cool the place down after an evening of hot ovens. She walked with purpose through the dark kitchen, lit by a single fluorescent strip over the grill that reeked of something burned. No workers in sight this late at night, but someone had to be around. Probably out on a cigarette break. She'd lucked out, and leaving the kitchen, she quickly found the hall to the guest rooms.

Landing in her room, the short yet comfy bed called to her. She dropped her backpack at the door, walked up to the bed and fell forward, and didn't rise until sunlight burned across her eyelids.

ROOM SERVICE DROPPED off a plate of fried eggs, fresh sausage, strawberries and some pale yellow juice that didn't look like fresh-squeezed oranges and had the thick, sweet taste of bananas, or perhaps plantains. After a shower, Annja sat on the bed, powered up her laptop and logged on to archaeology.net to scan for anything similar to the bull statue. It would help to be able to match it to others of similar design, yet she already knew where it came from.

That wasn't true. She knew where it had been dug up, but not the country of origin. It could have been brought to the dig site from anywhere. A museum was her best bet. So she did a search on robberies and entered the names of the museums in the Andalusian area.

The statue wasn't the key to this mystery regarding the dead man carrying stolen artifacts, but it was a starting point. The real mystery was what had been in the crate, because that had been valuable enough to commit murder.

The eggs were rubbery, but the savory sausage made up for them. Lying on her side and clicking through the Photos section on the vast online forum, she did find a few pictures close to what she'd found at the dig site and transferred them to her online cloud storage files.

Primarily a fertility god, when shown in human form, she was surprised to see Baal associated with the Illuminati. That was a new one to her, but then again, the Illuminists tended to lay claim to any number of symbols, including the Star of David.

The statue she had unearthed bore a remarkable re-semblance to an Iron Age bronze statue, but without the actual artifact in hand again, she couldn't date it.

Then she found a hit. In 1920 a cache of artifacts had been stolen from the Cádiz museum. It had been a bra-zen, daytime heist involving two patrons who simply walked off with a bag stuffed with artifacts, including a silver platter believed to have been a gift to Isabella of Castile from the French King, Louis XI, and vari-ous gold pieces.

"Wonder why James Harlow didn't know about that."

It was a brief article and Annja didn't expect a twenty-first-century employee to know the history of the museum, though an unsolved robbery may be something talked about over the years. But now she had an answer that didn't really move her ahead. They'd already suspected the items stolen. That's what had landed the pieces in the ground in Puerto Real. But who had stolen them recently?

She looked up Jonathan Crockett, but his credentials all checked out. She knew that already, having checked him out before working with him last week. He hadn't officially headed any digs since the 1990s, but she'd guessed that about him after an afternoon of chatter at the dig site. This was now a hobby for him, and he snatched up any digs he could, which were mostly small projects others couldn't be bothered to even acknowl-edge or to get funding for.

She couldn't find any criminal files attached to his

name, but that didn't mean he hadn't done the very bad something he'd offhandedly confessed to. A man usually had a good reason to avoid the police. *She* now had good reason to avoid the Cádiz police. The look on Soto's face when she'd described yet another dead body had been priceless.

Giving up on the eggs, she pushed the plate aside and traced her finger through the sausage grease before licking it off. Woman did not function by healthy eating alone. Protein must never be overlooked, even the rich, fatty stuff buried under gravy that tasted so good her ears hurt.

Checking her watch, she saw that it was still only 7:00 a.m. Too early to venture out to shop for a change of clothing. She wanted to wait until the streets were filled with tourists.

César Soto made her itchy for reasons she couldn't pinpoint. Annja knew that familiar itchy feeling never boded well for her future.

It made sense the local police would have no need of her expertise. There were many professors at the university who could help them with the archaeological details of the case. And the museum was filled with experts who far outranked her in degrees of knowledge.

Typing in *Diego Montera* on Google, she decided the search would be too broad, so added *guitarist* after his name. The search engine brought up more than sixty entries, so she went back and also added *Cádiz,* which narrowed it down to eight.

The first two entries were for men far older than
the man she had seen lying facedown on the hotel bed.
Mid-twenties had been her guess.

The third entry brought up the Gato Negra club in the
old city, which placed it dead center in the original part
of town. The link opened onto a photo of the nightclub,
which featured a black door nestled unassumingly in a
brick wall, no neon, no fancy signs. Looked as if you
had to know the secret password to enter.

She clicked on the Performers page. Pictures of half a
dozen guitarists were listed with short bios beside each.
Diego's picture was last, and since the names were not
alphabetical, she guessed talent or tenure ranked them.
Bright blue eyes beamed at her from the laptop, and his
curly dark hair had been tugged loosely behind his head.
Handsome and vulnerable in a manner that struck her.

His bio read "Diego Montera, 24, is a guitar prod-
igy who has been playing since he could hold the instrument. His family is the famous Granada Monteras
of toreros."

"Too young to die. Poor guy." And his family was
into bullfighting? She wondered what had compelled
Diego to study music instead. "Couldn't have been
easy," she said, thinking to herself the family tradi-
tions in this neck of the woods ran deep through their
culture like a vein of marble.

She suspected a guitar player in a city filled with
guitarists didn't command a high income, and if he had
no help from family it was possible he'd been lured to

criminal activity. And if the operation was small-time, they could hire out young and naive liaisons to transport stolen goods to buyers. Use the liaison a few times, pay him cash, then ditch him before the guy got too smart and nosy or attracted police attention.

And if the police were involved? Even more reason to use average Joes who needed to pick up a few extra bucks and who could be controlled by threat.

But what had been in the wooden crate?

The Cádiz police were probably working the same angle, checking the guitarist's background and following his leads.

Bookmarking the page, she then clicked through to read about the flamenco club. There were dozens of clubs like it in the city, commonly dark, cavelike respites for aficionados to slip away for a drink of strong whiskey and some music, song and dance. The origins of flamenco traced back to the caves that pocketed the mountains of Spain. To this day, Annja was aware Gypsies still lived in the caves. As well, they'd become tourist features, offering *casas-cueva* as hotels, and with amenities like electricity and water.

Clicking on the Gato Negra's Dancers page, she found three listed. There was a picture of the first, Marguerita Esperanza. She was probably in her forties and the photographer had captured her in a spin, her elegant red *bata de cola* dress splayed about her ankles in blurred motion.

Two additional dancers, Anastasia Samaritan and

Ava Vital were also listed. An ornamental capital *A*
served as place marker in lieu of a photo for Anastasia. And for Ava Vital an interesting symbol provided
her placeholder.

Annja clicked on the symbol to enlarge it, though
the one click only brought up a low-resolution, pixi-
lated version of the picture. It looked familiar. A wing
curled to a decorative ball on the longest feathered tip.
It resembled the symbol she'd seen on the dancer-cum-
sniper's wrist last night. She was sure of it.

"Really?" She sat up, staring at the symbol and cau-
tioning her active imagination from drawing conclu-
sions.

Ava Vital had a tie to Diego Montera, dancing at the
same club where he played. That didn't mean anything.
They could merely be coworkers who had no relationship beyond the club. Or they could be friends. Perhaps
he played while she danced. They could know each
other very well simply by sharing the music.

Would the man's murder be enough for a woman to
go vigilante and attempt to shoot another man? And
why? Maybe they had a bad relationship and someone
had an affair? Didn't make sense. That only worked
provided that Ava had had an affair with Manuel. Or
hell, it could be the other pairing. Annja had no gaydar
whatsoever. She doubted it, though. Didn't feel right.
And Ava had said she was going after a murderer.

No. The two working in the same place had to be a
coincidence.

Could Diego Montera possibly be connected to Manuel Bravo? Montera's family were toreros. But Spain was filled with bullfighters. Didn't mean they all knew one another. Though they would know the more popular names, and all matadors traveled, so those from Granada would know others from all over the country.

"Are you who I think you are?" Annja said to the symbol on the screen, wishing there'd been a picture of Ava to verify her guess. "I need to talk to you."

Typing in *Manuel Bravo* and *Diego Montera* brought up no links. She searched *Montera* and found the names of his brothers. None appeared to have risen in the torero ranks to fame, and she could connect none to Bravo's name.

Her cell phone buzzed and she turned over on the bed to grab it from the nightstand. Garin's voice greeted her and asked where she'd disappeared to last night.

"After returning to the stadium, I found I was invited to another date at the police station. Seems they enjoy my company here in Cádiz and can't resist inviting me over whenever they have opportunity."

"You've become such a social climber, Annja."

She laughed. "I managed to track down the sniper and thought it would be helpful if I gave the authorities her description."

"You tracked her down…and then let her go?"

"Not on purpose."

"Ah, so she got the better of you. Annja." The tutting sound he made was very unlike Garin Braden.

"She got lucky." With the help of some mischievous children and a laundry line. "Anyway, while I was being interrogated I helped the sketch artist to complete a perfect rendition of the mysterious sniper who may also be a flamenco dancer."

A flamenco-dancing sniper? How weird was that? Actually, it was kind of cool.

"I suppose you mentioned the body at the dig?"

"Had an ethical obligation to do so."

"I bet the Cádiz police have a file an inch thick on you by now, Annja."

"Pretty close. They don't like me much. I was given a police escort to the airport—do not pass Go, do not collect two hundred dollars. The police wanted me out of town, Garin."

"I'm reading from your tone you take that as strange. Yet I'm aware that you have been escorted from various places many times. Hell, happens to me all the time. But you're still here, so you take the forced escort about as seriously as I tend to."

"Yes, but why don't they want me here? I didn't give any indication I had a desire to meddle in the case."

"Yet you did, and you will continue to do so."

He didn't get points for the obvious. "I also provided a good likeness of the suspect."

"Maybe someone recognized her?"

"I did mention Crockett's suggestion that the police had murdered Simon."

"You didn't." He paused. "And?"

"No comment from the officer. He pretty much shoved me out the station following that."

"You think the police are covering up something?"

"Maybe. I don't know. I'm not investigating a murder—I'm trying to track stolen antiquities to their dealer. I don't think the sniper is a connection, either, but it's interesting enough that I can't set it aside. I still can't place how she would be connected to the bullfighter. She said something about going after a murderer. That can only be Bravo, but don't you think that's pushing the whole protest thing a bit far?"

Garin sighed over the phone line. "Why don't you let me swing by and pick you up for a leisurely day at Manuel's villa? He expressed concern over your absence last night."

"Leisurely does sound tempting, but I've got to head over to the museum this morning to complete my work with the medieval coins. Despite the distractions, I do take my work seriously. Give me the directions to Manuel's home and I'll get there this afternoon. I wouldn't miss an opportunity to learn more about him."

"That sounds strangely investigative. He's a good friend, Annja. I'll warn you to be respectful."

"I will."

He gave her directions and Annja headed off to the museum.

AFTER A FEW HOURS of taking notes on the coins and assuring herself there was nothing else she could do with the materials, Annja thanked James Harlow as he escorted her outside to the shady Plaza de Mina that fronted the museum.

"No luck on the investigation?" he prompted.

"A sniper has been added to the mix."

"Really? How does that tie in with stolen artifacts?"

"I'm not sure it does. It's an interesting added sideshow. And yet, I tracked the stolen bull back to this museum."

"How? When was it stolen?"

"In the 1920s. I found a brief article online. Stolen by two patrons who apparently just walked out with a shopping list of items. Obviously they didn't get very far with the artifacts if we found one of them in Puerto Real. But there were no linked articles detailing if they were ever caught."

"I'll have to look that up. That's an excellent reason to get the bull returned to the museum instead of routing it to the university."

He sounded as though he'd won a race, and he'd just spat on his competition. Harlow punctuated his satisfaction with a tap of his cane on the sidewalk.

"I'm glad you can use the information to lay claim to the stolen statue. I found a close match from the Iron Age. I'm sure it represents Baal."

"Iron Age? Do you think it's that old?"

"No. But again, I didn't handle it for long. I'd love to get my hands on the thing again. If you look it up, I'm sure the museum has records of acquisition."

"Good call. I'll head right back to do that."

"Has the museum ever sought to investigate prove-nance on articles they receive that are undocumented?"

"Of course, but there is only myself and a rotation of assistants, and as you've seen we're kept quite busy with the daily operational routine."

She understood. And tracking provenance on items was like searching for the proverbial needle in a hay-stack. Generally a fruitless venture, especially when dealers could draw up fake papers and letters.

"While we are very choosy about the items we re-ceive," Harlow said with a glance at his wristwatch, "it's difficult to refuse donations, you understand."

"Yes, and if one museum won't accept the donation, then the wealthy benefactor will simply turn elsewhere and mark your museum off their list for future dona-tions."

"Exactly. It's a wicked blade we balance."

"Made even more wicked when murder is involved."

"We did not receive any of the artifacts associated with that murder, Annja. Don't be so quick to pin that heinous crime on us."

"Sorry, I didn't mean it that way. But can you be sure you haven't received items previously from the same seller?"

Harlow sighed and winced. He stopped about ten yards into the Plaza de Mina, in the shadows from the tree canopy, to rub his thigh.

"Injury hurting you today?"

He nodded. "Injured my hip, but it manifests as pain in my thigh. It's been trouble for days now. Ever since you arrived, actually. Odd, isn't it?"

If she were self-conscious, Annja would take his comment as a subtle dig against her being in town, but she wasn't and so let it slide.

"I've heard skullcap is an excellent herbal remedy for muscle aches. It may be something to look into."

"Thanks, but cannabis is another excellent pain reliever. So you're leaving Cádiz, then?"

"Er…" He had suggested she look into the stolen artifacts, and yet everything he said spoke against that suggestion. "Not today. Heading out to El Bravo's villa, actually. I was invited there through a mutual friend."

"A marvelous hero for the city. You got to watch him fight?"

"Yes, he truly does deserve the moniker El Bravo." She shook Harlow's hand and again thanked him for the invite. "I'll check in with you on my progress regarding the article. And keep you posted if I get any closer to the looters."

"I'd be disappointed if you didn't. Good afternoon, Annja."

HE WAITED FOR THE TALL, pretty young archaeologist to enter the crowd milling in the Plaza de Mina before pressing his speed dial.

"Things go well?"

The voice on the phone paused, which was remarkable because he knew her to usually be staid and inscrutable. "I got the item. It's been processed. You should have it in your hands. What's the problem?"

"The problem is, it got filtered through the wrong hands. Why weren't you more careful?"

"I always use the guy on the docks. You knew that."

"Yes, and I was taking a chance on you that apparently failed."

"Hell, where is it now?"

"I believe you'll find the object much closer than you expect."

"What is that supposed to mean?"

"Don't take that tone with me. You promised to keep this quiet and it's become everything but."

"Well, if you'd stop being so cryptic maybe I could figure out what the hell you're talking about."

"The piece was found at the scene of a murder."

"The one in the hotel yesterday morning? Don't blame me for that."

"I'm not. And yet, there was another murder I know I can blame on you."

"James, just spit it out. Where's the piece?"

"It's been taken into police evidence."

She whistled, a common reaction to surprises that bothered James to no end.

"I want that statue," he said. "And I won't tolerate another mistake."

She blew out a heavy breath over the receiver. Probably rubbing her forehead and pacing, as she should be.

She was an amazing lover and an expert marksman, and he'd thought she had the operation under control, but this slipup made him nervous. And with Annja Creed nosing about, he wanted to quickly sweep this all under a nice dusty carpet deep in the bowels of the museum.

WHILE STROLLING THROUGH the old marketplace and admiring the stalls of colorful fruits and vegetables and handmade items such as baskets, shoes and clothing, Annja decided something a bit dressier than her cargo pants and T-shirt would be appropriate for her visit to Bravo's villa.

In a tourist shop hugging a stucco building that also boasted a pottery shop, she purchased a long, colorful skirt that wasn't too frilly. But it was a style a lot of the tourists seemed to wear, along with a red blouse with cap sleeves. Changing in the back room behind a blanket hung up for privacy, she twisted her hair back into a chignon and stuck a decorative jet stick in to secure it.

Not too costumey, and pretty. It would be respectable for dinner. Annja hailed a cab and took it out to El Bravo's villa, which sat at the western edge of Cádiz on the beach.

10

The matador's home was an unassuming whitewashed adobe villa at the edge of town, overlooking the sea. Magenta begonias lined the drive and the house, softening the bleak white structure. Seagulls circled in lazy turns out across the water and back toward land.

A thin man with a thick nose and equally thick, dark mustache who introduced himself as Manuel's butler greeted her at the door. "Señorita, Maestro Manuel is out back caping the calves."

That sounded too intriguing not to explore further. Annja thanked the man and followed his direction back through the house.

As she walked through the home, taking in the interior adobe style and clean, spare furnishings, her eyes fell on many Spanish artifacts from all time periods. The majority depicted bulls. A small ivory carving of a leaping bull looked Scythian in origin, but then she corrected herself. It was probably an ox. A bull-headed lyre sat in a recessed wall pocket under halogen lights, the horns ivory and the instrument made from wood she didn't have time to guess at as she followed the butler's lead. A teak statue of a matador posed before a bull had to be a recent creation, but the curvaceous form of it appealed to her.

Briefly she wondered if Manuel had interest in a bronze Baal statue, but just because he murdered bulls didn't make him a murderer of men. And besides, if he had been interested, he would have taken the statue along with whatever—

"Stop it," she muttered to herself. She was pinning the blame on the man without probable cause.

Annja paused to read the engraving on a modest plaque hanging at eye level. From the local St. Mary's orphanage, thanking Manuel Bravo for his charity. It was known that after the fight he bought the bull he'd slain and gave it to a shelter to slaughter and distribute meals to the homeless. It was one of the many reasons the locals adored their hero of the corrida.

The real spectacle was the patio behind the house, decorated with white-and-black paper lamps, strung from the palm trees that curved away from the sea. Add to that an unspoiled white-sand beach and it presented the perfect atmosphere for an afternoon siesta.

She spied a fenced barn west of the property. A few men were calling to a bull, likely a calf, because she couldn't see any animal movement over the hip-high fence.

At the butler's direction, she wandered across the sand that segued into dirt. She'd bought a cheap pair of flip-flops to accompany the skirt and wished she was wearing her hiking boots right now, no matter the fashion faux pas.

Bravo's property was an official ranch, though the acreage was small. Gauchos in blue jeans and cowboy hats were Spain's version of the American cowboy. Officer Soto must be a fan of the American version to judge from his headgear.

As she neared the fence, one of the men nodded to her and called to Manuel. The master of the homestead patted the rump of a white calf and sent it scrambling toward the open barn gates where another gaucho waited with a bucket of feed. What did they feed bulls? Food scraps? No, Annja knew cattle were grass feeders, yet there wasn't a lot of pasture nearby, only a narrow strip of grass that abutted the north side of the fence and barn.

"Annja!"

Manuel Bravo gestured for her to join him in the fenced pasture, and not seeing a gate, she hitched herself up on the fence beside a smirking gaucho and, clutching the skirt discreetly to her thigh, swung a leg over and jumped down. Dusty red dirt similar to the topsoil on the dig spumed up around her sandals. She hadn't anticipated tromping next to bulls in a skirt.

The matador's somber smile and long frame stilled her. He'd taken out the ponytail that he wore in the ring, and his thick, curly black hair was slicked along the sides of his head, yet the natural curl in it wanted to coil out above his ears. A dark shadow of stubble coated his jaw and halfway up his cheeks. He wore sleek gray trousers and a loose white shirt. Perhaps a welcome respite from the formfitting suit of lights the torero wore to work.

"Señorita Creed," he said with an easy smile, his eyes raking over her face. "You are stunning in red."

"Thank you. You've got a beautiful home. I noticed you have many artifacts depicting bulls. Are you a collector?"

"Yes, by matter of default, you might say. Every statue or bull object I own has been given to me by friends. That's right, Garin told me you are an archaeologist. I cannot tell you what the objects are worth or where they originated. I just know I like them. Perhaps later you can tell me a little of their history?"

"I'll give it a try. My expertise is medieval, but I recognized a few items."

Though, if he had no idea of their origins, she hated to break it to him that the objects were scientifically worthless. On the other hand, that shouldn't matter to him. Displayed as art, other collectors would place great value on his possessions.

"How are you, Maestro Bravo? I haven't had the opportunity to speak to you since the incident last evening. I was told the bullet didn't strike anywhere near you?"

"I felt it pass by my head, but no, it didn't touch me. I am invincible." He gestured outward with his hands, puffing his chest up in a classic matador's pose. "Be it horn or bullet, El Bravo defies them both."

Prideful, yet for good reason. It took a certain kind of ego to face death day in and day out during the bull-fighting season.

"I suppose the local news reported on it," she guessed.

"National news," he said with a gleam in his eye. "And you," he continued, "you ran off in pursuit of the shooter. Remarkable. So brave a female I have not before known. Señor Braden tells me you lost track of the shooter, though."

"Yes, I'm sorry. I tried. Though I did get a good look at her and gave that description to the police. I'm sure they've shown you the picture. Do you have any idea who she could be?"

"Me? Why should I? Aficionados far and wide love me. I am as startled by the event as everyone else."

"No enemies? Jilted lovers?"

"Ah…" His wince didn't go unnoticed. "I do tend to leave a trail of tearful lovers in my wake, but none so angry as to come after me with a pistol, I assure you."

"It was a sniper rifle. High caliber. And the shooter… Well, the shooter was positioned far enough away that he had to be an expert marksman. Or she, as is the case. I'm sure there are people you meet in your profession who are not always so pleased with your performances?"

"Do you suggest a poor showing in the ring should

prompt someone to come after me with a gun to end my life?"

"No, I didn't mean it like that. That would be an awful excuse for murder. But what about your private life? Something unrelated to the corrida?"

"You suggest there is something in my personal life that would attract a sniper with a death wish for me? And a *female,* at that?" He smiled and made a joke with one of the gauchos.

She shrugged. Any one of the artifacts in his home could start a small war if he'd gotten it from the wrong person. Give a man a valuable object and a reason to protect it and he would, to his death. That went for anyone who might want the valued object or have reason to believe it had been stolen from them. Criminal minds were small and stupid.

Could Ava have been hired by a former owner of one of the artifacts in Bravo's home? A dissatisfied seller? That wouldn't give her reason to be so vehement over the matador's death, to call him a murderer. And if she was a hired assassin she would do the job without emotion or concern for the target.

"I've nothing further to tell you, señorita. I am sorry. Is that what you've come here for? To question me as the police did?"

"No, sorry. I was curious. I'm sure the police have already gone over the details of the incident with you."

He bowed his head, but did not nod in confirmation. "So, an archaeologist. Sounds adventurous, yet...

boring…if you'll excuse my presumption. You like to dig about in the dirt for treasures?"

"I've been known to wield a trowel and boonie hat on many occasions. Not at all boring to me, but I can certainly understand how a man who faces death daily would view it that way. It's not all sitting about and brushing away fine particles of dirt. I'vc been on dives in the Adriatic, climbed the Himalayas and have even eluded pirates in the open seas."

"You are a woman of many talents, Annja Creed. Not in the least, the talent of charm. I have never seen a woman in a skirt leap a fence so gracefully as you just did. You want to learn to cape the bull?" he asked.

"That depends on whether the bull is the size of the one you fought yesterday afternoon in the ring or the size of that little one you sent back inside."

"A little larger than the white calf, who is only six months on his legs," Manuel said. "A yearling is best for practicing capework. Let me show you a few veronicas and then we'll bring out Brutus to test your skill, eh?"

Brutus? But the idea of learning more about what the matador did was irresistible, and Annja agreed.

"Cristo!" Manuel held out his hand. The ranch hand sitting on the fence like a sunbaked vulture tossed Manuel a small red cape, then leaned back against the barn wall and tugged down his hat brim to resume his snooze. "Cristo is my sword bearer."

"He carries all your swords to the fights?"

"That, and he tends to all my travel arrangements,

cleans and folds the capes and helps me dress before a fight. A personal assistant, if you will."

"I could use one of those."

The matador chuckled. "I was hoping you'd arrive before Señor Braden returns," he said, turning the cape in a swishing manner, not looking up at her. "I always prefer time alone with a beautiful woman."

"Thank you. You don't think the skirt will hamper the lesson?"

"It'll handicap you, but I've seen women perform capework while wearing much the same. Just don't allow a horn to hook the fabric."

As the torero moved the cape back and forth in graceful sweeps as if getting the feel for the fabric, Annja cast a glance over the estate. "So all this land is yours? To the sea?"

He nodded. "Family land for centuries. My father was a torero and his father before that. And before that, the Bravo family raised fighting bulls on land off the Bay of Cádiz. They weren't prime bull for fighting. Bad maternal blood gave them a habit of skittishness and cowardliness. Which is why the family switched to pursuing the cape instead of the bull."

"Garin explained you select the bulls you fight beforehand. How do you recognize a cowardly bull from a brave one before it enters the ring?"

"Ah, that's not so easy." He tucked the cape under an arm to use both hands to gesture as he spoke. "Usually both are quite similar before entering the ring. Only after the animal is presented with the challenge of the moving cape does it decide to either stand and charge or stir the dirt with a hoof and snort and put on a cowardly display. I do not like a gutless bull."

"Would make it difficult to do the job of showing the audience both your skill and the bull's skill."

"Oh, yes, very difficult." Manuel held the cape regally, arm out squarely and jaw lifted. "I enter the ring to show the crowd how brave the bull is. Everything I do is designed to display its bravery and give the animal the opportunity to defend its life."

"I saw that while you fought yesterday. And yet…" She wasn't sure how to ask without offending him, but curiosity niggled at her.

"Annja, ask. You have questions about the art of the bullfight? Doubts? Concerns? There is nothing I haven't heard."

"You know the bull is going to die when it enters the ring. You have that advantage."

"Not so. Man and beast enter the ring with equal chance to live or die."

"Okay. Yet how can the animal die a noble death when you and your assistants keep wounding it, wearing it down to exhaustion? There's very little competition."

Manuel gave her a look over his shoulder, yet he assumed a classic matador stance. "Am I not wearied, as well? Accompanying the physical strain, the mental toll is immense when a man must stand before his death daily. Yet if all goes as desired, both competitors give their all to the fight."

"But you've got to reserve your strength for the next fight, and the next. How many bulls have you killed during one corrida?"

"Six. They allowed me all six kills last year in Jerez de la Frontera during a celebration of my one hundredth corrida of the season."

"Congratulations."

He bowed, accepting the accolade with a wink. "I never tire of appreciation from a beautiful woman."

And she was beginning to feel his charm do its work. Annja wasn't sure how to take that. She wasn't here for a flirtation.

"Now to the lesson, yes?" He held out the red cape. "This is a smaller, practice cape. Take it in your left hand and hold it like this."

He stepped beside her to show her how to grip it and then moved her hand left to right until she caught on to the sweeping motion.

"It's not the color that attracts the bull?" she asked.

"No, it's the motion. They don't process color as we do, although bright colors do attract them. The *toro* has a central dead zone in their vision, so it's always wise to center yourself before the bull. Until it is released into the ring, the bull has never seen a man on foot. Often great bulls are sacrificed before even getting to the ring because some stupid kids have snuck into the field to tease them."

"Aren't the bulls many years old when they reach the ring?"

"Four or five years, yes. They are kept on secluded ranches and guarded well. See here. If I work my cape successfully, the bull will not be aware of me until the moment I wish to be revealed. I sweep it this way and that, back and forth, making many veronicas. Passes. Then I allow it to see my feet." He swept the cape slowly before him in demonstration. "Then my knees and up to my hips. Then finally, when I wish it, I reveal myself to my opponent, and for the first time, it marks me, a man. Standing before it, a target. That is why the torero must stand relatively still when closest to the bull."

"I was fascinated at how you seemed to embrace the animal as it swept past you, turning its body to curve before you. And your arm slid over its back, almost hugging it."

"Keeping my balance and also, yes, there is a fine moment when man and bull can be so close as to be one. The crowd cheers, but I no longer hear them. My heart pounds. I cannot hear anything but my life racing through my veins."

"I bet."

"It is a sacred moment all toreros seek. There is no other feeling like it on this earth. It is in that moment our love for death is fulfilled."

"I've heard matadors love death."

"Just a little bit," he said and winked.

Annja swept the cape before her, impressed with the swish she'd given it. "Like this?"

"Yes. And then a sweep to the side as you step to the right. Feet together and legs straight. Keep a good, strong line with your body. Hips and torso long and shoulders proud. That's very good, Annja."

His hand moved along her back as if to correct her posture and she straightened. But she realized the touch was more personal when his hand stopped at her shoulder and he leaned in to smile at her.

"Don't let the bull smell your fear," he warned.

She wasn't a woman who scared easily, even when faced by a gun-wielding terrorist, but animals weren't so easily confronted. "Isn't it impossible not to be afraid?"

"Yes, it is. A torero who is unafraid has lost his bravery. That's why we say our prayers before each fight and tend the *meada de miedo* right before going out into the ring."

"The big fear leak?" she translated literally, smiling.

He chuckled. "Exactly as it sounds. The big leak of fear that relieves us before walking out into the ring. Otherwise, we'd surely piss our pants when the bull charges. It all shows in those tight *trajes cortes* we wear."

"That's for sure."

He tilted his head at her, his eyes twinkling. "The women always linger on the pants. You are all much alike in your hearts. Ah, but I love women. Just wish it was easier to have a relationship during the season."

"I imagine you're a bit of a rock star on the corrida circuit."

"I fight at least every other night during the season. No time for more than a one-night stand. Not that there's anything wrong with that."

He winked at her a third time, and then he whistled over his shoulder. Cristo snapped awake, jumped over the fence and disappeared inside the barn.

"Let's see what you've got," Manuel said. "You ready for the bull?"

"No." He'd only given her a few minutes of instruction. All she could do was turn the cape this way and that. "This bull doesn't have horns, does it?"

"Yes, but they're small and blunt. We keep them that way for the boys who come to practice on the weekends."

Horns. Great.

But if mere boys practiced with these bulls, Annja wasn't about to show cowardice. On the other hand, who was she kidding? She'd take a jungle guerrilla wielding a machine gun to a bull bred for violence.

She gripped the cape and eyed the barn door where she saw the head of a dark-faced calf scamper along behind the fence. Scampering was good. Yet it was much taller than the calf that had just been in the ring.

She took a step toward Manuel and wasn't afraid to silently admit relief when he remained close beside her.

"I admire a woman who is not afraid of new challenges," Manuel said as the calf burst into the ring, trotting toward the opposite side of the fence. Its black shoulders were broader than most cows she'd seen.

"That's not a yearling," Annja said.

"Brutus may be closer to two years. No worries, Annja. I'm right here. Perform the veronica I showed you. Use graceful, long movements. And keep the cape to the side of you in case the calf should charge aggressively."

Manuel whistled sharply, bringing up the bull's head. The beast trotted toward them, playful in its steps, but as soon as Annja flicked the cape to the right, it dodged right and headed toward the fluttering fabric. Its short horns skimmed the cape and he made a whole pass on her right.

"I did it," she said, quickly turning to attract the bull on the other side. Again it charged, and again, she easily steered it around her.

"Olé!" Manuel clapped, as did the ranch hand who had set the bull free. "Now try it without moving your feet so much, Annja. Hold your body straight and glide along the bull's body."

The calf's head was as high as her shoulder, and this time she stood, legs together, and her side facing the charging beast. Waiting until the last moment, she flicked the cape to the right. Except the calf didn't veer right. She stumbled, seeing it coming right toward her, and stepped wrong on her foot.

Swept from her feet, a strong arm clasped her under her breasts and swung her around and away from the charge of the bull. "I have you," Manuel said, still cling-ing tightly as he set her on her feet. "You steady?"

She nodded, but he didn't release her.

"Guess I got a little cocky with that one. I'd better stick to the basic moves and running for my life when the thing gets too close."

Manuel laughed and squeezed her in a hug. His cheek brushed hers and she registered the scent of his spicy aftershave. Catching a glimpse of Cristo, who rolled his eyes at the flirtation he'd likely seen many times before, she shoved herself out of Manuel's grip and handed him the cape.

"I think that's enough for today."

"Yes, the bull got the better of you. But no worries. There's always tomorrow. You didn't feel the hoof?"

"The hoof?"

He pointed to her leg. Lifting her skirt, she saw a dusty red smear of dirt from her knee to her ankle. The bull must have almost stepped on her foot. And in these sandals, that could have resulted in broken bones. Not good.

"It's nothing." She tried to brush the dirt off, but it clung to her. "Your dinner guests will think you pushed me."

"Ha-ha! I like you, Annja Creed." The matador turned and blocked her against the barn, putting both hands to the wall over her shoulders and pressing his body against hers.

Annja reacted by drawing up her knee. He gave a small hiss and relented, but didn't step back.

"To be bedded by El Bravo is a great victory," he muttered quietly. "Let me show you how I tame American women."

"I kinda like remaining wild and free. I'm sorry, Señor Bravo, if I've given you the wrong impression. I'm just here as a friend of Garin's."

"Are you his lover? I should have asked him." Manuel stepped back, taking in Annja's figure through the skirt and red blouse that now felt gaudy and not at all comfortable. "He is a very lucky man."

"Garin and I are not…" Lovers. Or friends. Or even allies, at any given moment. "I should freshen up before he returns. Thank you for showing me your—" moves "—capework, Señor Bravo."

She liked him. But nothing more. She had no desire whatsoever to strike another mark on her bedpost just because he was a celebrity. Besides, Ava's accusation stuck in her brain. A man capable of slaying an animal for a crowd's enjoyment could also be capable of murder.

"Go ahead and use the washroom in the villa," he said, gesturing to the house. "The butler will show you where it is. I'll be right in."

THE MUSEUM'S DATABASE was packed with information but not easy to search on as the ancient operating system never seemed to merit an update come the biyearly budget reviews. Only over the past decade had the museum taken to transferring the older paper records to digital format, and that was a slow go considering it was a one-man job. With such a vast filing system—and most of it in archival boxes in the basement—not everything was electronically searchable. But James Harlow managed to find what he was looking for after forty-five minutes of attempting one search keyword after the next.

The image on the screen was of a black-and-white photo of the bronze bull statue. A document detailing the acquisition of the small item and postulating its origins as seventeenth century, representing a pagan god of fertility, was also included. It was a small trinket in the overall scheme of statues and totems. The museum had only placed it on the floor for display in 1921. It was stolen not three weeks later.

"Well, I'll be. It really does belong to us."

James Harlow sat back in the creaky desk chair he would never get rid of. Just because something wasn't smooth and polished didn't make it useless. The picture of the bronze bull statue was grainy and black-and-white, having been taken in the early part of the last century.

Now that he had a clear picture of it, his brain was jolted with recall of what, exactly, it was. Years ago he'd been given information on this little bull. At the time it had fascinated him; history had virtually lost all information pertaining to the prize. Hell, even the archives hadn't had the proper details.

Well, they hadn't held it long enough to do proper research on the acquisition. With a scan over the document data he verified the acquisition date. Harold Wilson—a name that had no significance to Harlow— had donated it after returning from a trip to Guatemala. It wasn't at all Aztec in nature, and there was no certificate of provenance. But that didn't mean much. If what Harlow had been told about the object was true, it had originated in Spain. The museum apparently had accepted the donation with a blind eye.

He typed in Harold Wilson's name and found a few more donations over a ten-year period. A gold neck plate that did feature Aztec hieroglyphs. No certificate of provenance. A silver tea service that was completely modern, and Harlow thought perhaps it was the beaten old set in the cafeteria. Could be. They used a desiccated elephant tusk to hold down papers in the IT department. If you could label a staff of one an entire department.

"This should make it easier to get it returned," he said and hit Print.

Someone had to have known exactly what the statue was when it was stolen in 1921, Harlow postulated. Yet they hadn't gotten far if Annja Creed had dug up the booty in Jerez.

"Or maybe they hadn't had a clue," he murmured as he tugged down a scruffy notebook he'd labeled neatly with a Sharpie marker in the upper right corner on a piece of medical tape: London, 1995.

The year he'd met Rockford LePlante, a man who made Indiana Jones look like an amateur. He'd traversed every inch of the world, including islands rumored to be populated with headhunters. If issued a challenge, he jumped. If given a deadline, he beat it by hours or days. He was known to wield a machete and semiautomatic at all times and could judge a poisonous snake from a harmless viper at striking distance. He was currently on a quest for the Fountain of Youth, and Harlow wouldn't be surprised if the man found it. LePlante might have gotten along well with Annja Creed, but he wouldn't have appreciated her morals interfering with a devotion to the quest.

The things Harlow had learned from Rockford could fill volumes, and as luck would have it, Harlow took notes about everything. He paged through the moleskin notebook, one of the few he hadn't allowed his assistant to transfer to digital format. There were some things a man must keep to himself. Secrets about treasures, namely.

The page he recalled flipped over and he traced a finger over the pencil sketch of the statue Rockford had drawn as he'd been describing it. The man had once seen the bronze statue, and then it had been lost. A small trinket, he'd said. No one would ever know its true value or that its real treasure was in the belly of the bull.

"The belly of the bull," Harlow muttered. "Clever."

Through the centuries many a valuable treasure had been hidden inside innocuous artifacts to transport them through customs and shipping ports without alerting authorities. Sometimes people innocently displayed the outer shell in their homes for centuries without ever being the wiser about what it held inside.

In this particular bull's belly there was rumored to be an exquisite jewel far more valuable than the Hope Diamond. Rockford hadn't been clear on what it was exactly, but he'd thought it wasn't a diamond. Perhaps a ruby, maybe an emerald. He had hoped it was a ruby simply for the effect it would have. The blood it would represent. And should the statue ever be cracked open, well, then, it would be quite the find. The adventurer believed the thing had been created in the seventeenth century, as a gift to King Louis XIII from Philip III of Spain on the eve of his daughter Anne's marriage to the French king. But the carriage the future queen had been riding in had been looted en route, possibly by the very guards escorting her. The statue had been passed through the centuries, no one ever the wiser to what might lie in its belly. The only proof was Rockford having seen some designs for statues by a little-known seventeenth-century artist who had once produced some jewels for Philip III's wife, Margaret.

"Yes," James muttered and slapped the notebook shut. "Quite the find." And yet it had been passed over and left behind near a dead man's body. "Interesting."

11

The matador's house was a marvel of modern design accented with various ancient artifacts placed in recessed nooks and standing on the floor in the corners of most rooms. Annja passed a bronze bull displayed under LED lights in the hallway and paused to look it over. About a sixth the size of the so-called calf she'd learned to cape, its sinuous lines and smooth surface leaned toward a modern sculpture. The horns were tipped with silver and one of the ears was pierced with a silver ring featuring what resembled Celtic ribbon work around the circumference.

Nice, but not old, she decided.

She had no idea matadors made so much money they could afford such rare relics, but then again, Manuel had said everything he owned had been gifts to him. The man certainly had generous friends.

Searching for the bathroom, she strolled past an open door and peeked inside. It wasn't the room she was looking for, but the low lighting glowing off the walls tempted her to walk inside the simple, small window-less room.

The plaster walls were illuminated by a stretch of halogen lights tracking across the ceiling. Nothing decorated the walls, except for trowel swishes in the plaster beneath the muted ocher paint. A simple damask-padded bench fashioned from dark-stained wood sat against one wall.

The wall opposite the door hosted a shrine of sorts, or possibly an altar. A dark wood table rose before a cushioned prie-dieu. On the altar, a few candles and an incense burner sat on a white cloth edged with elaborate white tatting.

The most fascinating votive crowns hung over the altar. Two of them, suspended from delicate gold chain link. Visigothic in origin, from the seventh or eighth century, if her guess was correct. They had once been fashioned by kings as gifts to cathedrals. Particularly valuable and rare.

She had only seen one, in the Madrid museum years ago—part of the treasure of Guarrazar—and didn't believe there were many others out there. Not in museums, anyway. Many had been lost over the centuries, and probably hung in the homes of the wealthy, and perhaps…one suddenly intriguing matador.

She stood on tiptoe to inspect the larger of the two. The crownlike circle of pounded gold was dotted with rubies and sapphires. Another gold circlet was suspended above the first on elaborate gold chains, to give it the votive appearance. The double crown was rare, as the single was most common. The Visigoth kings once sat beneath them on their thrones—they hadn't actually worn them as crowns. Letters around the base sometimes spelled out a king's signature. And one of these crowns did have letters. It read in Latin "Given by Alaric."

"A Visigoth king?" The name sounded familiar. If he'd ruled in medieval times she would have known for sure.

How El Bravo had come to possess two votive crowns baffled her. More generous friends?

"They should be in a museum," she whispered and lifted a finger, but then stopped. It felt sacrilegious to touch it. "No, they can't be authentic." They had to be copies or fakes.

"Did you touch them?" Manuel asked from the doorway.

Unaware he'd been watching her, Annja slid her hand around behind her waist and shook her head. "No."

How long had he been standing there? And she, a guest in his home, had been caught snooping. Even with the dirt still streaking her leg, it was obvious she hadn't been looking for the bathroom.

"They're beautiful," she offered.

"This is my private sanctuary. I never allow people inside."

"I'm sorry. The door was open, and I was looking—"

"Come out of here now. Please." He'd lost the teasing charm he'd shown her in the practice ring.

Annja knew most matadors kept prayer altars. They never stepped into the ring without honoring the ritual of asking for blessings.

"Forgive me, please," she said as he closed the door with a hard click of the lock behind her. "I was drawn to the votive crowns. The only one I've ever seen was in the Madrid museum."

"And now you have seen two more."

"They aren't authentic, are they?"

"The washroom is next door." He gestured ahead without meeting her eyes.

And then he shoved her shoulder against the wall, and his dark eyes found hers. Heartbeat racing, Annja felt like the bull standing before the torero that intended her death. "Tell me truthfully. Did you touch anything?"

She shook her head.

"I don't like it when people touch my things. Especially my sacred things."

"No, I didn't. I was going to, but I didn't. I swear it."

His fingers squeezed her shoulder close to her neck, pinching the artery painfully, but then he let up and, with a bow, gestured she walk ahead of him.

She made quick work in the bathroom, washing off the red dust on her bare leg and splashing water on her face. Staring at her reflection, she wondered what the matador was involved in.

She'd feel him out during supper, but she'd be wary. Manuel Bravo could prove more deadly out of the ring.

GARIN HAD ARRIVED while she was washing up, and Annja joined him and Manuel in the sitting room outside the dining area. Both men puffed on cigars, and when offered, Annja accepted a Cuban Churchill. A few puffs opened up to rich notes of caramel and hickory, and relaxed her—and helped to assimilate her into the men's club. That club was often impenetrable, and she didn't count sexy blondes who hung on a man's arm and pretended to inhale as having infiltrated it. To be in the club, not quite a member, you had to stand alongside them and engage in the same conversation and not give a damn about your shoes, hair or dress—but still be able to look good.

Manuel sneered at her. He actually sneered. His demeanor had grown decidedly cold as he poured a finger of brandy into a tumbler for himself and leaned against the mahogany bar. Still thinking about the votive crowns, she felt sure.

As was she. If authentic, they had not been obtained legally.

"So, Manuel tells me he gave you a few lessons on fighting a bull?" Garin asked. He wore a cream linen suit again today. Hemingway, look out. "If there's a woman out there who can stand against a bull, it is Annja Creed," he added over his shoulder to the scowling matador.

"She was a bit skittish," Manuel said. "But she has potential. Of course, women should not be allowed to fight professionally."

Annja was aware of a few professional female matadors. Most were forced out of the profession because of lack of interest in their fights. Blame it on Spanish machismo and the idea that a woman's job was in the kitchen and cradling a *niño* in her arm while she checked the oven.

"Why is it nothing frightens you, Señorita Creed?" Manuel's question pulled her from the nightmare image of a woman in an apron standing over a smoking, burned meat loaf. "First you chase a sniper, and next you stand before a bull with no training in the cape whatsoever."

"You had said the bull was just a yearling. And I did have you right beside me. I was afraid. You said fear was necessary in the ring."

Garin began to shake his head, but Manuel joined them, cigar smoking in the fingers that clutched the brandy glass. "It is. A torero who enters the ring without fear and a cocky attitude will take the horn or fight poorly, it is guaranteed."

"Does the bull feel fear?" she asked. Cigar smoke curled around them, wafting the delicious scent above their heads. "Can you see that?"

"Only the cowardly ones do. A brave bull charges without pause. Fights to the finish with honor."

"Exactly how does a bull display honor?"

Manuel smirked and touched her at the back of her neck. Tap, tap, with the blunt end of one of his fingers. "If I were to prick you here with the banderilla. And here." Another tap wrapped chills around her spine. "And again. Could you stand and, focused only on the cape, continue to charge?"

"It would be difficult. Painful. Plus, I'd be bleeding out."

"And yet, the bull does so. The bull challenges me to step up my game. To face death alongside it."

"You do love death," Garin commented.

Manuel grinned. "It is necessary, no?"

"No," Garin said. "Well, yes, for your profession it is. But for me, I don't favor death or even the idea of it."

His glance to Annja brought images of Joan's broken battle sword to mind. He'd been convinced of his immortality before the pieces of the sword had been collected. But now that the sword was whole? Who knew? A man who had experienced such a long life wasn't willing to concede it to mortality.

"What of you, Annja?" Manuel narrowed his dark gaze on her, the smoke curling about his head taking the appearance of diabolical coils. "Do you fear death?"

"Not at all. It is a natural thing we must all eventually succumb to." She returned Garin's glance. "But I admit I hope my death isn't painful."

"Ah, but that is the only way to die," Manuel stated. "No glory without the pain, eh? I should show you the wound on my abdomen I took from a horn last year.

They carried me out to the infirmary, stitched me up without anesthesia, and less than half an hour later, I was back in the ring to finish off the bull. Ah!" He gave a grand sweep of his hand.

Machismo at its finest.

The cigar smoke was beginning to make her woozy by the time the cook announced dinner, and Annja heard Garin's audible sigh. She caught his sorry shake of his head, as if to say "don't bait the maestro," but ignored it.

The men walked ahead of her, making it apparent she hadn't breached the men's club, after all. Stubbing out the cigar on a silver tray, she followed them into the dining room.

The elaborate meal consisted of five courses and two wine vintages. She'd learned something about wine, but would never consider herself a connoisseur. By the time dessert was brought out Annja had begun to wonder where both men put it all. Especially the matador, whose costume showed every ounce of excess body fat. He had none.

"This must be fuel for your next fight," she pondered as she set aside the tempting vanilla custard and instead reached for the glass of pansy-garnished water.

"Not at all," Manuel said, "I fuel up on protein in the morning and have a light lunch before heading off to the fight. It may not appear as though I work that long in the ring, but the nervous energy alone requires a hearty meal."

"And all the sweat," Garin commented. "The suit of lights you wear must be a bitch in the sun."

"It is not the most comfortable attire. And the jacket doesn't allow for ease of movement. But tradition demands the heavy costume. I appreciate the elaborate embroidery on the jacket when it deflects a wayward horn. Now the shoes, they are a bit feminine, I must admit." The two laughed heartily.

While the men discussed the merits of bespoke leather shoes, Annja let her eyes roam over the wall behind Manuel. It was plastered with tickets to bullfights and posters advertising them, most of them, she noted from the names listed, fights El Bravo had appeared in. But others were older, dating back decades. Perhaps fights he'd watched when he was younger or even fights his relatives had appeared in.

When Manuel noticed her interest, he turned to stretch an arm along the wall. "My history."

"It's fascinating." Folding the cloth napkin on the table, she got up to examine them more closely.

"What is a *novillerado?*" she asked, bending to read the details on a ticket.

"Novice fights," Manuel explained. "The bulls' horns are blunted and they are often used many times in the rings, which would never be allowed in an official corrida. Once a bull has been in the ring it's no good for future fights because it begins to learn defensive tactics or to be fearful. The *novillerado* offers opportunity for aspiring bullfighters to appear before the public and hone their skills with a more docile animal. They are often some of the most interesting fights you will see."

"Are there many injuries?"

"Not so many as you would suspect." Manuel joined her, and she felt as though his anger over having found her in his sanctuary had finally subsided. "This was my first." He pointed out a yellowed poster, which featured four fighters' names, his in the smallest font and on the bottom of the list.

"That must have been exciting. Are your parents alive? Do they attend your fights?"

"My mother is ailing, but she comes out once a month, along with her girlfriends in their fancy shawls and *bata de colas,* the flamenco dancer's dress." To illustrate he performed a quick stomp of his feet, a flamenco dance move. "I always dedicate my kills to her. My father is traveling with my brother right now. Renaldo is rising in the ranks as matador. It won't be long before he surpasses me. He's already started to pic his own bulls. Soon enough, he'll have mastered the kill. But for now he's still leery. Tends to jump too high, for fear of the horns. He'll come around."

Annja ran her gaze down the many Spanish names on the posters, and one in particular jumped out at her. "César Soto?"

She glanced at Garin, who crossed his arms and frowned at her. What was that about? He was very pouty this evening. Had the butler made him check his gun at the door?

"Isn't he the chief inspector of the Cádiz police?"

"You've met him?" Manuel nodded. "The man was once an aspiring torero. About the same time I started. He was no good. Had no leg strength and was always stumbling before the bull could even reach the cape. No bravado." The last comment was made in a tone of disgust.

"He's very keen on his job," she replied. "And I noticed he has a limp."

"Which is why he is not a torero today."

"He was the one I spoke to after chasing the woman who attempted to shoot you and…" He didn't need to know about the murder at the dig site.

"César Soto is on the case? Well, then, I'm sure the matter has already been solved."

The comment was meant as a means to dismiss the conversation. Annja could feel the tension stiffen Manuel's lanky frame beside her. He didn't like talking about César Soto. But apparently he knew him well enough to judge his former fighting skills.

They looked about the same age, late twenties or early thirties. Was it possible they held an animosity toward each other? Perhaps César, the failed matador, couldn't care less who had taken a shot at his former rival? Or had reason to see someone did?

"The sun is setting," Garin interrupted. "Let's take our brandy out on the veranda."

And without another glance from either of them, the men wandered out, leaving Annja searching for Soto's name on the other posters. She didn't find it. The two were tied together in a manner she couldn't quite piece together. But she would.

12

The computer screen flashed through three different profiles, each an employee of the Cádiz PNP. César Soto paused on the one he deemed most likely to be the double-crossing thief who was looting artifacts from the Puerto Real site. Had the suspect also murdered the guitarist?

Soto wasn't betting the farm on that one. He had his suspicions. Hell, he had a very clear idea of the culprit. And that was without taking fingerprints from the scene or standing in watch while forensics had done their work.

He wanted to nab the dirty cop. He oversaw this division and wouldn't tolerate such a blatant flick of the finger at his command.

It was a good thing he'd sent Annja Creed out of the city. He didn't need her interference or a leak to the media regarding the possibility of a dirty cop. She'd gotten too close to the truth, and he had the distinct impression she was too smart to let things go.

He picked up the sketch of the sniper's face Creed

had made adjustments to after the sketch artist had finished.

"How are you involved?" he asked. "Don't make me come after you, Ava."

ANNJA TOOK A CAB back toward the old city, but got let off a few blocks from the Hotel Blanca. The streets were alive with tourists and she wasn't in the mood to return to her room. At the aroma of spiced, savory meat and the sweetness of plantains, her mouth watered. Despite the five-course meal she'd packed away earlier.

It had been a while since she'd smoked Cuban with Bart McGilley back in Brooklyn. Bart worked for the NYPD and occasionally served as her contact, providing information only he could access in the police database. But first and foremost, he was a friend. She decided she'd call him the moment she returned to the States and set up a boxing date at Eddie's gym. The strains of a flamenco guitar lured her through an inconspicuous black door and into the Gato Negra's cool darkness, and that was without a secret password. Annja found a table at the back of the curved room in close confines with the tightly placed, small circular tables that seated one or two patrons nursing shots of wine or whiskey. The walls looked carved from stone, but it was just an effect on molded plaster, and the graffiti along the bottom hid a few chips out of it.

Alone beneath a single spotlight on the dark, narrow stage, the dancer began slowly, marking the *compas* with her footsteps, confident and stolid. She stretched up an arm, twisting her wrist in a graceful, compelling movement that demanded everyone watch as she interpreted the music.

Mixed with influences from Spain and the Moors, flamenco music had begun with the Romani Gypsies who expressed their fears, their heartaches and hardships through music. Flamenco had originally been focused on the singer and the dance. The guitarist was a later addition and was generally viewed by aficionados only as accompaniment. But now guitar soloists had made quite a name for themselves worldwide, though often the music was considerably altered beyond the influence of *flamenco puro*.

The dancer was familiar because Annja had made a few touch-ups to her sketch earlier that day. Funny how her expression possessed more murderous intent while dancing than it had when she'd faced Annja down in the alleyway in a battle of strength. Fiercely intent in her movements, Ava Vital pushed out anger through her precise steps, weaving raw emotion into the fast rhythm of the dance.

The audience clapped *palmas* and an old man seated at the table next to Annja stomped his feet, performing a few fancy footwork moves himself. Annja almost wished she had some Spanish heritage herself because the mood and energy proved darkly alluring.

Thinking to use the dancer's performance as distraction to look around, Annja walked to the back of the club and noted the hallway at the end of the bar where the performers came and left the stage.

Checking that no one was watching her, she slipped past the bartender, who was busy pouring shots for a noisy trio of college girls—one of whom attempted her own flamenco dance with a lift of her übershort skirt to the mockery of the elder drinkers around them.

The hallway was dark, lit by lamps that glowed above doors and rooms blocked by strands of hanging red beads. Out in the club, the music had changed pace, and Annja heard a woman begin the haunting strains of a sad song.

Annja was grabbed from behind by the ponytail, her head jerked back sharply.

"What the hell are you doing here, señorita?"

A blade touched the side of Annja's rib cage, and she followed the woman's directions down the dark hallway. She was led past a dressing room no larger than a closet and through a dented metal door outside into a dark alley. The dancer shoved Annja against the brick wall. Fine rain misted the air. The crisp coolness was welcome after the smoky club.

Spinning around, Annja put her hands on her hips. The woman's knife wavered before her, but the distance Annja had just gained would allow her time to dodge. "Happy to see you again, too, Ava."

"Why are you following me?"

"Can't a girl watch a show?"

"Not you. Not this club."

"I see." Annja nodded toward the street. "I didn't see my name posted on the door with a big red X through it."

Ava spun the dagger in her fingers, obviously trying to intimidate her. She spun the blade as if she'd been doing it since she was a toddler. Most impressive, but Annja bet the woman would gape if she pulled her battle sword out of midair. Not the time for it. Yet.

"We need to talk," Annja said. "Without giving each other bruises. Is that possible?"

The dancer gave her a disgusted once-over. "How do I know you're not working for the police?"

"You don't, but I'm not. I've developed a distinct dislike for the police since I've come to Cádiz." Still, she hadn't decided to believe Professor Crockett's claim that the police were dirty until she'd seen actual proof. "I need answers about Diego Montera, Ava."

"How do you know my name?"

"The internet is a marvelous place. There's no picture of you on the club's site, just that interesting tattoo of yours."

The woman crossed her arms over her chest, dagger tip tapping at her chin as she considered Annja's suggestion. "Diego was a friend of mine."

"And now he's dead."

"I did not do that."

"I didn't say you did. He was involved in something I believe was well over his head. Please, just a few minutes of your time to ask some questions. You can keep the knife pointed at me if it makes you feel better."

The woman tilted her chin up in a defiant gesture. "You're either stupid or telling the truth. There's a tapas bar down the street. You're buying."

She followed Ava, dressed in full flamenco regalia, down the alley. Where the woman kept the dagger hidden was beyond Annja, but she had to say the ruffled-danger look really worked for Ava Vital.

But it didn't intimidate her in the least.

INSIDE THE RESTAURANT lit by green lights and decorated with kitschy palm trees, the dancer ordered tap beer and fresh prawns soaked in lemon and sage. She possessed the command of a man ordering dinner and taking charge, which Annja found familiar. A wise female alone in foreign countries on digs should always present confidence.

"Who are you?" Ava asked after the waiter had dropped off the plate of appetizers and two beers. "Why should I trust you?"

The beer was warm but had a spicy kick Annja suspected was clove. She put down half the mug before speaking. "I'm Annja Creed. I'm an archaeologist, and I was working on a dig in Puerto Real before coming into Cádiz to spend a few days at the city museum inspecting some Egyptian-found coins."

"You're from New York," Ava said.

"Is my accent that obvious?"

"I used to date a guy from Brooklyn."

"That's where I live, but not where I was born. I guess the accent does affix itself to a person."

"Guy was an asshole." Ava tilted back her beer and set the mug on the wobbly wooden table with a sharp thunk. Propping her elbow against the back of the chair, she lifted her posture defiantly. She had perfected the cool, don't-mess-with-me stare. "You mentioned Diego?"

"I was the one who found him dead in his hotel room."

"You were there? How did you find him? Did he invite you in?"

"No, I had rented a room and happened to see his door open, and, well…"

"And how did you learn he was connected to me? Is that why you chased me last night?"

"I chased you last night because you took a shot at the matador. I had no idea, at the time, that you had ties to Diego until I found the website for the Gato Negra. Interesting how life doesn't serve up coincidence, but rather clues to the greater picture, isn't it?"

"I just want to know why you've been following me."

"I know Diego played guitar at the Gato Negra and assume you danced for him."

"I did. As did the other dancers in the club. We all work together. Diego has excellent *compas*—he keeps the rhythm…. Kept the rhythm. But once in a while he tended to get carried away with flourishes. Distracted from my dancing, you know?"

"I can imagine. The guitarist is not the soloist. The dancer is."

"You've got that right."

"But were you two close, away from the club?"

Ava set back her shoulders and crossed her legs, kicking out a black velvet shoe.

"Look, I don't mean to pry into your personal life," Annja said, "but you present an interesting twist to this case."

"The case? You said you weren't with the police. I knew you were lying to me."

"I'm not with the police," Annja rushed out. "Just sit back and let me explain. I'm an archaeologist. And an occasional host of a cable television show that show-cases monsters throughout history."

Ava's frown deepened.

"I travel a lot and on occasion join digs, as I did in Jerez. I'm not trying to solve Diego's murder or even get the sniper who shot at the matador arrested. Not at the moment, anyway." They exchanged serious stare time, and Annja served her most damning glare. "I'm involved because there's an artifact I've had my hands on recently that showed up in Diego's room. Stolen. More than half the artifacts you see in museums are obtained illegally."

"I don't go to museums."

"Yeah, I would have guessed that about you." Probably spent most of her time in gun shops pricing rifle scopes. "Still. Besides being concerned about the looted dig site, Diego's death was senseless, and I do care about justice for him."

"The Cádiz police can take care of that."

"I spoke to the dig supervisor this morning, and there's been another death."

"Probably not related," Ava said too quickly.

"What makes you say that? What do you know, Ava?"

The dancer bounced her foot furiously, but then with a heavy sigh said, "Diego got involved with the wrong people, but they are not directly related to your archaeological dig."

"How can you know that? You must have been close to Diego to know what he was involved in off-club hours."

She shrugged. "We worked together, shared a beer once in a while, but that was it. Though I suspect he had a crush on me. He had that puppy-dog look that always made me uncomfortable."

"Who was he involved with? Was he picking up side jobs? Perhaps delivering artifacts to buyers? There was something missing from his hotel room. An artifact, I suspect."

"I don't know names or anything like that."

"What can you tell me?"

Ava ate a few pieces of shrimp, then made a show of wiping her hands on the cloth napkin before leaning across the table. "All I know is Diego was trying to make extra money. Guitarists don't make a lot, and he didn't work every night at the club. My guess is he got involved with a shady group. He never mentioned anything about it to me, but that's what I piece together from what you've told me."

"Did he mention where he was going that night or who he intended to meet?"

Ava shook her head. "Like I said, I wasn't as close to him as he would have liked me to be. He was mostly moon-eyed around me. Didn't give me a lot of personal details of his life. If what he did was illegal, do you think he would tell me? No."

"So what makes you so sure it's not related to the murder at the dig I mentioned?"

She sighed. "I don't. You make me nervous. I don't like you, *loco Americano*."

"I'm having trouble finding your appealing qualities, too. Especially since you've got a blade tucked at your back."

"A blade I can handle well."

"I'm sure you can. Are you a dancer first or a sniper?"

She jutted her chin disapprovingly and looked aside. Shouldn't have expected an answer to that one.

"I suspect the police are covering up for something. Someone. Probably the killer."

"Now you're getting smart, Brooklyn." Ava pushed aside her beer mug and leaned forward, tapping the table with an insistent finger. "And now you understand why I won't be giving anyone information. Not even a curious archaeologist with bad fashion sense."

Annja looked over her colorful skirt. So she'd bought a stupid skirt.

"Just leave me alone, and I'll leave you alone," Ava said with the biting vitriol of a threat. "Diego's killer will pay."

"You say that like you know who the killer is."

"I do."

"Then you know who stole the artifact."

"No. I only know what I feel in my heart, and my heart tells me Diego got in the path of one very bad man."

"You took a shot at Manuel Bravo. You think he killed Diego? That would imply you believe he stole the missing artifact." Annja pulled the plate of lemon-soaked shrimp closer and stabbed one with her fork.

Ava remained tight-lipped, arms crossed even tighter.

"Did Diego tell you it was Manuel he was going to meet? Ava, if you have information, I need it. The police need it."

More silence.

So she tried a different approach. "How does a torero get involved in theft of artifacts?"

"I don't know what you're talking about."

But she did. The woman could cast all the threatening gazes she wanted at Annja—it only confirmed she held some information that might help her piece together the parts.

"And how much is it worth it to you, a seemingly innocent flamenco dancer, to take another man's life in revenge for one seemingly innocent guitar player? You say you didn't have a relationship? I'm having trouble believing you in the face of such vengeful emotions against the matador."

The woman narrowed her eyes. "You don't know anything, Brooklyn."

"I found Diego dead on the bed. But the artifact he had with him was still in the room."

"What was it?"

"A bronze statue of what may be a Baal god."

"I don't understand what the hell you just said."

"A small bronze bull. That statue wasn't stolen. There was a wood crate in Diego's room, as well, and that was empty. I don't believe the statue had been transported in that. You're sure you have no idea what else he'd been carrying? It could be a means to pin the murder on the matador."

The woman stretched taller, meeting Annja's gaze. She tilted back the beer, then stood and nodded to an elderly man who complimented her on her dancing as he passed their table. "Stay out of it, Brooklyn, or you're going to get hurt."

Annja also stood and let out a soft chuckle. She put her hand to the woman's shoulder. Ava roughly pushed it away. "We can get more accomplished if we work together."

"I don't think so. *We* are not together. I work alone."

"As a sniper? You've been trained. And your fighting skills are expert. Who are you?"

"Who are you?"

Annja held out her hand and said, "Annja Creed. Want to try this over? You are Ava Vital. Dancer. Sniper. Professional assassin?"

The dancer moved quickly, dragging Annja away from the table and slamming her against the brick wall. She turned up a roundhouse and landed her heel against Annja's gut. They were only noticed by a couple of men sitting three tables away at the back of the restaurant. The men didn't move to stop the scuffle.

Not willing to throw a punch and attract more attention, Annja got up from the kick. "You've had martial-arts training," she said. "Or is the roundhouse kick standard in flamenco dance schools?"

"I've always been a dancer. I was born with the rhythm in my blood. It is duende."

Annja had heard the term before. The natural rhythm born to dancers and musicians.

"The desire to kick ass came later." Ava slammed her palm to Annja's shoulder, pinning her to the wall. Annja relaxed, unwilling to cause a scene. "I served in the Special Forces a few years, but I found spying more interesting. I was given more training, but too quickly the entire training program was disbanded. I was left unemployed." She released Annja and shifted her hips to a more powerful stance, hands fisted at her sides.

"So you're using your skills to commit murder?"

Through the restaurant's speakers, a guitarist played a mournful tune and a singer punctuated the song with a low and lingering bellow Annja felt vibrate in her gut.

Ava asked, "Did you enjoy the bullfight?"

She wouldn't bother to ask how she knew she'd been to a fight.

"It was…a new experience for me. First time I've witnessed a live fight."

"Did you approve?"

"Of the spectacle? To a degree."

Ava shook her head. "Americans."

She stood ready to deliver a fist or a kick, but sensed the dancer had used her silly threat and wasn't going to attack again. "Spaniards," Annja replied.

That curled the corners of Ava's lips into a smile.

"I need your help," Annja said. "I want to find out what was worth killing Diego for. What was in the crate. And who, in fact, stabbed him in the back to get it."

Ava studied her. Working out the pros and cons of revealing all that she knew, Annja guessed. For someone who had publically attempted to murder a man, it was a wise pause.

By rights, Annja should make a citizen's arrest and haul her into the police station. But she wasn't too sure César Soto would arrest Ava or instead slap the handcuffs on Annja. After all, he'd had her escorted from the city and thought she'd be in London right now.

"Have you considered the method of killing yet?" Ava asked with a sly glance to the stage where the dancer marked out the *compas* in alternating steps and claps.

"A stab to the back. Are you aware of that?"

"It was on the local radio," Ava explained. "I'm wagering Diego's death is similar to another stabbing here in the city not a month ago. Guy was found on the beach bleeding out, but by the time they got him to the hospital he was dead. The stab wound was made from above the head."

"That information couldn't have been relayed on the radio."

"Rumors have circulated," Ava said. "If you're a performer in the old city, you hear things. Do you want me to tell you this, or are you going to continue to question my sources?"

Her hands akimbo, Annja nodded for her to continue.

"The blade was delivered over the head, into the spine at an angle. A method of placing the blade that is very familiar to some in the city. You understand?"

Annja pondered that, trying to figure how or why the murderer would stab in such an awkward manner. To go in over the head, he would have had to approach the man from the front, to allow him to see what was coming, instead of knifing him in the back from behind. It was a bold move, much like…

When it came to her, Annja met Ava's eyes and the woman nodded in acknowledgment.

"The *estocada?*" The moment of truth during the bullfight when the matador thrusts the *estoque* sword into the bull.

"But is that possible with a human?" she continued. "To sever the aorta from such an angle? The anatomies of a bull and a human are completely different."

"Does it matter? The act of placing the blade was the same as a torero to the bull. Now do you have to question if it was El Bravo who killed Diego?"

"Of course I do. I have no proof he was in the Hotel Blanca that night. There are any number of matadors in the city. And just because a move associated with the torero was used doesn't mean the murderer actually was one."

But truly? A matador had murdered Diego Montera?

"Who told you this?"

"Not important," Ava said. "Think about it. You look like a smart woman. You'll put the pieces together."

The dancer who would be an assassin strode out, grace evident in the swing of her shoulders and the sturdy placement of her steps. A few admirers followed her exit, including Annja.

Ava believed the bullfighter had killed Diego. What motive could he have?

The walls of El Bravo's villa had been lined with artifacts depicting bulls. He'd said they were gifts. But wouldn't a man interested in bull paraphernalia have taken the Baal statue from Diego's room?

And why was Ava so determined to take revenge against him? She had implied she and Diego weren't close, had no sort of relationship outside of the club. Hardly reason to want revenge against a man she suspected had killed a fellow worker.

On the other hand, Annja should never judge what pushed a person to murder.

She needed to get back to the hotel and check online to see if anyone had replied about the photos she had uploaded.

13

Annja entered her hotel room, opened her laptop and went online. There was an entire page of replies to her uploaded pictures and she scanned through them. Most replies suspected it was an effigy of Baal, but had no proof and hadn't seen the exact object before. One suggested it was a party favor for one of Hugh Hefner's blowouts and thought she should try to crack it open to see if a room key fell out.

Not everyone lurking on the loop was helpful or, apparently, sober. Annja had to chuckle at that.

One reply stood out, addressed from Rockford LePlante.

She'd heard that name before. Some kind of Indiana Jones who lived off the land and refused to take money for adventures or movie deals. "Must have a trust fund," she figured. How else to support a habit of world travel and dangerous adventure?

She read his email.

Miss Creed, it is a pleasure to communicate with you after hearing so much about your adventures, and yes, I admit, I follow your television show whenever I'm near electricity (which isn't often). The pictures you've posted may seem to represent just another bronze statue, but I am especially excited to see an actual photograph of it. So much so, I'd rather not discuss details online. Could you please give me a ring? I'm traveling toward Pukapuka and will be in and out of cell-phone reception, so do try to make contact today if possible.

The email had been sent six hours earlier. He listed a phone number, which she promptly entered into her cell phone and pushed Send. The call was answered on the second ring with a scatter of static.

"Miss Creed! Wish you would...called...sooner." Each word was punctuated by horrible static. "—entering dead zone."

Pukapuka, one of the first islands to be sighted by the Europeans, was a coral atoll in the Pacific Ocean's Cook Islands. Extremely remote, it was barely more than three kilometers of land area so she wasn't surprised at the lack of reception.

"Thank you for giving me your number," she said quickly. "You know about the bronze bull statue I posted online?"

"Ye—" a long buzz indicated he had entered a dead zone, but as quickly sound returned "—won't believe what's hidden inside. Or so I believe."

"Inside the statue? Our connection is awful, Mr. Le-Plante. Maybe I should call back later?"

"No! —off grid for a month. Take this down. Louis XIII. Austrian princess. Dowry."

Annja started making notes as his words came through between a scrabble of static. "I got it. Anything else?"

"—idden treasure—uby."

The line went dead, and she waited but he didn't return. That was all she would get from Rockford Le-Plante.

"Have fun in Pukapuka. Wish I was there." In one of very few places that was still generally untouched by civilization. Though even then the island did have a small air-landing strip.

She tapped the pen on the notepaper. "Louis XIII? And his Austrian princess?" She thought over what she knew about the French king who had ruled in a time when Versailles had been considered the capital of France. The princess Anne of Austria had been daughter of Philip III of Spain. It was a time when Cardinal Richelieu reigned more than the king and musketeers went on daring escapades for the queen.

A hidden treasure? Inside the bronze bull? But what was *uby?*

She muttered the nonsense word over and over until it came to her. "Ruby. There's a ruby inside the statue?"

This case suddenly got very interesting.

She had to look up Louis XIII and Anne of Austria.

Somehow the bull statue was related to those two, and that LePlante had said *princess* instead of *queen* indicted they'd not yet been married.

She slid a finger across the mouse pad when a ninja yell erupted outside on her patio. Annja sat upright on the bed.

The patio door slammed open and suddenly two hands clutched her neck, painfully squeezing her carotid artery. The attacker knew what he was doing. He didn't need to apply too much pressure for more than five or six seconds, before she would pass out.

She swung her backpack up and managed to clock the attacker in the side of the head. It was enough of a surprise to loosen his grip. With an elbow to his ribs, she gained her freedom, lunged forward to land her palms on the end of the bed and pushed back forcefully, spinning around with a roundhouse that connected with his jaw.

He wobbled, but with a shake of his head, grinned and pulled out a nunchaku. The tiny olive-skinned man with a bad case of acne performed a flashy figure eight with the weapon. Tricks were tricks. And Annja wasn't about to take a hard oak nunchuck to the side of the head.

He backed her toward the bed. She leaped onto it, which caused the laptop to slide off and land on the floor with a crunch. No time to lament the lost technology as she lured him around the side of the bed, then jumped off the opposite side. As she did, she called the leather-hilted sword to her grip.

A nunchuck whooshed by her ear. Annja swung around, cutting the air and a few inches of hair from her attacker's stick-straight buzz cut. Using his small stature to his advantage, the attacker ducked and swung out the nunchucks, sweeping low so Annja had to leap to avoid taking them to the side of her knee. He came up holding both sticks in one hand and blocked Annja's sword with one of them. A good, solid blocking weapon, she decided as the blade reverberated back to the hilt in her hand. She wondered if he was aware the weapon had originated as a farming tool to thresh wheat. He probably didn't care.

"Who sent you? Why are you here?" she demanded. She immediately guessed César Soto, for reasons she couldn't quite justify.

Her next swing caught him on the shoulder, slicing cleanly through his loose-fitting leather jacket and spattering blood across the pale bedspread.

The man yelped, yet did not drop out of attack mode. He swung and hit the back of Annja's thigh with the hard wood as she jumped to the floor.

"Get out of Cádiz!" he cried in Spanish.

"Says who?" She swung up the sword, not under his throat, but instead pressing the tip into the gaping slice in his shoulder. "Tell me who sent you."

The man rammed his shoulder against the blade. It was such an incredible move, Annja dropped her guard.

In that second the nunchuck swung around and hit her against the back of the head. The inertia of the blow spangled stars in her vision. She wobbled, but maintained consciousness. She'd been lucky it was the back of the skull and not her nose or jaw. Sweeping the blade blindly, she managed to block another oncoming blow.

Adrenaline coursed through her system, working to eliminate the blackening effects of the intense hit to her skull. On a high, she dodged the next blow and managed an undercut to the man's rib cage. This time he gripped the wound and stumbled toward the open patio door. He ran out the doors and, with a kamikaze yell, leaped over the balcony.

She raced to the wrought-iron balcony and saw that he'd landed on the back of a trailer stacked with cardboard cartons of melon. Rolling off onto the street in a clutter of broken cantaloupe, he took off running, leaving a trail of blood-spattered melons in his wake.

"Time to find a new hotel," Annja muttered, rubbing the back of her head. "And some aspirin. Ouch."

Swinging out her sword arm, she dismissed the blade back into the otherwhere and went to gather up her things.

ANNJA SLID ONTO a patio chair at the café across the street from the Hotel Argantonio, which wasn't far from the museum and the Plaza de Mina. She intended to check in at the hotel, but first wanted to gather her wits about her. Besides, she was hungry after the tussle at the Hotel

Blanca. She was gradually moving up in hotel class and stars, which she hoped would deflect further in-room fights with unknown hit men. Powering up the laptop—which wore a new dent on the corner, among many other dents, but which was also no worse for wear—she decided to cybersurf before she completely forgot what Ava Vital had told her earlier.

Sipping coffee while she waited for her meal, she looked up the bullfight, the final act, in particular.

The faena was a series of passes made before the bull, to square it up in preparation for the kill. To make the kill, the matador thrust the *estoque* between the bull's shoulder blades, which must go through to the aorta or heart. The act must be made by charging head-on toward the bull and allowing as close as possible connection to the horns while avoiding getting gored. It was the moment when most matadors did get gored.

A quick, clean death was preferred, and the crowd would let the matador know with boos or seat cushions tossed into the ring if he hadn't placed the sword well. Placing the sword was called the *estocada,* as Ava had referred to the act that had killed Diego.

Sometimes, if death was not instant, the matador would perform the *descabello* with a second blade to sever the spinal cord. Annja had seen that done during the fight yesterday afternoon. If that failed to kill the bull, then the matador's assistant must move in for the coup de grâce with yet another cut to the spinal cord at the base of the brain.

The bedspread had barely been wrinkled in Diego's hotel room. Someone not experienced with placing the blade certainly may have struggled with his victim. On the other hand, a professional would have worked quickly and cleanly.

Annja paused to let the idea of an actual matador having killed Diego sink in. Such a man, who would kill for an artifact, would likely already have many artifacts of immense value in his home.

Had it been a business exchange gone bad? Why would the matador kill the delivery person and then not take both artifacts?

"He'd only wanted what was in the wooden crate," she murmured.

Pressing a palm to the back of her head, she felt the tender bruise, which had started to swell. She was lucky she hadn't gotten a cracked skull out of the deal.

Her thoughts went immediately to the votive crowns in Manuel Bravo's sanctuary. They were the right size to fit the crate. Which would make Ava Vital's assumption correct. But that still didn't explain why the dancer had it in for El Bravo.

Or how a bull statue possibly containing a valuable treasure was connected to it all. She switched her search to the seventeenth century.

"Louis XIII and Anne of Austria were both fourteen when they were married. Tough luck, kids. I can't imagine representing a nation so young, and to be forced to the conjugal bed? Ugh."

Anne's father, Philip III of Spain, sent along a dowry of jewels and a wardrobe worth half a million crowns.

She searched for more information on the dowry, perhaps a list of its contents, but there was nothing like it online.

Anne of Austria had traveled in a caravan from Spain to Versailles, where her future husband met her. The retinue possibly carried the dowry, but it could also have been sent by an armed guard preceding or following that first ostentatious meeting, Annja decided.

She clicked over to a Rumors of History site and after sorting through the bibliography of seventeenth-century articles was thrilled to find a scanned sketch very similar to the bronze bull. The article had been written by Rockford LePlante himself and stated the bull was merely a delightful ruse, which hid an even greater treasure. Anne's father, Philip, had enjoyed puzzles and secrets and often had valuable objects made that hid inner workings or treasures. The piece could well have been intended as a gift to King Louis XIII.

The scan was of an old document, so it didn't look like something LePlante could have drawn in contemporary times, and it was intricate even though the actual statue was rather plain. It indicated an open belly in the bull, which hid something inside. The scan was blurred there, and Annja bit her lip because she couldn't make out exactly what was inside.

"A ruby?" she wondered.

Her cell phone rang. When she picked up, James

Harlow started right in, expressing his surprise she was still in town. He kept saying that, as if she should have left already. Why did everyone want her out of town?

"I'm just trying to help," she said. "But it's hard to do that when strange men wielding nunchucks jump me in my hotel room."

"Are you all right, Annja? Did you call the police? Where are you now?"

"I'm fine, though the back of my head hurts like a mother. I suspect the police wouldn't be too pleased to hear from me again."

"Any idea who sent the guy? Did he say?"

"No. Between dodging his weapon and watching him leap over my balcony to make his escape, he didn't take the time to mention who was behind his visit. I tell you, people have lost all etiquette nowadays."

"At least you're not hurt seriously. You aren't, are you?"

"I'll survive. But I may need to wear a crash helmet for a while."

"Ouch, that sounds bad. Did you go to the emergency room?"

"I'm exaggerating. I'll be fine."

"Good." Hardly an empathetic response, more rote, if anything. "Where are you staying?"

Providing that info didn't feel right. Not to someone who seemed to want her out of town as much as the next guy. "I'm looking for a new hotel at the moment."

"So no luck on your search?"

"No luck, but a bit of serendipity. I spoke to the woman who tried to kill El Bravo."

"I'm ever surprised by the circle in which you travel, Annja. How did you manage that meeting?"

"I have my ways. She's led me to believe Diego Montera's killer may have been a matador or a man with the skills of a matador. And there's a certain local matador who has an amazing collection of artifacts displayed in his home."

"Manuel Bravo," Harlow said. "I've been to his place."

"I wasn't aware you two were friends."

"Acquaintances. A few years ago I was invited to a party and only spoke to him briefly. Did you see the Scythian Baal god he's got in the main room? You can't lay your hands on those anymore. He admires the bull as totem as much as I do."

"You don't seem too upset the man has a collection of illegal artifacts."

"That's only an assumption, which is probably true. But what can I do about it? To speak against a local hero would be insanity. You watch yourself, Annja. El Bravo is loved by everyone. Don't throw stones unless and until you've got facts. Do you have facts?"

"No. And don't worry, I've no intention of accusing the man of anything. Have you had any luck locating possible warehouses where the bronze statue may have passed through?"

"I apologize but I've been busy with work."

"Of course." Though when she'd been in the museum photographing the Hercules coins, Harlow had spent most of his time walking the museum floor, chatting with patrons, and he tended to take a couple hours for siesta. "Does the name Rockford LePlante mean anything to you?"

The pause on the line indicated yes, so Annja was surprised when Harlow bluffed his way to a no.

"Why do you ask?" he finished.

"It came up while I was doing some research on the statue online."

"Wait a minute, perhaps I do know about him. Some kind of adventurer, isn't he? A crazy, live-off-the-fat-of-the-land archaeologist who would rather dance with pygmies than hold a civil conversation."

"Sounds right." She was about to mention her phone conversation, but didn't. The vibe she was getting from Harlow cautioned her, and she always paid attention to her intuition. "It didn't net any information, but I thought his background was fascinating."

"Indeed. Though I can tell you more about Jonathan Crockett."

Annja felt Crockett wasn't related to the artifact theft and had struck him off her list. Yet Harlow continued to keep him front and center. He was deflecting the conversation from LePlante. That was curious. "Go ahead."

"I did a deeper search on the internet. The most recent scholarly article he published was in 2002. It's as if he'd fallen off the earth after that. He left the Uni-

versity of London to go 'on sabbatical.' Which probably means he'd gone through a nasty divorce and was
now living it up with a younger woman, had decided
dirt-sifting wasn't for him and was swabbing decks on
a luxury cruise line, or he'd gone off the grid and was
living with the pygmies in Africa."

None of which was true. As far as Annja knew.

"Professor Crockett has never been married," Harlow
confirmed, "so we can rule that out as possible means
to gain income. Divorce payments are a bitch, coming
from someone who knows. He's been working on small
digs around the Cádiz area for at least two years. A few
digs were financed by the university in Madrid, which I
verified with Roberto Aguirro in acquisitions. Or rather,
his assistant, since Aguirro never takes my calls. There
are a few digs that don't list the contributor."

"That's not unusual," Annja said. "I sense Crockett
has a ready supply of funds, perhaps a personal fortune."

Usually operations like this tended to get shady, she'd
learned from experience. So why hadn't she suspected
as much during her few days on the dig?

She'd been in the zone. When squatting over freshly
dug dirt, trowel in hand and boonie hat shading her
eyes from the sweltering rays, Annja Creed left the real
world and found her Xanadu. She could pass an entire
day without uttering a word to her fellow dig mates, and
that day soared by like mere hours. Weeks moved by
swiftly, and she always regretted leaving a site, no mat-

ter if it had been a successful dig or muddling through broken pottery pieces.

"That's all I've found, Annja. Sorry. It's been over a decade since Jonathan and I worked alongside each other."

"Right, Egypt."

"Yes. I did chance to speak to him once at a fundraiser a few years ago. I found him droll as ever."

The two men were exact opposites, Crockett being laid-back and seemingly private, while Harlow was the epitome of button-down, yet fiercely protective of his work and the museum. Of course Harlow would find Crockett offensive to his very nature.

"Okay, thanks. One more question. Have you ever had the opportunity to see any Visigothic votive crowns pass through the museum?"

"Only when I was working at the Madrid museum. Gorgeous things. Why do you ask?"

"I saw a couple in Manuel Bravo's home."

Harlow whistled in appreciation. "They can't possibly be authentic. Acquiring even one of those would be quite a feat."

"Yes, and perhaps worth murder."

"Annja, do take my warning about pointing the finger at a local hero seriously."

"I do, and I will. You're probably right. They couldn't possibly be authentic. Thank you again for the invite to view the coins, James. We'll talk soon."

So, she'd missed something key about the dig. Someone was funding Professor Crockett's efforts near the city to keep him close by. Because no matter if he found nothing on his digs, maybe he was a front for bigger and better things.

Such as whatever had been in the wood crate in Diego's hotel room. A round object, a little smaller in circumference than a basketball.

"Like a votive crown," Annja muttered.

Sitting up on the hard iron patio chair and stretching out a leg before her, she typed in *Visigothic votive crown*. Google images brought up pictures of the gold votive crown displayed in the Madrid museum. It had been designed by the Visigoth king Recceswinth in the seventh century and donated to the Roman Catholic Church. The crown had a circumference that could very well be similar to a basketball.

Annja sat back, crossing her arms. Fitting the crown into the wooden crate worked like a *How to Smuggle Artifacts* tutorial video in her mind. She replayed it over a few times, and it continued to fit snugly into the brown packing paper shreds.

She brought up all the information she could find on the Visigothic votive crowns. There weren't many pieces circulating through the museum system at the moment. The most famous were included in the Treasure of Guarrazar, dug up close to Toledo, Spain, in the mid-nineteenth century. It comprised twenty-six votive crowns and crosses offered to the Roman Catholic Church by the Visigoth kings in the seventh century. The medieval treasure had been divided over the years, and many pieces had been lost—which Annja interpreted as stolen or sold to private collectors. There was only a nineteenth-century lithograph drawing of a few of the Visigothic crowns, no actual photographs, so Annja couldn't get a good idea if the crowns in Bravo's sanctuary resembled any from the Guarrazar collection.

The National Archaeological Museum of Spain, in Madrid, actually listed six crowns in their possession. As well, the Musée de Cluny in Paris featured two, one of which had been bejeweled with pearls.

She found a gorgeous picture of a gold crown decorated with sapphires and precious stones that once belonged to King Recceswinth in the second half of the seventh century. The elaborate filigree design featured a dangling Byzantine pendant cross, along with the Latin words *RECCESVINTUVS REX OFFERET,* meaning "King Recceswinth offered this." A truly remarkable piece.

Annja tilted a look at the crown. It seemed more elaborate than the ones in Bravo's home, but his had been decorated with sapphires and the one had letters on it that read "Given by Alaric."

She transferred a jpeg to her cell phone, then looked up King Alaric. Much earlier than Recceswinth, Alaric was fourth century and had been the first Germanic leader to take the city of Rome. His name meant "king of all" and he had been known as King of the Visigoths. He sacked Rome many times and liked to stage sieges, which was nothing new for the time period. There were no references to a votive crown in his biography, but that didn't rule out the possibility that Alaric had one fashioned. His apparent lust for requesting outrageous ransoms led her to believe he would have surrounded himself with fine things, including a gold crown or two.

"I wonder if one or two crowns have been reported stolen within the past few years."

After another fifteen minutes spent searching, she stumbled on a brief article listing the Cluny museum as having reported a crown missing six months earlier while in transport to the University of London. Police had investigated and had quickly traced the diverted shipment to a British man, who had been found dead in a warehouse of stolen artifacts. A local man, he was named as a police informant and had committed a laundry list of minor criminal activity. No name was mentioned—and the article stopped there. The case had just stopped.

"Weird. And yet…"

Annja had a hunch. A local London man who informed about stolen artifacts? She knew a guy like that. Russell Jones was sixty going on twenty and had never met a stolen chunk of pottery he didn't like and couldn't sell. He was also keen on tracking the nonexistent paper trail of artifacts and knew everyone who had ever touched looted goods, from decades of looting in every country under every condition. He was the last of the wild and crazy pothunters from a generation that had come before the dawn of the big-business organizations who operated by gun and threat.

Picking up the cell phone, she scanned through her contacts, pleased to find she still had Russell's number. He changed it often, so she didn't expect it to go through, but when a female answered, she asked after Russell, using the code name he expected.

The woman sniffed, and Annja heard her sit roughly on what must have been a creaky metal folding chair.

"Is he all right?" Annja asked. "He's a friend. I haven't spoken to him in years, though, and had a question about a Visigothic crown."

"That damned crown!" the woman wailed, and the sound of her sniffling followed.

Bingo. Annja could guess Russell Jones had touched the votive crown at some point. But was it either of the crowns in El Bravo's sanctuary? The one stolen from the Cluny? "Can I speak to him about it?"

"He's not here." More sniffling and a very unfeminine snort.

"Can I leave you my number so he can return my call? It's important. I'm trying to track the origins of a specific votive crown and determine the current buyer."

"He's dead," the woman said and snorted loudly. "Because of that stupid crown. So you won't get any answers, and I don't know who you are—"

Sensing she was going to hang up, Annja spoke quickly. "I'm so sorry. Do you happen to know where he sold the crown or even where it was shipped?"

"Are you going to find the guy who shot him in the back of the head?"

"I...uh, did you report it to the authorities?"

"They were the ones who found him dead when they were investigating the crown. He was going to marry me, you know."

"Oh. Sure. Again, I'm sorry. But..." Not exactly a delicate question to put to the grieving fiancée. Matters of the heart always angled just by Annja's common sense.

"I think it was Spain," the woman blurted. "I'm sure of it because I like the curly stuff they have on their interior design. Russell called it Moorish or something like that. I wanted to visit but he said we'd have to wait for the honeymoon."

"Spain. Thank you. That helps me a lot. Uh, if you've records...?"

"If you're a friend of Russell's you should know better."

"I do." All the man's records were in his head. He would never risk putting anything to paper. "And I thank you. Goodbye."

Annja hung up. The setting sun flashed across the hotel's glass-topped tables.

Two men who handled the votive crown were now dead. No, make that three, if indeed the crown had been inside the crate in Diego's hotel room. Everyone who had touched the crown was dead or missing. So whoever held it now was either next on that list or the one responsible.

As well, Ava had mentioned something about a man being found dead on the beach with a stab wound to his back. She typed in the info to bring up a search and found an obituary for Salamandre Riche, no family, and a stab wound to the back. Deemed a derelict, that was all it mentioned about him.

Might he have been used as a liaison to deliver a valuable gold crown?

Hmm...

"I wonder if a certain person gets so upset when people touch his stuff that he's willing to murder for it."

14

Manuel waited patiently as Cristo unwrapped the bolero jacket from the crisp tissue paper that kept it pristine while traveling from stadium to stadium. The jacket was stiff and even when off him retained its shape due to the starch and elaborate beadwork. After each fight, Cristo brushed it clean if there was no blood on it and repacked it in tissue before hanging it in a special traveling wardrobe case. It had to be soaked in cold water overnight if it had taken on blood.

He preferred the light blue *traje de luces* because it had brought him luck over the years. Much better than the purple suit he'd been offered by a wily tailor last year. The fabric had been the color of a coffin lining. Very bad luck, should he wear that. Though he didn't believe in luck in the ring, facing down the bull, he welcomed it most other times.

Luck had not brought Annja Creed into his life.

There was something about her he didn't like. She was beautiful and smart and curious—that was it. Her curiosity offended him. She'd no right to enter his sanctuary without permission.

"Arms," Cristo said.

Manuel stretched back his arms and received the bolero jacket. The entire costume weighed around thirteen pounds. A weight he had borne through the years to entertain the masses—at the risk of his life. Not an easy thing to wear in the hot Spanish sun, but he'd grown up wearing a smaller suit designed by his mother. He was more comfortable in the suit of lights than in the casual clothing he wore outside of the ring.

Cristo adjusted the narrow black tie at the front of Manuel's neck and then left, knowing Manuel's routine required a half an hour to himself before loading the capes and swords in the van and leaving for the corrida.

To another dance with death.

Striding out from the bedroom with his flat black leather shoes, he made no sound on the tiles as he entered the sanctuary's plaster walls. He bowed before the altar and crossed himself, shoulder to shoulder, then forehead to chest. Kissing his curled knuckles he offered blessings to the Virgin Mother.

Kneeling on the prie-dieu, he whispered the Lord's Prayer and then said thanks for all the blessings he had received and was yet to receive. He didn't think to bless his brother, Renaldo. Rather he did consider it, then decided he would not.

He tilted a look up at the votive crowns, gleaming in the circle of candlelight. The rubies set into the pounded gold on the first crown winked, as if the very eye of God approved the task before him.

Another piece of his soul ransomed for the cheers and adulation.

Standing, he ran his fingertips lightly around the base of the largest gold crown. Closing his eyes, he thought to feel the energy vibrating from kings centuries past. Without their strength, he could find none for himself.

And yet, he didn't feel the positive energy so strongly tonight as he had on previous days. Annja Creed had touched the crown; he knew it. She'd lied about touching it to cover her crime. She had stolen the energy for herself.

Over the years, women, more often than not, had proven his bane.

He couldn't allow Creed to keep his power.

Blowing out the candle, Manuel lingered over the smoke, inhaling the strong rosemary scent. It cleared his head and narrowed his focus. Now he would get in the van and ride to the stadium, but he must remain in his body, unaffected by the cheers and jeers from the crowds, the protestors, the hangers-on who wanted to touch him. He would maintain this peace until he entered the ring.

A peace made fragile by the reduced energy of the votive crowns.

THE PRIVATE ROOMS assigned to the matadors were behind the bull stable. Manuel liked when he heard nothing on the other side of the wall. To hear snorting and the clacking of horns meant the bulls were edgy and fearful. No torero preferred a cowardly opponent.

He paced the short stretch of the narrow room, avoiding the bottled water set out as a courtesy because he'd just taken a piss. He didn't want to risk voiding his bladder should he be grazed by a horn or, worse, gored. He wouldn't be gored. He was too quick, too agile. El Bravo was invincible.

He was first to fight this afternoon, and last. He liked those positions. Fresh out in the ring, he was the first to capture the audience's admiration, and in the last position, he could win them completely after watching the other toreros' performances, and learning from and avoiding their mistakes.

The door opened, and as he turned to demand solitude, he saw César Soto with his hands shoved in his front pockets. The man broadcast the image of the laid-back cowboy Manuel had seen in American Westerns. He didn't like the cocky attitude, though some might claim the toreros walked the same arrogant walk.

It wasn't cockiness but confidence.

"You know I don't see visitors before the fight," Manuel said. He was cautious not to allow his voice to cut like the blade he wielded so expertly. He walked around César as if the man were a ring-bred bull who hadn't seen a man on foot.

"I came to wish you luck."

Manuel nodded, but he wasn't buying the lie. "And so you have."

"You have no right to be quick with me, boy."

Boy? They were the same age. And really? Manuel stood much higher on the social ladder than Soto did. He liked to use his badge as a means to belittle people. Fortunately, Manuel could rarely be cowed.

That didn't mean he wouldn't exercise caution.

Manuel lifted his chin, his jaw tightening. He eyed César, and the man matched his stare with a cool, straight gaze. He possessed a lanky ease about him, again like the gunslingers on the television. His body language was difficult to read, and Manuel didn't know when the cape would be necessary or when a dash for safety behind the barrier was the wisest move.

"What do you want?" he asked. Adjusting his tone, he struggled to prevent his frustration from spewing out. "The money is gone. I work my body weary each season to meet the blood price my father has been paying on you far too long."

"I've never expected anything from you," César said in his slow, sure tone. "Yet we remain tied by bonds that sicken me."

How dare the man insinuate such a thing? "No one asked you to become my keeper."

"Is that so? Then I should stop covering your tracks? Just let the detritus fall where it may? Splayed out in the open like a dead man for all to see?" César grabbed

Manuel by the wrist, but he wrenched away from the presumptuous intimacy.

"Don't touch me."

"Right." Soto rolled his eyes. "Don't touch your things. Don't touch you. You're a freak, Bravo."

Clenching a fist, Manuel ran it along the lower edge of his jacket, scraping his skin along the gold beading to distract him from his anger.

"Have you spoken to the female archaeologist?" César asked.

"The gorgeous, green-eyed one? Of course."

"Right. There's not an attractive woman in the country that hasn't lain beneath the great El Bravo's horns. You screw her?"

"Why is that your concern?"

"Because she's trouble. She's been looking into things. Asking questions."

A suspicion Manuel had already begun to entertain. "Then get rid of her."

"I tried that already. She's bounced back onto my radar. Which means you had better lay low and keep your horns tucked."

"I can't keep her from approaching me. You know how the women—"

"Yes, don't I know it. Avoid her, Bravo. If you know what's good for you."

"You have no idea what is good for me, Soto."

"Is that so? Well, it's not that woman. You have another fight in a few days?"

"I get to kill all six bulls. It's the grand exhibition in my honor."

"Right. Your one-hundredth corrida. How did I let that one slip from memory?" César stroked a hand along his holstered gun, then opened the door. Outside, Manuel's team waited in full regalia with capes and hats, lined along the hallway, quiet yet anxious. "The archaeologist is bad news, Manuel. She's getting close to touching things you'd prefer remained untouched."

"She's already contaminated something I hold precious."

"Well, then. You know how to take care of people who touch your things."

Manuel lowered his head, nodding resolutely. He didn't like it when Soto presumed things about him.

"To the bulls," Soto said and left.

Manuel punched the wall. "You will see what I do with the bulls, you bastard."

15

Garin's call came as a surprise. Annja was walking along the shore, checking out a row of warehouses edging the south side of the city. Could one of them be hiding illicit antiquities? She had her eye out for armed guards after sighting one at the corner rooftop of a brick building half a block from the nearest dock.

"Manuel mentioned your interest in some crowns he has hanging in his sanctuary?" Garin asked.

"If you call spotting stolen goods an interest, then yes. Is he angry about that? I don't think he believed me when I told him I hadn't touched them."

"On the contrary, he said if you liked them so much you should get one for yourself. He got the replicas at a little shop in Cádiz off San Pedro."

"That's not far from the hotel where I'm staying. But a replica? Hard to believe El Bravo would place a cheap trinket in a room he calls his sanctuary."

"You didn't go *in* the sanctuary, did you, Annja?"

"I was lost. Looking for the bathroom."

Garin sighed heavily. "Annja, don't do this. Not

everything that looks like an artifact is valuable. You of all people should know that. Some items simply hold personal value."

"And some friendships blind people to the truth."

She had no right to prod him. It wasn't as though Garin Braden was redeemable at this stage in his long and notorious life.

"I'm passing along the message. Bravo thought you might be interested in owning one for yourself."

"So what are you up to this fine sunny day?"

"I'm getting ready to watch the fight."

"I'm not invited to join you?"

"Not this afternoon. I've got another friend on my arm."

"I bet she's buxom."

"That she is. And she doesn't wear khaki like it's going out of style. Luck with antiques shopping, Annja."

"Thanks. I think I will check out the shop Manuel suggested."

So Manuel claimed the votive crowns were cheap knockoffs. The two crowns in his sanctuary had been the real thing. Annja felt it instinctually.

She'd handled too many valuable artifacts over the years to guess this one wrong.

Garin had given her an address, despite having told her that El Bravo said the crown was a replica. Something must be worth checking out.

THE COBBLESTONE STREETS in the old city reminded Annja of paintings made by starving artists that depicted a mood but not necessarily a real place or event. Brick walls on either side of the narrow street sandwiched her in. Strung here and there were clotheslines flying laundry—sometimes bright and garish, sometimes all whites, bras, boxers and stockings. Moorish influence showed in the decorative tiles around window frames. Iron staircases hugged the walls, and rickety tin planters were overflowing with gaudy flowers. Graffiti she deemed worthy of an exhibit at a museum taunted her with the challenge to *Speak out!* and *Be Real.*

The yellow-tiled cupola of the baroque Cádiz cathedral loomed high above the street. The cathedral had taken one hundred and sixteen years to complete and a person could sight the cupola from virtually any position in the city. She had to take a trip there before leaving town.

She pushed open an intricate black wrought-iron gate, taking a narrow alleyway toward San Pedro. She could hear the calls from shops and stands for "Fresh sausage!", "Two for one!" and "Cold beer!"

The thermometer was pushing toward one hundred. A cold beer sounded great. She headed toward the vendors but kept an eye out for the house with the antiquities knockoffs.

She stopped dead when she came face-to-face with a massive bull. A real, live, very big bull. It had the blackest pair of eyes and black horns tipped with striated white bone. Its hide was red, which made her think of the Hercules coins. Hercules's tenth labor had been to steal red cattle from the monster Geryon. The bull flicked its tail in the classic manner all animals used to broadcast anger.

Its shoulders were as wide as a draft horse and it stood in the middle of the street, eyeing her as if she were a magenta-and-yellow cape. Where it had come from was impossible to guess. She hadn't heard hooves on cobblestone. The last turn she'd taken had been through the gate—that gate was now closed.

No time to wonder who had it in for her by closing her in with a thousand-pound beast. An uncaged bull stood staring her down. Its size and the huge *morillo* muscle at the back of its neck told Annja it had been bred for the ring. A bull bred to fight for its life and to use its horns against anything it deemed a threat. And if it truly were corrida bred, this may be the first time it had seen a human on foot. Any movement would act as the cape to the bull's targeting eyes.

Heart pounding, Annja flexed her fingers and cautiously took three steps backward, remembering movement was what the bull saw, not color or, in this instance, the lack of color in her khaki pants.

Who would waste a bull on her? Couldn't be bred for the corrida—had to be one of those bulls used in the *novillerado* fights for amateurs. A bull that had seen a person on foot and had developed a healthy respect for the danger a biped presented.

She could hope.

The instinct to draw her sword was strangely absent.

This threat was not premeditated on the bull's part. It was innocent.

The bull charged.

Feeling the ground thunder beneath the bull's hooves, Annja knew it would gain on her—and it did. She smelled the manure and animal musk close up behind her. Dodging to the right, she sensed the bull followed. She was the target. It went after what moved. So she should stop.

Except she wasn't stupid.

Pumping her arms, she leaped and grabbed the bottom step of a second-floor iron staircase attached to the side of a limestone building. Something skimmed her boot, twisting her ankle painfully. A horn.

The bull clattered to a stop. It turned and snorted, searching for her—anything that moved—while she held her knees up tight to her chest, dangling above its massive bulk.

Clotheslines fluttered three feet above Annja's head. The bull would never be distracted by the distant movement. She wasn't even sure it could lift its head that high to notice the movement.

A heated yet whispered conversation between two men caught her attention. Annja noticed them at the same time the bull's head swung around.

"Get out of here!" she yelled.

The men took one look at the bull and crept slowly back into the connecting alleyway. The bull charged them.

Annja eyed the laundry. A fluttery red-and-pink skirt

would prove just the thing. Pulling up into a biceps curl, she kicked out and flung her body upward. She grabbed the skirt by the hem, and it tugged at the line as she dropped to the ground. The clothespin didn't release the skirt and instead the whole line fell, blanketing her with clothing.

Above, a woman's head popped out the window and she bulleted angry Spanish at Annja. Annja tugged the clothes off and yelled at the bull, which couldn't fit its broad shoulders through the narrow alley where the men had escaped.

The bull snorted and whipped its tail angrily. It trotted away from Annja and down the street. She didn't mind that the animal was moving away from her, but she did care if any unsuspecting people got caught in the bull's path. They could be injured or even killed. She wasn't about to let that happen.

"I hope this works."

Dashing down the street and alongside the bull, she sped up beyond it by five yards and swirled the skirt to get its attention. The bull sighted the flash of fabric and veered toward it.

The little Annja knew about caping the bull had come from her impromptu session with Manuel. He'd taught her a basic veronica. How to lure the bull toward her and sweep it beyond her body while avoiding connecting. Capture the bull's attention and mesmerize it with the cape.

She didn't have time for style or swagger.

Sweeping the skirt aside and high, then flicking her arm behind her body, the bull passed wide on her right side, a safe four feet away from her.

Twisting, she called to the bull, which hadn't turned to search for the cape again. "Hey!"

"It is 'huh,' señorita!" she heard someone call from behind and to the side. One of the men who had fled the bull's path lingered in the alleyway. "Huh!"

The bull swung its head toward where the man hid. It could turn quicker than a polo pony despite its massive bulk.

"Huh!" Annja called to redirect its attention. It worked. "Call for someone who can manage this," she yelled in Spanish. "I'll try to keep it in one spot."

"Already done. I sent my friend. A retired bullfighter lives not far from here. Watch out, señorita!"

The bull thundered toward her, horns down, and aimed for her leg, because that was where she held the skirt. Quickly she flicked out the fabric and at the same time jumped to the side to put her body out of the bull's line. Not exactly a matador's calm, defiant stance, but she was no torero.

A horn snagged the fabric, pulling it out of her hand. Not optimal. Not even the best of the best worst scenarios she could imagine.

Annja now stood alone in the alley with a bull, which was shaking its head in an attempt to dislodge the bright cloth flapping from its horn. On its flank she noted the brand. A half circle above a bar. If she survived, she intended to track down the bull's origins.

Adolescent cheers caught her attention. Down the alley, where she had turned to enter the street, a klatch of young boys had pushed open the iron gate and skipped and tugged on a rope they each held with one hand. Unaware of the bull, they took up position at the end of the street and laid out the rope in preparation for some sort of game.

"No!" Annja yelled. The bull was still struggling to free itself from the skirt. "Boys! *Chicos!*" she called.

They didn't hear her.

"Is the torero on his way?" she called to the unseen man.

"I haven't heard from my friend. I will try to find another cape!"

"No, don't—" She took a breath to alleviate her panic. He couldn't help her. She didn't want to involve anyone else in this incredible danger.

She didn't need the man's help.

The bull stomped a hoof down on the skirt and with a shake of its head finally tore it off its horn. It dropped to the ground in shreds. The animal looked down the alley and shifted its back legs.

It had seen the children.

Without a thought for her own safety, Annja ran alongside the bull, which was beginning to move. This time, she called the sword out from the otherwhere and without hesitation stabbed the bull in the bulging muscle behind the neck, much like the mounted picadors did with their long spears. The bull grunted and twisted its head in aggravation at the small stick that had penetrated its thick hide. It slowed to a stop.

Annja didn't have the time or skill to perform precision moves of weakening the bull with repeated stabs to the swollen *morillo*. And the bull wasn't about to stand around and wait for her to learn.

It charged her, head down and left horn aimed for her thigh. She leaped and rolled in the air, landing with both feet planted behind the bewildered bull. Her athletic abilities had improved ever since she'd first held the sword. She could perform some remarkable feats when necessary.

"Huh, huh!" she taunted the bull, waving her free hand, but its attention was no longer on her.

It lifted its head, the leathery black nostrils sniffing the air. The boys playing at the end of the street jumped over the rope on the ground, picking up stones as they landed on one foot.

A woman's shriek finally alerted the children, and when they saw the bull, they panicked and backed against the iron gate that blocked the end of the street.

Annja again bypassed the bull, running toward the children, who had been accompanied by an adult she only now noticed. Panic widened the woman's eyes. Annja stopped thirty feet in front of the children and turned. She waited for the bull to come to her. Was this what it was like to stand in the corrida and face down death? But this was no spectacle. Innocent lives were in danger.

The bull walked a few steps, its hooves marking hollow clicks on the cobblestones and its tail flicking fiercely. It was assessing its opponent.

Adrenaline racing, Annja waved her hands and walked toward the danger, angling slightly to the side. She hated leaving a path open toward the children, but if the bull followed movement, then perhaps she could lure it away.

With a snort, it charged.

She stared down a locomotive that couldn't be stopped. The only hope to alter its path was derailment.

Gripping the sword with both hands, she raised it high above her head, blade pointed down. The battle sword was much longer and wider than the *estoque* employed in the ring, but it would serve the purpose.

The matador placed the blade between the shoulder blades at the back of the neck muscle. Perfect placement slipped the blade in smoothly, to cut the aorta and ensure almost instantaneous death. It was a move made so quickly the crowd often never registered the kill—the moment of truth.

Annja jumped high as she felt the heat of the bull gain on her. She brought the sword tip down and pushed it hard into the bull's back, slightly left of the spine. She didn't hit bone.

Landing with a hand on the bull's side, she pushed off from the sweat-slick red hide and again landed against a brick wall bracing herself with her hands. The bull remained standing. She may have missed the aorta completely. A coup de grâce at the base of the brain might be necessary.

Turning, she waved her hands to keep the bull's attention on her and not the screaming boys.

She slapped its side and it whipped around to charge her. The battle sword remained deeply embedded in the bull's back.

Annja dodged and changed her trajectory to the right. The bull managed to follow her, its tongue lolling and blood spilling from the sword's entry point.

She miscalculated the distance and ran right up against the rough wall. The bull was on her, its hooves punishing the cobblestone. Its hot breath on her arm, she turned to meet the bull's forehead and nose as it butted up against her stomach—gently.

The acrid scent of blood and musk nearly overwhelmed her. Toes pushing upward, she couldn't gain another inch of space between her and the beast. She pressed her palms against its forehead but it was as if she was pushing an iron statue cemented into the ground.

The horn tips scraped the brick on either side of her torso. The bull lifted its head weakly, dragging its wet nose along her hip. And then it faltered, wobbling backward. A horn tore her pant leg, pulling a strip of fabric away from her thigh to hang shredded above her knee.

Annja pushed against the flat head. The bull's legs

shook. Drool spilled out of its open mouth. Its eyelids shuttered. It was dying—because of her.

The world rushed back in on her in a fury of sound. Screaming children. Shouting men. Close by, the honking of a car horn. The bull's irregular panting prodded her conscience.

The bull fell to its knees, releasing her from the horned prison against the wall.

Annja stumbled forward and, in a moment of clarity, grabbed the sword hilt and pulled it out of the bull's back. She released the sword to the otherwhere.

The bull's head dropped. It tumbled to its side, hooves clacking against the cobblestone.

Shouts of "Olé!" and clapping erupted around Annja. Her shoulders were jostled as men congratulated her on defeating the bull and her stunning prowess.

Her eyes tracked to the children who were being claimed, one by one, by adults, who swept the boys to safety.

Annja lowered her head and pushed through the crowd that had begun to circle the fallen bull. She nodded, offering a weak smile to the people who continued to congratulate her.

When she cleared the street and turned the corner to stand against the door of a closed candy store, Annja exhaled.

16

Annja slammed her hotel room door behind her. The message light on her cell phone flashed. Mindlessly, she punched through the buttons and checked the messages. One from Doug Morrell, her producer at *Chasing History's Monsters,* one from Garin Braden and another from an unlisted number.

The unlisted number intrigued her. Tossing the phone on the bed, she sat on the edge and stretched her back straight, straining her well-used muscles. Only now did she remember the tear in her pants and, for the first time, noticed the blood. On closer inspection, she found a six-inch abrasion across her upper thigh. The bull's horn had gotten her and she hadn't even been aware of it.

A much lesser cut than the one she had given the bull.

Digging through her backpack, she pulled out some prepackaged alcohol swabs and cleaned the wound. She'd survive.

Calling up the sword, she sat on the bed clasping the hilt in her lap. The blade gleamed. It wasn't bloody.

It never came back to her hands showing any sign of damage.

She had killed with this sword. It had been necessary for her survival and to protect innocent people. She never dwelled on that. At least, she tried not to.

Roux claimed that the sword had chosen her. She believed that to her marrow. She wasn't Joan of Arc reincarnated.

But she had never killed an animal. Well, did a shark count as an animal? And there had been a pack of wild dogs… While her life and the lives of the children had been in danger, it hurt her to consider what she had done.

Where had the bull come from? Someone had to have opened the gate she'd closed behind her and pushed the bull through. Without her noticing.

The image of the bull's brand haunted her, but she couldn't bring herself to pull up a search on the laptop.

She had pressed her palms to the bull's head and had felt its end. It hadn't chosen to be used as a weapon. It had never chosen a life that would see its first freedom the final steps toward its death.

She pressed the flat of the blade to her forehead. The cool steel was a balm to her. Today she felt she had abused her power.

ANNJA WOKE TO the sound of a slamming door. She sat upright in bed. A woman in a red-and-black flamenco dress leaned against the door. Annja still held the sword.

"That's some big steel," Ava Vital commented, crossing her arms over her chest and arrowing her patented glared on Annja. "Don't worry, I didn't come to duel. Though that would be fun, wouldn't it? Dueling. Whatever happened to dueling?"

"It went out during the Enlightenment when drunken fops battling to the death tended to walk themselves into their enemies' rapiers." Annja stretched her neck to the side, easing out a kink.

"We would never have dueled drunk. When we call someone out, we mean business."

Realizing it would be risky to send the sword to the otherwhere now, Annja set it aside on the bed. "And who has wronged you that you would call out?"

"Let's not rehash this, okay, Brooklyn?"

"Right. The matador."

"I heard you killed a bull with that sword. Rescued a couple of kids."

Annja shrugged. "News travels fast."

"Faster than the internet in this old neighborhood. A man can slap his wife and walk out the door and by the time he reaches the end of the street, a posse of housewives wielding cast-iron frying pans stands waiting for him. So how does it feel?" Ava asked quietly. "To kill?"

"Not right."

"Good. You're a better person than I had initially thought."

"I'm not sure I need the points right now."

"Especially not from me, eh?"

No, especially not from someone who had a death wish for the matador.

"You let yourself in. You must have good reason." Annja stood and paced to the balcony door, aware that Ava had approached the bed to look at the sword.

"Looks a couple centuries old, but I'm no expert. A battle sword isn't an easy weapon to get through customs."

"No, it's not." Annja left it at that. "So, the reason for your visit?"

"I'd thought you'd left the city. Why are you still here?"

The only reason anyone would assume she had left would be because they knew she'd been escorted to the airport. Only the police were aware of that, and James Harlow. Which shone a new light on Ava Vital. Who did she know?

"I like the sun." Annja grabbed the pitcher of water from the dresser and poured herself a glassful. She offered one to Ava, but the dancer refused with a shake of her head.

Her dress swished as she strutted across the room, her hands on her hips. A member of the Spanish Special Forces as well as a dancer. If the woman hadn't tried to kill Manuel Bravo, she could imagine them getting to know each other better, perhaps even becoming friends.

And since when do you worry that your friends have murderous impulses? Her conscience always made her face her truths.

"Have you come to tell me to leave Cádiz?" Annja asked. "I'm not keen on threats."

"I guessed that about you. But I will warn you to stay out of my way."

"And that way leads to Manuel Bravo?"

Ava leaned against the patio door, her elegant form silhouetted in the setting sun. Annja realized she must have fallen asleep for a few hours. "The matador is in deeper than he can imagine. In the ring he is a maestro. Outside the ring, he isn't very smart."

"Sounds like you have more against the guy than the suspicion he killed your friend."

"Diego wasn't a friend. Just a guitar player."

"Who are you?" Annja finally blurted. She was beyond frustrated trying to figure out all the players in this game and their positions.

"I'm a dancer." She lifted her skirts at the hip and pounded out a few steps that beat the dust up from the hardwood floor. "You didn't notice the costume?"

"A dancer who carries a knife at the back of her skirt and who shoots a sniper rifle like the Special Forces she is and who has a very close relationship with the police."

"The police? I don't think so." She wrinkled her nose.

"Then why haven't they arrested you? I gave them an exact description. Including that tattoo. If I found you, the authorities shouldn't have any trouble."

"The police are stupid."

"Do you know César Soto?"

The dancer looked down her nose at Annja, but didn't

answer. Annja couldn't judge whether it was because she did know him or wanted to maintain her dominance by refusing to answer another question.

"Tell me about the tattoo on your wrist. I wasn't able to find reference to it online."

Ava moved her arm up in a sinuous glide, flicking her wrist in a classic flamenco move to display the tattoo. "It's my tribute to Nemesis."

"The goddess of divine retribution?" Greek vengeance. Often depicted with wings. Annja couldn't believe she'd missed that. Though the tattoo was a single wing. "A strong female warrior."

"Why the label? Can't she simply be a strong warrior? Like Boudicca, or Althena, or Joan of Arc."

Annja glanced at the sword on the bed. "I'll grant you that. You get the tattoo after being trained in the Special Forces? Doesn't really fit with army standards."

"I had the tattoo done after—" She glanced aside. "A bad breakup."

Bad romance and a retribution goddess? Made sense.

"It was the matador's assistant who set the bull after you," Ava blurted.

Annja tilted her head to eye the dancer. "Cristo?" How could she know that?

Ava nodded. "Did you see the brand?"

"Half circle above a bar."

"The bull was from Cristo's ranch. El Bravo considers his bulls unworthy of the ring. The two argue incessantly about that."

"Yet Cristo works for Bravo. He was there the day I was out to his villa. I didn't notice any animosity between the men."

"Cristo can't sell his bulls to the corridas—they share Bravo's opinion—so he needs the money. I believe the man thinks someday the matador will use one of his *toros*. A twisted relationship, if you ask me."

"Why would Cristo set a bull after me? Because Bravo asked him to?"

Ava nodded.

"Manuel Bravo strikes me as someone who never asks others to do his dirty work for him."

Yet, he believed she had touched the votive crown. The man wouldn't actually kill someone for touching one of them, would he?

No, that was ridiculous. He'd have to be a psychopath to let such a small affront affect him.

"He removes obstacles in his path," Ava said. "With a sweep of his cape, El Bravo can direct a charging bull toward death. He does it for a living, Creed. You cannot trust him."

"I think I can't trust you. Or the police."

"Never trust the police. Especially not regarding the corrida. Are you aware of César Soto and El Bravo's relationship?"

"Were they once competitors?"

Ava laughed. "Soto would never have been considered anyone's competition. He has weak ankles. He could never stand before the bull without his legs shaking. He was injured badly."

"I've noticed his limp."

"El Bravo's father had been training César when it happened. A bull gored him in the thigh. Went all the way through and damaged the muscles permanently. Manuel's father could never get over the guilt. He's been supporting Soto since."

"Really? Like, paying his rent?"

Ava nodded.

"His bills?"

"Everything. Except now the burden has fallen on Manuel's shoulders. He is now the primary supporter of the family. And in this country, family pride is everything."

Ava waited in silence as Annja considered what she'd said. So Manuel Bravo was working not only to support himself, but also César Soto? Over a wounded leg? When did such a guilt payment end? Would he pay Soto's way forever? That certainly gave the matador a reason to be angry. But not Soto. She still couldn't see how that gave Bravo a reason to murder Diego.

"Does Soto return the favor by overlooking El Bravo's indiscretions?" Annja posited.

"Now you're using your brain," Ava said. She spun, the move flaring out the skirt of her dress.

"How do you know so much about the torero?"

The dancer lifted her chin. "You haven't done enough

computer research, clearly." Ava sighed. "Remain in Cádiz at your own risk."

Annja's shoulders stiffened. "Is that a threat?"

"Not at all." Ava strode to the door and opened it. "I'm dancing at the Gato Negra in a few hours. Stop by for a drink."

Annja raised an eyebrow.

"Now, *that* was a threat." Ava sauntered down the hallway, leaving the door open.

Annja's skin crawled. She felt as if Ava had cursed her.

Soto and Bravo were indebted to each other.... Interesting. And that Ava knew so much about their relationship added a new twist to the mystery. Somehow, the three were tied together. Clearly one of them had been her lover. Is that why she'd taken a shot at Bravo?

17

Garin glared at the guard standing in front of the steel door to the seaside office. The neckless lackey had been placed there to pat down everyone who entered, and Garin understood that it was his job. He locked eyes with the bruiser, who stood as tall as he was. "Drake expects me."

The guard let his gaze, hidden behind dark sunglasses, drop to Garin's chest, where he could be concealing a weapon—and was. He favored a Heckler & Koch Tactical lately. With a nod, the guard stepped aside and opened the door.

"Braden!"

The enthusiastic welcome came from somewhere beyond a forest of ferns and palms set before a panoramic window with a breathtaking view of the Atlantic Ocean. Garin strolled into the luxurious office, waiting for the door to close behind him, then unbuttoned his suit coat and shrugged his shoulders. He'd been going casual the past few days, so suiting up this morning felt restrictive.

"I've made tea," Drake called from within the forest. "It's brewed. Help yourself. I'm almost finished."

The palm-tree fronds shivered and Garin heard the sharp clip of snippers. He poured a cup of tea that filled the air with sharp punches of cinnamon, clove and anise. Settling into an armless leather chair before a massive granite desk, he nodded when the thin, tall man appeared, his sleeves rolled up. The red silk shirt he wore matched the red in his cheeks. An extreme sun allergy, Garin knew, which is why Hannibal Drake did all his gardening indoors.

The man pulled off his gardening gloves and tossed them onto the desk. Gesturing to the miniature forest, he said, "I think I've been watering them too much. Rot is setting in. You like the brew? I have it sent from Nepal."

"Spicy. Heats the throat going down."

"Indeed, and it's good for the circulation."

Garin set the fragile teacup on the desk in front of him. "So you're into gardening and tea now?"

"It calms me. Or it's supposed to." He moved the gloves to a steel table on wheels that was stocked with garden supplies, and poured himself a cup, adding an unhealthy dose of sugar. "My physician says I'm to cultivate serenity in my life."

"How's that working for you?"

"Not bad. Not bad at all." Hannibal Drake sipped, then winced. "This stuff is awful. I can't get the knack for tea. It always tastes like weakly flavored water with bits of stick in it. Don't tell me you actually like it?"

Garin shrugged. "I've tasted better brews, and usually bearing a wax seal that promises it's been aged for decades."

"Right." He veered toward the wet bar behind Garin. Glass clattered as he poured two tumblers of brandy neat. "If anything will bring me serenity, it's this."

Garin tilted back the golden spirits Drake handed him, and guessed it was some fine stuff. Smooth. Sweet, smoky and sultry. Exactly like the perfect woman.

"Portuguese," Hannibal said. "Sweeter than the Macedonian stuff I usually serve."

"Send me your supplier's information," Garin said. "This is worth stocking up with a few cases."

"I will. Hell, I'll send you a case. You catch a fight while you're in town?" Hannibal asked as he opened a desk drawer and pulled out a flat wooden box.

"Wouldn't miss one. El Bravo is a good friend."

Hannibal set the box on the desk and met Garin's eyes. "Ah, yes, I know the torero. That's excellent. You choose your friends carefully."

"As I chose you. So what do you have for me?"

The man slid the box across the desk and sat back without a word. He swirled the tumbler, watching as Garin lifted the lid. Inside, arranged carefully on black velvet, lay a necklace that had been crafted in the late nineteenth century during the Art Nouveau period. The metalwork was hand-chased brass, pounded and polished to represent acanthus leaves and ivy. A few flower petals skirted the edges. Rubies highlighted the curved motion of the piece but did not overwhelm it. They were only there to catch the light and draw the eye to the pendant.

As a centerpiece, the ivory pendant was half as large as Garin's palm. The porcelain oval had been hand-painted. He knew this without question. It depicted a Rubenesque woman with titian hair spilling down her shoulders, eyes closed. Her lips were parted and she held a ribbon across her lower lip. An expression of ecstasy no man would ever mistake.

"Is it the one?" Hannibal asked.

Garin touched the pendant, careful not to press too hard or get the oils from his fingers on the paint. A piece this old, in watercolors, could easily be damaged. He traced a finger along the woman's face without touching the piece. He'd forgotten those lips.

No, he hadn't.

Garin rubbed a hand along his thigh, keeping his expression neutral. Some days he did forget. The centuries moved slowly. When people entered his life for years, it felt like mere moments. He remembered some. Few he recalled with such accuracy he could bring up the scent they had worn or their exact gestures and speech inflections.

This necklace stirred the memory of her mouth, curved on the one side in laughter. Just waiting to be kissed.

"Yes," he said and closed the lid. "This is the one. How much do you want?"

"From a friend?" Garin doubted the man hadn't already decided exactly how much he could snake out of him before he'd arrived. "One hundred thousand."

Not worth that much. Unless it had been painted by a master of the time period, such as Mucha or Toulouse-Lautrec.

Garin nodded. "Deal." He placed the box on his lap and pulled out his cell phone. "I'll wire the money to you. Give me the account number."

In less than five minutes, Garin had a new trinket. No, not new, but a familiar piece he'd lost long ago.

"A pretty piece," Hannibal said, rising and gesturing for Garin to follow him to the window.

With the box tucked under his arm, Garin joined his friend and marveled at the view. A white-sand beach intersected with a shipping dock to the left of Hannibal's office. The dock couldn't obscure the blue water, which glinted with sunlight.

"I often study the objects that pass through my hands," the dealer said, "especially the ones with portraits. What do you think the name of that woman was?"

"No clue," Garin said. Some memories he had to keep sacred.

His attention was diverted to the left. Sunlight glinted off a warehouse fronted by a parking lot crowded with rusted shipping containers when its steel doors rose to admit a forklift driver. Inside, a bustle of workers moved around crates of a certain size and shape that Garin suspected contained guns. Along any shoreline around the world you could find that kind of underhanded operation. Hell, it served a man well to have a few such places on his contact list. You never knew when they might come in handy.

"Not what you're thinking," Hannibal said, interrupting his thoughts. "No guns in that warehouse. But if you're in the market for weaponry…?"

"Not at the moment." He respected the relationship he and Hannibal Drake had cultivated. They could discuss almost anything and not fear that the other would share it with anyone else. "If not guns, what are they moving down there?"

"Artifacts. Small-time. Bunch of junk, if you ask me. Though they do bring in the occasional treasure. I have first pick, which pleases me to no end because that leaves—well—someone else in the lurch."

"First to the treasure walks away with the spoils," Garin agreed.

"And in this town you'll find a whole nest of vultures eager to pick through the spoils. Most of the hypocrites work for the university or the local museum. Now, if you're looking for something a little older and more interesting to display in your office…?"

Garin chuckled and slapped Hannibal across the back. "I've already put a small fortune in your pocket today, Drake. It was good to see you. Thanks for this."

"I've been watching for what you described for years.

Glad to know I finally found what you've been seeking. I'll send the brandy to your place in Berlin."

"Looking forward to it. Good afternoon, Drake."

Garin left the office and decided to drive around the building to get a better view of the warehouse. The workers shuffling around outside weren't very covert, though at a glance someone might guess they were merely shipping crated goods. He picked out an armed guard on the rooftop, a semiautomatic slung over his shoulder. Again, not covert at all.

"Artifacts," he said. "And Annja Creed stuck in the middle of some kind of mess, as usual, that involves stolen artifacts. Should I or shouldn't I?"

He weighed his options.

Her insinuation that El Bravo could have something do to with the guitarist's murder had insulted him. Perhaps after a cigar and another brandy back at the villa he would decide what to tell Annja. If anything.

18

The plaza the museum was on was lined with palm, locust and banana trees. The narrow, tight streets in this island-bound city all led to big, beautiful plazas. Elizabethan architectural influences were everywhere. Pair that with the Moorish tile work and a blend of Gothic, Baroque and Renaissance, and a girl could get lost in her admiration of a cupola here or an arched entrance there.

So Annja didn't notice that the car on the street heading toward her didn't swerve to avoid her until the front fender was just six feet away. Sensing the driver *did* see her and was actually aiming for her, Annja leaned into the parked car to her right. Gripping the hood with her fingers and using the flat yet sticky-from-the-heat metal surface, she levered herself up. She did a somersault over the hood of the car as the moving vehicle whisked by.

Landing on the sidewalk in a roll, Annja came up into a kneeling position and jutted her head up above the car's hood to scan the area. The dented green luxury car that had just tried to kill her stopped and began to back up.

"Definitely not an accident."

Taking off in a run down the sidewalk, she heard tires squeal as the car made a backward turn in the middle of the street. The museum entrance was to the right, so she went straight, heading out of the plaza. Civilians could be put into a dangerous situation there.

The car behind her gunned it. With a glance over her shoulder, Annja saw it jump the curb. The wheels tore up the landscape fronting the museum. Its tires spun in the soft ground, spitting up clods of grass in the vehicle's wake.

Pumping her arms to increase her speed, Annja couldn't outrun the car, which was getting too close for comfort. To the right lay the museum grounds. To the left, the street—and a very familiar rental Jeep. The driver honked and waved frantically.

Once again, the man's Annja-radar saved the day.

She dodged right, and the car behind her followed along with the change in direction. Garin drove slowly, marking her progress. She leaped into the open back bed of the Jeep. The car following her rammed into the back of the Jeep and Garin put his foot down hard on the accelerator. Annja clutched the roll cage bar as the momentum slammed her body hard against the side of the bed.

"Not surprised," Garin said as she climbed into the

front seat, "and only a little offended you didn't invite me along for the chase."

"You're here now. Stop complaining. Turn right. Take this scuffle away from the crowded plaza."

"Ever concerned about the innocents." Garin turned a hard right, the Jeep lifting high on its outer wheels, before gunning it down a narrow street. "Who are we evading?"

"Not sure."

"Did you look at him the wrong way?"

"I was minding my own business headed to the museum when he almost crushed me against a parked car."

"Hardly the way to pick up a beautiful woman."

"I'll say. Some men have no manners whatsoever."

"I'll lose him down by the docks."

Annja focused on the green car coming up close behind them. Looked like an old-model Mercury with a long, flat body. The license plate was obscured by mud, and the fender looked as if it had taken more than a few hits. The driver wore dark sunglasses and a bandanna over his hair. She couldn't pick out any remarkable features. He had found her outside the museum, so she could guess someone had known where she'd been headed. But she hadn't told anyone. He must have followed her from the hotel.

"Much less threatening than the bull," she muttered as the Jeep increased the distance between it and the tail. Garin took another sharp turn.

"What bull?"

"I narrowly avoided being gored a few hours ago."

"What? Where? You were at the corrida?"

"No, I was on my way to the antiquities shop you suggested I visit. Which makes me suspicious now. You were the one who sent me there."

"A bull came after you while you were shopping? Heh. So the whole bull-in-the-china-shop thing…"

"Not as funny as you think it is. It found me before I found the shop. Had to take it out before it trampled down a bunch of kids."

"Good going. Where'd it come from?"

"I have an idea. A certain sniper visited me afterward to let me know the bull had come from Cristo's ranch."

Taking another sharp turn, the Jeep shot under an iron bridge. Here it was darker and the smell of oil and industry made it hard to breathe.

"You know Cristo?" she asked. "Or for that matter, do you know someone who might have Cristo sic a bull after me?"

"Annja, I hope you're not implying what I think you are. I thought I'd made it clear—I trust Manuel."

"I know. You two are friends, and you choose your friends carefully. But why would Cristo want me dead?"

"You're not dead. Are you sure the bull didn't escape its cage while being transported through the city?"

She stared at him and knew he got the message even though he didn't turn.

"All right, all right," he said. "I sent you off shopping,

and it led you into danger. That is suspicious. Want me to ask Manuel about Cristo for you?"

"I don't understand how the ranch hand could be involved. Unless he sells illegal antiquities and felt I was getting too close to discovering it was him."

"Cristo doesn't strike me as the discerning sort who would be interested in bits of pots."

"The votive crowns in El Bravo's sanctuary are not pot bits. And just because he sells them doesn't mean he has to have an interest in their aesthetic qualities. Yet if he's that desperate for money, as Ava implied, that he was involved with the sale of the crowns, he couldn't be that bad off now. No. I don't understand the assistant's involvement."

"Lost him." Garin pulled the Jeep to a stop near a chain-link fence in front of a stretch of warehouses along the shore. "You're sure it was one of Cristo's bulls?"

"It had a half circle above a bar brand."

"That is Cristo's brand." He adjusted the rearview mirror to keep an eye out behind them. "I'm not keen on your involvement in this particular adventure, but I'll look into it."

"Thank you."

"I have a price."

"Not willing to pay."

"Come on, Annja, don't be like that."

"I know better. Your prices are too steep, and that's without tapping into my bank account."

"Fine. You'll owe me one."

He drove onward, navigating a turn that took them beneath a streetlight defaced with red-and-white graffiti. They had driven far from the tourist areas or any festivals. Annja peered over her shoulder, making sure the tail was nowhere in sight. A wooden box in the backseat caught her eye. "What's in the box?"

"A trinket."

"Can I look?" She reached back and pulled the flat, wide box into her lap.

"Don't you even want to hear what you're going to owe me?" He flashed her a bright, white crocodile smile. Lesser people had fallen shaking to their knees before that duplicitous grin, she felt sure.

Annja rapped her fingers on the box, vacillating between the two curiosities.

"You're thinking about it," he teased. "I love a curious woman."

"Does it involve you dressing me for an event that has me tagging along awkwardly?"

"Dressing you I've done. Door number two or what's in the box?"

She smoothed her palms over the box's polished wood surface. It was stained dark and stamped with the maker's mark—two crossed swords inside a circle. She didn't recognize it. Door number two involved doing something for, or with, Garin Braden. It could be as innocuous as attending another corrida, or it could involve an excursion that involved weapons and stealth.

It might even be a weird kind of date that meant getting dressed up and meeting legitimate dignitaries at a charity ball. The man's interests were eclectic, to say the least.

"Door number one," she muttered.

"It's a research thing," Garin said. "Some dusty old artifact I put my hands on recently. I thought you could take a look at it for me."

"Is it in this box?"

"No, that's just a trinket."

"Hmm… Seems like every time I take a look at an artifact for someone, bullets fly. Not to mention the local authorities develop an extreme dislike for me."

"Is that a no?"

"What is it? This artifact you want me to look at."

"It's unique. I don't have it with me, but will look forward to your visiting me in Berlin to assess it."

Annja pressed her shoulders to the back of the seat, curling her fingers around the box. She knew he couldn't possibly ask her for a favor without requiring she go to him and meet him on his grounds. Wouldn't be Garin Braden if it had gone any other way.

"Deal. Next time I'm in Germany, it's a date."

"A date? I wasn't suggesting we go that far. So I have to buy flowers and prepare you a meal, too?"

"Sounds about right. But skip the flowers. An unnecessary expense. Now do I get to look in the box?"

"It's not locked."

Running her fingers along the edge, she prolonged

lifting the cover as her mind sifted through the possibilities of what might lay inside. To Garin, a trinket could weigh fifty carats and have once hung around a queen's neck. Or it could be a solid-gold pistol from the eighteenth century embossed with Garin's name or even the name of a past king. Or why not a biological weapon he'd picked up for a song because he could?

He chuckled. "It's not going to leap out at you."

"Was it obtained illegally?"

"Annja." He mocked a pout, which answered the question in the positive.

Pushing open the lid, she was initially relieved it was only a piece of jewelry. Then she was disappointed it didn't glitter with priceless jewels. It was an elaborate Art Nouveau piece, but the metal was bronze, in need of a polish, and the ivory pendant featured a hand-painted portrait. The woman's face had been done in the style of Alphonse Mucha, but she sensed it wasn't the great master's work, though she surmised the artist had once designed pieces for Fouquet, the famous jewelry designer.

"Pretty," she offered as the Jeep rolled along a coastal street, catching flashes from the intermittent streetlights. "You a fan of the Art Nouveau style?"

"Not really."

"Then it must be the woman in the portrait," she guessed. "Who is she?"

Garin almost ran into a bicyclist loaded down with

wicker baskets. He had to quickly spin the wheel to the left.

"Well, well," she remarked. "She must have meant something to you."

Braden remained silent. And she had guessed correctly. He knew the woman in the portrait. Or likely, *had known* her, to judge the piece. It was well over a century old. Certainly the man had a long list of conquests. Could this woman, with the red hair and sensuous mouth, have stolen his heart?

She wouldn't ask. "Where we headed?" she said and turned to place the jewelry box on the backseat.

"We're here." He pulled the Jeep in front of a warehouse sided with bleached wood slats warped from the sea air. "I was shopping in the area earlier—"

"There are no stores in sight, Garin."

"I bought a pretty necklace. Anyway, listen, I noticed this warehouse and thought it might hold some interest for you. Want to take a look inside?"

"Will I like what I see?"

"Knowing you and your morals, probably not. There are usually only two workers here during the evening according to— Ahem. Let's go through the side door beyond the chain-link fence and greet them."

"Have you previously introduced yourself to anyone inside?"

"No. I took a drive around after I was done—"

"Shopping."

"Exactly."

Garin walked beside Annja, his hand on the gun he wore concealed under his left arm. He strode with the confidence of a man you didn't want to mess with, especially if you were involved in bad things in an unassuming warehouse by the sea.

They vaulted over the chain-link fence with ease. "Is this a guns-blazing scenario?" she inquired as they neared the dented, rusted tin door. A glance over her shoulder ensured the area was still and quiet. "Or a silent reconnaissance mission?"

"I think a little of both. You cool with that?"

"Always."

Garin winked as he gripped the door handle and waited for her to signal her readiness with a nod. He lifted the door upward so the tin panel didn't scrape the asphalt and pulled it open far enough for Annja to slip inside. The setting sun didn't reach this area, but inside hazy streaks of light beamed through cracks in the sea-and-wind-damaged tin roofing.

Annja's fingers tingled to hold the sword. It had become a sort of sixth sense, but she only drew it out when faced with real and imminent danger. The warehouse was dark but she heard no sound.

Garin gestured for her to walk ahead, down an aisle of steel girders boasting vertical rows of empty steel shelving. It was difficult to guess what the warehouse may have originally been built for.

Dust tickled the back of her throat and she closed her mouth to breathe shallowly so as not to sneeze. In

her backpack she kept a small Maglite and drew it out,
flashing it from side to side.

A curious scent lured her forward, toward an open
area. She recognized it as formaldehyde. A good indication that there may be artifacts ahead. Unless some-
body was embalming bodies.

Annja paused. Here, near the end of the steel-girdered
row, wooden packing crates of varying sizes lined the
shelves haphazardly. As well, some pottery and even
random human bones were laid out as if awaiting cataloging. Nothing stood out as particularly valuable. No
gold or silver or anything she could immediately place
with certainty to a specific time period or age. Nothing was tagged, and most of the objects had been set
down carelessly to judge from the broken pottery. But
that didn't mean the valuable stuff hadn't already been
sorted out. These girdered racks could merely be where
all the detritus ended up.

Her assessment? Most definitely an antiquities operation. But the variety of artifacts baffled her. Had all
this been dug up in the Cádiz area? Couldn't be possible. She recognized a potsherd as ceramic. Whatever
it had been used for, it wasn't Spanish in origin. The
warehouse must also be receiving from other locations.
As well as shipping out? A shipping-and-receiving hub?

Garin's hand on her shoulder made her turn around.
She held the Maglite between their faces. His expression
to her indicated he'd follow her. Which she appreciated.

A metal conveyor belt snaked through the center of

the warehouse, starting near the tin garage doors and ending at a line of tables, obviously used for sorting. The tables were stacked with crates and scattered with Styrofoam packing material. In the midst of the white Styrofoam pieces jutted a small bronze fertility statue Annja recognized as Mayan.

Taking in the surroundings, she tracked along the walls and the girders. She ran her gaze along the upper floor that featured a walkway across the nearest wall that must lead to offices and possibly roof access.

No one around? Didn't make sense, unless they'd stepped out the back door on a coffee break. It was beyond siesta time yet she suspected this place didn't hold to normal work hours. Security was a must with an operation like this, so she remained alert.

Before she could step out from the girders toward the tables, Garin's grip on her upper arm tightened. She turned to follow his gaze. Smoke billowed from under the door through which they had entered. Bright orange flames licked along the base of the empty girders close to that door.

The fire had started behind them. Someone had been keeping an eye on them.

Crashing through the closed double garage doors, a white van spun to a stop beside the tables. Three men wielding machine guns leaped out and started to toss the artifacts into the back of the vehicle, seemingly oblivious to Annja and Garin's presence not thirty feet away.

Garin raised his arm, aiming at one of them. They hadn't yet been seen, or perhaps the fire had started because someone *had* seen them enter, but it was apparent they were claiming all they could before the place ignited into an inferno.

"No." Annja slammed Garin's arm down with her fist. "I want to get up into the office and see what I can find."

"The building is on fire. Let me take them out, and then you can reclaim the treasures."

"I'd rather find documents on previous sales and trades. Besides, what's on the tables doesn't look valuable."

"What about that statue?"

"I have no idea if it's authentic. They're too busy gathering junk to notice we're here. Cover me."

With a nod, he reluctantly pulled up his aim. She slipped along the aisle of steel girders, aware she was completely in view of the looters, but sure they were more intent on grabbing what they could before the flames made it to the tables.

Jumping onto the bottom step, she winced and ducked down when her hiking boot clanged against the loose iron.

The looters didn't pause and swept all the articles into the van in such a manner that nothing could have survived without sustaining damage.

Tracking up the stairs, she found the door to the office locked and timed her kick to match the slam of the vehicle doors as the looters closed the back of the van. Inside, the room was empty. Slatted plastic window shades hung broken, revealing a slash of illumination from the bright yard light.

Annja ran out to the next door, kicked it open and found yet another empty room.

"Nothing."

Who would leave the place unguarded? Either this operation had been in the process of clearing out or someone else had overtaken them. Probably the same men who were ransacking the place.

And yet, someone had been keeping an eye on it to be able to charge in and save what they could. Why hadn't they stopped her and Garin from entering? Had they arrived moments before the others?

Or had someone tipped them off about her visit? Impossible, unless Garin had done it. But he didn't want her dead. Not today, anyway.

The only answer was that they were not aware of Annja and Garin and had set the building on fire, and were quickly clearing out the evidence.

Backing out of the room, Annja spied something behind the door and grabbed it. A cell phone that still held a charge. She clicked it on, but no home information showed. Checking the contacts, she scrolled through a dozen Spanish names and a few she recognized as Egyptian in origin, and—she landed on a familiar name.

"James Harlow?"

Interesting. Tucking the phone in her pocket, she backtracked down the steps as the van revved its engine.

"Now can I shoot someone?" he called as she arrived by his side. He shoved her hard, and she went down on all fours, as did he. Bullets ricocheted over their heads, pinging the metal conveyor.

"Go for it."

He popped his head up and fired the Heckler & Koch. The van swerved as a bullet nicked but didn't blow the tire.

"Follow them!" She tried to get a look at the driver, but the van had already cleared the loading dock.

They raced out to the Jeep and got in.

"What was inside the upper rooms?" Garin asked as he turned on the ignition.

"A cell phone with a list of contacts."

He turned the Jeep around and trailed the van, which picked up speed and swerved into traffic on the boulevard that paralleled the sea.

"You think they destroyed their own operation?"

"Possible," she said. "But I'm of the belief another operation looted this one. On the other hand, there were no signs of struggle and not a single dead body. The offices were bare, as if someone had wanted to remove all evidence. And the guys in the van seemed completely unaware of our presence, so I think they wanted to make a fast getaway."

Glancing back to the flaming warehouse, Annja didn't regret not attempting to save any of the artifacts left behind. There hadn't been too many items of value. Was that enough to burn an entire warehouse to keep hidden? Yes. An illegal operation would destroy what it had to cover its tracks.

"They had to be trafficking in artifacts from all over. There were too many random items."

"Could have been."

"Wish you'd taken a picture before, when the place was intact."

"I'm not your cameraman." Garin twisted the wheel and avoided an oncoming truck. "I was doing you a favor by bringing you here."

"Which I will repay, apparently, next time I'm in Berlin."

"Glad you haven't already forgotten our deal."

She clutched the overhead handgrip as they swerved onto another street, this one cluttered with market stalls. They slowed to a crawl.

"Garin, if you were inside earlier, you know that implicates you."

"In what? I didn't go inside. I drove around the place. Ah, hell."

He stopped abruptly, shifted in his seat to look over his shoulder and began to back up.

"What?"

"You know where we're headed?"

"No, I—" She eyed the building ahead. It was familiar. She'd been inside it twice already. The white van drove around behind. "They were with the police?"

If the police had been out to the dig site and had murdered Simon Klosky, then this was an obvious connection to the same dirty dealings.

And yet…why would they return to the police station, knowing they were being followed? Not very smart if they wanted to keep it hidden from the station.

Behind them, the white van passed on the street fronting the station.

"They were taking us on a goose chase," Annja said.

"Maybe." Garin shifted and turned the Jeep around.

Annja pulled the cell phone she'd found out of her pocket. James Harlow had commented how the police were always helpful whenever he'd needed them. She had no proof whoever was in the white van was the police. And if it had been, the snatch at the warehouse could have been an official seizure.

No. If that were the case, they would have gone in with badges and guns.

"You've got yourself in a fine mess." He backed the Jeep into an alley. Garin shifted and drove out the opposite way from the police station. Behind them, the hum of sirens, gaining on them, prompted him to flash her the evil eye. He tightened his jaw and stepped on the accelerator.

19

Garin swerved down a side street and gunned it, neatly avoiding a woman carrying armloads of shopping bags. The sirens followed.

"Maybe they alerted fellow officers we were on their tail and that's why they led us right to the station," Garin said.

"Doesn't feel right. That would imply the entire department was dirty."

"Yeah, I guess not." Garin pulled the Jeep over to the curb.

A red fire engine blazed past them, followed by two patrol cars. Not in pursuit of them.

Garin blew out a breath and chuckled with relief. "Never a dull moment with you, Annja."

"It's why you like me."

"It is one of many reasons to like you. And yet…"

She caught his look in the rearview mirror. Twisting, she spied the white van gunning down the street.

"I don't think they're police," she said.

"You could be right. Hold on!"

He swerved the Jeep sharply, turning down yet another dark alleyway.

"Here." Garin handed her his Heckler & Koch, the standard weapon issued by the Spanish army. "Aim for a tire."

"Got it." Annja didn't bother to check the chamber. The gun was loaded. She rolled down the window and leaned out. A bullet pinged the Jeep's trunk. She adjusted her position to use the roll bar as protection across her chest, and fired.

The van swerved but corrected its front wheels and came right back in line with them. Return fire took out Garin's side mirror.

"Change in tactics," he announced and gunned the accelerator.

"Why don't you pull over and face them down?" Annja suggested.

Garin flashed her a smile. "I like your thinking. But I'm protecting a passenger, so no go."

"I can protect myself."

"Not to judge the weaponry in the car behind us. They're not cops. Probably were from the warehouse, taking down the place and covering their tracks."

"Maybe they think we were the ones looting the place?"

"Could be. Sit tight, Annja. I'll get us out of here."

"Then don't turn—"

Garin turned onto a dock. He was too busy concentrating on getting away and swerving from bullet fire to realize he was now driving right toward the sea. There were no turnoffs, and the van had taken the same turn.

"Hell. I don't know this area at all. You want to jump or ride it out?" he asked.

Annja eyed the car on their tail. If they jumped, they risked getting shot. If they rode it out, there was only the sea to catch them. It wouldn't be deep close to shore, but deep enough for ships to moor. The impact wouldn't kill them, and then they'd have a chance to swim for safety under the dock.

Anna pulled the seat belt across her lap and buckled it. "Ride it out, Thelma."

"Sure thing, Louise."

Garin jammed his foot on the accelerator and the Jeep sped toward the end of the dock, past the warning signs not to drive farther. The van tailing them skidded to a stop, and the man in the passenger seat popped his head out to watch as Annja felt the Jeep's wheels leave the end of the wooden dock. She gripped the seat belt strapped across her chest and hit the window button to roll it down while they soared through the air. Garin did the same.

The impact compressed her shoulders and spine against the seat. The front of the Jeep had hit the water grille-first, which Garin had intended. They plunged straight down, the tug of the water sucking the vehicle in like quicksand.

"You okay?" he yelled.

"Yes!"

She unlocked her seat belt as the sea gushed through the open windows and swallowed them into the cold water. Her head went under, and the surprising chill punched her in the lungs.

Grasping the top of the door, Annja twisted and pulled her shoulders and torso out through the window. Something stopped her and had a secure grip on her foot. She gasped in water and choked. Her boot was hung up on something. The seat belt.

She wiggled and tugged, but as the Jeep sank it pulled her down with it. She didn't have time to take another breath and her ears popped as she struggled for release. And calm. She wouldn't get free without remaining calm.

Garin would take care of himself and wouldn't know she was in trouble until he'd surfaced, and even then, he might suspect she had swum toward shore. The Jeep was sinking quickly. She twisted in the open window, trying to get a new angle, but only succeeded in wrapping the seat belt around her ankle. She felt the squeezing pull of the strap.

She could hold her breath underwater longer than the average swimmer, but not so long as a free diver, which was two or three minutes. Her mammalian diving reflex would allow her to achieve apnea, suspension of external breathing, which would allow her more time.

Did Garin keep a knife in the glove compartment? She scrambled to reach the compartment, but inside felt only paper and one of those spring-loaded center punches for knocking out the window in case of submersion. The irony of it was not lost on her.

Something snaked around her calf, and she felt her body being pulled down. Initially panicking and kicking—ridiculous thoughts of octopus tentacles and sea monsters sprang to mind—Annja relaxed when she realized it was a hand. The seat belt slackened and her ankle was twisted free. Her hind end was given a shove to push her completely out the window and up toward the silvery glow of the surface.

Her breath was gone. As she neared the surface, instinct reminded her that she couldn't simply pop her head up. Whoever had forced them into the brink was likely waiting above with their guns aimed. The darkness would provide some cover, but the moon was high and a glint on her water-soaked head could reveal their location.

She angled a shoulder toward shore and kicked, propelling herself through the water at a depth of about ten feet. She breathed in water through her nose but remained calm, resisting the urge to gasp. Arms cutting through the murky waters, she finally made it to darkness and determined she was under the dock.

Arrowing her head upward, she kicked, rising slowly, and broke the surface without a gasp, but instead a deep intake of breath through her nose.

Garin followed, submerging with the eerie and foreboding presence of a Navy SEAL beside her. Water slapped a steel dock piling five feet away. Overhead, the dock boards blocked any oberservers' view.

"You must have iron lungs, Annja," he commented.

"I suppose being immortal, you could have wandered around underwater for hours?"

"Longer than most. Hell. I forgot the necklace." Garin swam out and dived.

"Don't go back!" She grasped for his foot but missed it by a mile. "Stubborn medieval warrior. Whatever you left behind isn't worth it."

Annja swam over to the piling and wrapped an arm about it. It was coated with slimy seaweed, but it anchored her to one spot. She was able to stop kicking and collect her breath.

Listening for footsteps overhead, she heard the crack of tires rolling over the planks, away from the end of the dock. They must have decided the job had been successful. Except they couldn't expect that she and Garin had died in their plunge. Interesting.

But Garin still wasn't out of trouble. What was he doing?

The necklace's sentimental value must have been greater than Annja had guessed.

After nearly ten minutes, a head surfaced thirty yards out. Garin swam toward shore, using long, sure strokes, and then passed by her position. She followed, and the twosome climbed up onto the smooth head-size rocks lining the beachfront and sat. Wet clothing slapping her skin, Annja felt the evening breeze chill through to her bones.

Garin slammed the jewelry box onto the sand beside the rock he'd sat on and swore.

"It should be okay," she said. "It wasn't under for long."

Annja picked up the box and opened it up. Seawater poured out. The necklace wasn't inside.

"It's not in there, is it?" He wiped both palms over his face, his gaze on the horizon that blended the sea seamlessly into the moonlit yet cloudy sky.

"Sorry."

He let out a wet, dismissive chuckle. "Easy come, easy go."

"It meant a lot to you. I can go down with you for a few more dives before it gets too dark."

"The shore drops significantly thirty yards from here. I must have dived sixty feet. It's lost. I'm sure the water has already damaged the paint on the porcelain." He rose and shook his arms, which splattered water over her head. "I'm out of here. I should have driven you straight to the airport on the mainland instead of that warehouse," he said, finding purchase on the tumble of rocks lining the shore. "You're barking up the wrong tree, Annja. El Bravo isn't your man. And even if he were, you're not the police."

"I don't suspect he's involved with the stolen artifacts in the warehouse. But the votive crowns were obtained illegally."

"So are seventy-five percent of the artifacts on display in peoples' homes across the world."

"Listen." She tracked after him, squeezing the water out of her T-shirt. "I respect that you have a friendship with Bravo, and perhaps your perspective of his morals is a bit blurred. I won't ask you to do anything that would jeopardize that friendship."

"No, you won't. Because I won't be seeing you again until it's in another country, on another adventure. And I suggest you leave town as fast as you can find a flight because the police might be chasing you."

"How do I know they weren't after you?"

He smirked. "You've got me there. You don't know that." He scanned the shoreline, narrowing his eyes to take in the buildings.

"It wasn't the police. They would never have risked taking us around behind the police station. And I'm not leaving Cádiz."

"As suspected. Annja, just…stay away from Manuel Bravo. Promise me that."

"Can't make that promise."

Garin spun on her and gripped her by the upper arm. He squeezed hard enough to make her wonder if he could snap her humerus bone with a simple wrench of his wrist. She knew he could.

"You're hurting me."

"So make me stop. Slash your pretty little sword toward me and—"

She kneed him in the thigh. Her energy had been

depleted from the swim, but she made contact with the femoral artery, and it was enough to make him grit his teeth and wince. It broke his grip from her arm. Bringing up her elbow, she smashed it under his jaw. She followed with a roundhouse that connected with the back of his arm but didn't cause him to falter.

He gripped her by the back of the head and shoved her. Her boots, slick and the laces untied, tripped her and she tumbled onto the stones, catching her palm against a sharp corner and tearing open the flesh.

Annja huffed and spat to the side. The desire to draw the sword would only give him a satisfaction she didn't want to deliver. Instead, she studied her cut palm. "You don't get to win this one, Braden."

"I'd say it's been a pleasure," he said, "but that would be a lie."

Nodding, she tugged her wet hair back and squeezed out the water. "Thanks for the warehouse information, Garin. If you talk to Roux, tell him I said hello."

He didn't acknowledge her and turned to stomp away across the sand.

He was wrong about Bravo. But his friendship, and the way the man's mind worked, could justify anything the matador had done as right to Garin. Even knowing it wasn't right was still justified by the man's twisted values.

It didn't bother Annja as much as she felt it would others, because what you saw was exactly what you got with Garin Braden. He never claimed to be upstanding. She could take him in small doses. And getting a glimpse into his nostalgic heart earlier settled her need to badger him further. He was a man. He had a heart, like her. Things didn't always go right for him.

She wouldn't push.

But the two of them would never come up even on the scorecard. And she preferred it that way.

GARIN STALKED UP the beach, crossing through a block of warehouses, and hoofed it back to the seaside strip's hotels. Best place to hail a cab.

With a few shakes of his cell phone, the thing actually powered up. Waterproof to one hundred feet. Nice. He dialed Hannibal Drake and got an answering machine. He tried a few more numbers, Drake's cell and another cell, getting the same result. Before he could tuck his phone away in frustration, it rang.

"I saw your message," Drake said. "I only get one call."

"One call? Don't tell me."

"I'm sitting in the bloody brink. The police have arrested me on charges of illicit antiquities trading."

"Damn. I was calling to warn you that the warehouse next to your office went up in flames, but I guess you already know that."

"The police swarmed the area like bees. You stay away from there."

"Too late. We were followed. Be careful, Hannibal. The police may not be clean."

"Good to know. But I'm clean, which is all that matters. Well, basically. I'll be out of here as soon as I give them James Harlow's name."

The name sounded familiar to Garin, then he recalled why. "Is he a professor?"

"Works at the city museum. My nemesis."

Meaning, the other guy was Drake's competition in tagging the prime goods that arrived on shore.

"Is there anything I can do for you, Hannibal? Lawyer? Bail?"

"I've got it covered. Thanks, Braden. Enjoy the necklace."

The phone clicked off and Garin smacked a fist into his open palm. This time, Annja Creed had pushed him too far.

20

The walk to the hotel was uncomfortable as her cotton khaki pants dried and the seawater made her skin itch. In her room, Annja stripped bare and wrapped a towel around her torso, but didn't immediately jump into the shower. Garin's insistence that El Bravo was innocent rubbed her the wrong way.

Had one of the matador's votive crowns come from the seaside warehouse? There was no way to know, without tracking down the source. The bronze bull statue could have come from there. Again, she needed a source. Whoever had looted Crockett's site may have been located in the dock warehouse. They could have handed off the booty to a dealer or arranged for the delivery of the statue directly. And if Diego had been carrying both artifacts, the conclusion seemed obvious they had held both the bull statue and the votive crown she knew had been inside the wooden crate.

So the bull statue traveled from outside Jerez to a warehouse to Diego's hands. Or from Jerez directly to a dealer's hands, who then gave it to Diego to deliver—

to whom? Obviously not the same person who stole the crown from the crate.

Annja was aware of two people who had an interest in collecting bull-related artifacts: Manuel Bravo and James Harlow. And after finding Harlow's number on the cell phone in the warehouse, she wasn't certain anymore that El Bravo was the key player.

They could both be involved. Bravo had wanted the crown, Harlow the bull. Really? After she'd shown him pictures of the bull statue, had that piqued Harlow's interest enough to send looters out to the site to steal it? Was he capable of murder, whether or not he had been the triggerman?

She didn't see it, but then she didn't know him well. About as well as she had known Jonathan Crockett. And Harlow seemed determined to place blame for some kind of criminal activity on Crockett. To deflect the blame from himself?

And how did El Bravo play into all of this? A man who insisted all the artifacts he owned had been gifts. Had he obtained the crowns through others? She hadn't found the replica shop and couldn't know if that had been the truth. She suspected it was a lie, and walking up to a thousand-pound bull had pretty nicely cemented that lie.

"Time to pay the matador a visit and get to the bottom of this. I hope Garin decided to go club hopping this evening instead of visiting his friend."

AWARE THERE WAS NO fight this evening and that it was late, Annja wasn't sure if she'd find Señor Bravo at home. He'd indicated that besides bullfighting, women captivated his interest. He could be out carousing or seducing a beautiful woman right now. He could have someone at his villa.

Didn't matter. She was through with tiptoeing.

She wasn't sure of protocol. Could she knock on his door and expect to be admitted? Tomorrow was the big exhibition honoring the matador. He was supposed to kill six of the bulls in the fight. It would also bring him to his one-hundredth corrida of the season.

She'd worried about protocol for nothing. The butler let Annja in and offered her lemonade out on the patio under the glowing paper lanterns while he got Manuel, who was in contemplation. Most likely staring at the gold votive crowns, she decided. Contemplating their value? Or the life a man had paid to deliver one to Manuel's hands?

Twenty minutes passed before the lithe matador appeared, buttoning up a loose white shirt. He wore slouchy jeans that wilted over his bare feet, and he would have looked like a regular beach bum if it hadn't been for the slicked-back black hair and the cigar chomped at the corner of his mouth.

"Creed," he said around the cigar as he sat and put his feet up on the wicker table.

He was using just her last name now? Not so friendly anymore.

"How's the lemonade?" he asked, wincing as he looked directly at one of the paper lanterns. "Tart enough?"

"It tastes fresh squeezed."

"Of course it is. I always demand the finest. What are you doing here, and so late?"

"I was wondering if you'd allow me another look at the Visigothic votive crowns you display in your sanctuary."

"Why?"

His curt response took her off guard. The response "because I asked" wasn't going to cut it, she suspected.

"As I've told you, I'm an archaeologist. I study medieval arts. It's my specialty. The Visigothic crowns date back to the seventh century and earlier. At least, most of the ones in existence do. I've only ever seen the crowns in museums. I didn't get a chance to look closely at the ones you own when I was here the other day, and...well...I'm a curious girl."

"They are replicas. I cannot understand why they would prove of scholarly importance to you."

"I know you believe them fakes. Garin gave me the address to the antiques shop in the old town. But I wasn't able to find it. You said the artifacts you own are all gifts. What about the crowns?"

"I don't recall. I own so many pieces, you understand." He tapped the side of his head with a finger. "It's late."

"I know. I apologize. I had plans to fly out tomorrow after the fight, and I'd hate to leave Cádiz without knowing if I could have had a chance to examine the crowns more closely, perhaps even take a few pictures."

She tossed out that last statement to bait him. If he didn't allow pictures it would mean he had something he wished to hide.

Manuel tapped the cigar on a silver ashtray riveted to the wicker chair arm. He closed his eyes. "I thought I made it clear to you, Señorita Creed, I don't like it when people touch my things."

"I won't touch them. I promise. I have latex gloves with me. Carry them wherever I go." She pasted on her friendliest smile, which was not so garish as her beaming you-like-me-so-don't-shoot-me smile or so sly as her sexy smile (rarely used unless she was desperate). "Please?"

Cigar smoke curling around his head, Manuel eyed her through narrowed lids. Everything about his attitude toward her had flipped on its head. No longer charming and interested, now he was guarded and cold. Once again, she felt as if she stood before a bull. Without a cape.

Out back by the fence she saw a figure stride along the side of the barn, shadowed to a black silhouette in the darkness. "Is that your assistant, Cristo?"

Manuel shrugged but didn't turn to look. "He's teaching a novice tomorrow. Doing some last-minute prep tonight."

"You don't do that? I mean, teach."

"I don't have the time. Cristo is a matador. He's my best banderillero."

"I understand he owns a bull ranch on the mainland?"

"It is something his family has been doing for decades, breeding *toros*. They are substandard."

"You'd never stand before one in the ring?"

The matador shook his head, dismissing the suggestion as ludicrous. A puff from the cigar swirled fragrant smoke between the two of them.

"I was chased down the street by a bull as I was looking for the antiques shop," she said. "I think the brand on its hindquarter was from Cristo's ranch."

That got his attention. He sat forward. "Is that so? A bull was loose in the streets of Cádiz? Where? When? Are you all right?"

"I'm fine. But there were children in the area. They almost became collateral damage."

"You say that as if you believe someone set the bull on you."

"Señor Bravo, how often is it that a bull suddenly appears in the street?"

"Around here? More often than you would guess."

"And yet there's no stadium in Cádiz."

"There are a few ranches along the coast. But Cristo's ranch is on the mainland. It couldn't have been one of his. I'm glad you weren't harmed, and to hear that the children are safe."

"Thank you. The bull's brand was a half circle above a bar."

He flicked the ash from the end of his cigar, but it missed the silver tray. "That's quite startling. That is Cristo's brand."

"Believe me, it was startling to me to find myself standing before a full-size bull who apparently had not seen a person on foot before."

"You think it was a ring-bred bull?"

"It charged movement."

"As would most any bull."

"I caped it with a colorful skirt. The *morillo* was large."

"I see." Manuel nodded. "I'll speak to Cristo directly." He stood, setting down the glass of lemonade next to the ashtray.

"About the votive crowns, first. Would you mind?"

With a heavy sigh, he nodded. "I sense you will not give up otherwise."

"I can be very determined."

He gestured that she follow him inside the house. He turned on no lights, so she navigated down the dark hallway with a palm against one wall.

"Soto says you've been poking your nose into police business," he said over a shoulder. "Why is that?"

So he had talked to César Soto recently. "It wasn't something I set out to do. I witnessed a crime that needed to be reported to the police, and did so. That crime, a sniper taking a shot at a famous matador. If that's called poking my nose into things, then Officer Soto has a strange perception of right and wrong."

"He doesn't like you," Manuel said.

They arrived at the door to his sanctuary, but he didn't open it. A light from the dining area glowed down the hallway, making it possible to see his face, though it was still shadowed.

Annja shoved her hands in her pants pockets and kept up the hopefully endearing-yet-curious act. "You and César Soto are friends?"

"As I explained when you were here the other night, we once were. Now we are not. But I run into him at the fights. I appreciate you trying to help, but this isn't your concern. I trust César will track down the shooter and take care of the matter."

But she already knew the shooter's identity and had even shared drinks with her. What was so difficult about tracking her down?

She stepped to the side, bringing him around so the light fell on his face. "Do you know Ava Vital, Manuel?"

The matador tilted his head at her. "A dancer? I've heard of her. Why do you ask?"

"You two have never spoken? Perhaps after a fight or a party?"

"I find the question strange and prying."

"I'm sorry. I met her at the club where she dances, and she mentioned the great torero El Bravo. Just wondering if you two had met. So. The crowns?"

Manuel pushed open the door and ushered her into the room ahead of him. A flip of the light switch turned on the line of halogen lights above the altar, but the room remained low-lit and peaceful.

Annja fished out a pair of white latex gloves from her backpack and held them up in question. He nodded, then crossed his arms and leaned against the door frame. Not about to leave her alone, of course.

She sensed he was lying about Ava. But why?

The first crown was smaller than the one to her right. Annja made a cursory inspection of it, but she was eager to look at the bigger one that featured the letters dangling around the base.

It was suspended from a gold hook linked into a short length of chain. She followed the chain up to the ceiling. The screw holding the first crown had been painted white to match the ceiling, obviously installed when the room had been decorated or the ceiling had been repainted. It had been there a while to judge from the gray coating of dust.

The second screw hook was shiny gold metal. There were flakes of wood dust on the inner curve of the hook.

"This one must be a recent acquisition."

"Why would you assume that?"

She shrugged. "Looks like you've recently put it up."

"Sometime this year," he offered casually. "I lose track of dates and time when the season is upon me."

Uh-huh. Yet the fresh sawdust indicated this addition could have been as recent as a few days.

With a glance first to Manuel, she then carefully touched one of the gold letters dangling from the base of the crown. The capital *A* and next to that a capital *L*. Altogether, it spelled out "Given by Alaric."

She had a match. This crown had been stolen early in the twentieth century from the Madrid museum, and hadn't been seen since. Until now.

She traced a fingertip over a sapphire the size of a dime and sensed Manuel's posture by the door shift. She was touching his stuff. And he must know that if anyone could have an idea if this item was genuine— and possibly stolen—it was her.

Which put her in a bad situation if the man was as violent as Ava Vital had intimated. He was a trained killer. Artistic as Garin claimed that skill to be, she wouldn't let down her guard.

But she couldn't stop herself from pushing a little harder. "These aren't replicas."

"If you say so."

"I'm sure you're aware these couldn't have possibly been obtained legally."

"I'm not privy to the intricacies of the law regarding ancient treasures. What are you accusing me of, Creed?"

"Nothing. Yet."

"I acquired these from a secondhand party in the little shop I mentioned to Señor Braden."

"So, they weren't gifts. Earlier you couldn't recall if they had been gifts."

"You're making this sound like an interrogation. I

have no idea regarding the origin of those crowns. Nor do I care if they are authentic or merely copies. They have a sacred meaning to me. Though every moment you are near them you draw away some of their sanctity."

Uh-huh. Whatever. "If authentic, and I believe they are—at least this one here—these crowns were once owned by kings. This says 'Given by Alaric.' Do you know who that was?"

Arms crossed tight over his chest, the matador shrugged.

"He was a Visigoth king in the fourth century."

"I am not a big fan of history. I have heard how kings once fashioned the crowns to give to churches. They are made by royalty and with holy intentions. It is why they are sacred to me."

"Yet if you acquire them from a shop that sells replicas, how can you believe them real?"

"I like to believe they could be real. I do not question."

"If I am not mistaken, this very crown went missing from the Cluny museum a few months ago. Actually, it was being shipped to the museum and got lost in transport. By lost, I mean stolen. You've got stolen property in your possession."

"Have you proof?"

No. There were no photos online, nor did any of the research indicate King Alaric had actually fashioned a crown, but many historical details had been lost over the centuries. And not every single moment of every historical figure's life had been recorded. The words surrounding the bottom of the crown were the proof she needed to request the crowns be authenticated.

"You going to report me to Soto?"

"For some reason, I suspect Soto would arrest me instead of you. Besides, artifact theft should be reported to the local museum, as well as the authorities. Did you hear about the man who was murdered a few days ago in the Hotel Blanca?"

"My focus is on the ring. It would prove deadly if I littered my mind with every little problem in the world. War, terrorism, senseless killings and natural disasters."

He was deflecting the topic.

Annja removed the latex gloves and tucked them in a front pocket. "The man, Diego Montera, was killed with a knife or sword run through his spine from a position above his head. Similar to the *estocada* delivered by the matador to the bull during the faena."

"There are as many toreros in Spain as there are rock stars in your America."

"You have to admit the method of killing is unique."

"A stylish move."

"Stylish." She tapped the gold crown with a fingertip, then remembered his extreme annoyance over having his things touched. And she wasn't wearing the gloves. "Sorry."

El Bravo's jaw stretched so tight his cheeks had

blanched and his eyes should have blazed a hole through her heart.

"Creed, you are poking about for something. You dance around your suspicions like a matador plying the cape to a frisky yearling. I am a matador, not an *asesino*."

Murderer of people.

"My whole life is the bullring," he continued. "I have nothing else besides it. I live, eat, sleep and dream the corrida. Because of that dedication, my soul requires something else." He gestured to the crowns. "Salvation. Peace of mind away from the world. You know? I kill for my supper. *Kill*. Do you think salvation can ever be mine?"

"I, uh…" She was no one's confessor.

"These splendid effigies—real or fake—offer me a bit of that salvation I seek." He held an index finger before the crown, right where she had tapped it. "But once it is tainted, it no longer gives salvation. The energy has been weakened, diluted by the careless touch of another."

He stared at her as if squaring her up for the delivery of the *estoque*. "You've tainted it."

"Didn't even leave a fingerprint. Besides, it wouldn't be wise of me to leave fingerprints on a stolen—"

Annja turned to find a dagger a foot from her face, the tip directed toward her eye. The matador wielded it with cool élan. The blade was shorter than the *estoque* he used for the killing stab and must have been concealed in a pocket. His eyes defied her to make her next move.

"Seriously? You're going to cut me for touching the votive crown? An object you claim may not even be authentic?"

"You've tainted my salvation."

"And you are a nut job."

She backed toward the door, but the matador beat her to it and slammed it shut. His face had grown even paler, and malevolence brightened his dark gaze.

"You want to taint your sanctuary with my death?"

"Death brings me honor."

He slashed the dagger at her and she dodged, luring him to the right toward the altar. Annja stepped up onto the prie-dieu and tapped the crown, setting it wobbling. Gasping, Manuel's attention became glued to the artifact. It gave her time to grab the door handle and rush out of the room. She didn't want to fight the guy.

As she ran through the dark hallway, she realized she'd taken a turn into the bedroom—not the exit.

Calling forth the sword, it filled her grip with a solid reassurance. Annja held it hilt-up at her chest, blade beside her head, shoulders against the wall, as she waited. If she ended up injuring the bullfighter, César Soto wasn't going to go easy on her, that was sure. Neither would anyone in Cádiz and likely all of Spain. Not to mention she'd bring down Garin's wrath.

She eyed the window, which was shuttered with an elaborate Moorish-style dark wood screen. Just as she dashed for it, Manuel entered the room. She heard the sweep of his blade cut the air. Hooking an elbow about the bedpost, she swung around with the sword.

"Where the hell did you get that?"

"Does it matter? Girl's gotta protect herself from *loco* toreros. This is how I do it."

"Oh?" He strolled toward her, the blade held high and tilted downward as if positioned to enter the back of the bull's neck. He held the erect posture of a matador defying his opponent to charge. "Then show me what you have, Annja Creed. You think you can bring this torero to his knees? Deliver me the coup de grâce."

"I just want to walk out of here in one piece and with as little bloodshed as possible."

"You know too much. That's unfortunate, since you are so pretty." He slashed the blade toward her, and she stepped to the side, both hands around the sword hilt, but still unwilling to take a swing at him.

"So my suspicions about the votive crown are true? Where did you get it? From a local seller?"

"As I've said, I go through a dealer. I never wish to know the origins of the items I purchase."

"You had something to do with the bull being released in the street."

"I had nothing to do with that."

"It was Cristo, then. Does he look after his maestro's best interests? Issue threats to those who might learn too much? I've been told you and Cristo have a rivalry."

"Even more reason I would not employ him to do my dirty work."

"No, you do it yourself. It was you in Diego's hotel room that night, wasn't it?"

He lunged, and Annja jumped back. Backing toward the window, with a quick glance she saw the latch was secured with a hook. She tapped the tip of her sword up under the latch, and the curved mechanism slid smoothly out of the lock.

"Did you go through Russell Jones to get the crown? In London? You know he's dead."

"Never heard the name."

"And the man killed on the beach a month ago using the same method Diego Montera was murdered?"

"You are tossing out accusations like flowers into the ring. I crush them beneath my heel." He made an abrupt stomp of his foot, like a flamenco dancer ending the dance with flair, then sliced the blade at her.

Annja leaped onto the bed to lure him to the opposite side of the room. She jumped to the floor and met him with a clash of steel against steel. She didn't swing hard, because she didn't want to injure him. Out the corner of her eye she spied a small silver effigy of Baal on the hearth over the fieldstone fireplace. Another gift?

"Do you kill everyone who touches your things?" she countered. They matched each other, circling with blades pointed toward each other. "Did Diego Montera touch the votive crown when he delivered it to you?"

"I don't know what you're talking about. I never met the guitarist."

"How did you know he was a guitarist?"

"The news stations reported it."

"I thought you didn't pay attention to the media during the season. And why didn't you take the Baal statue?"

"The bronze bull?"

He abruptly shut up. As far as she was concerned, he'd just confessed.

Annja dashed to the unlatched window. "I will see justice is served. Those crowns don't belong you."

Sliding a leg through the window, she jumped out the first-floor window, landed on her feet in a patch of fuchsia begonias and burst into a run toward the gates that were open out onto the main street.

She heard Manuel call to someone in her wake not to follow her, to let her go. Great. But the fact remained, he'd killed Diego.

Now, if she could get an audience with the police without getting arrested.

CÉSAR SOTO SLAPPED his cell phone shut. He kicked the leg of his desk, upsetting a manila file that scattered the papers inside it to the floor.

"If she talks to anyone, I may never be able to pin down the dirty cop."

And he was this close. All he needed was proof that the alibi during the warehouse fire was false. There had been no prints at the dig site where Klosky had been murdered, but he suspected the gun used was still at large.

He picked up the phone and sorted through the contacts he rarely used. Top of the list was *A*. He hit Dial and then cursed Bravo for his indiscretion.

21

Annja hopped off the bus a few streets away from the hotel. It was close to midnight and the humid night air was filled with the sounds of dance, laughter and shouting. An American heavy-metal tune hammered out of a boom box at the corner of the intersection and a group of teenagers were krumping. Yet right alongside the modern dance moves, girls in flamenco skirts performed earth-punishing *golpes* while their graceful arms swept the air in rhythm. The mixture of the two dance styles brought Annja to a standstill to watch.

She recognized the zapateados in the dance, the rapid, percussive footwork a Mexican influence. The male partner worked his rapper moves, insinuating the street style into the traditional dance, while the female hipified the Spanish dance with an attitude that would have knocked over any gangsta rapper. A cardboard box had been set out and the appreciative audience was tossing in euros.

After her escape from the matador's blade, Annja needed to clear her head and take stock. She sat on the curved lip of a public fountain. The cool spray misted her shoulders and back of her neck.

"That man certainly does not like it when people touch his stuff," she muttered.

Touching her upper thigh below her hip, she felt the sting of the injury she'd gotten from the bull. It had cut through her khakis but hadn't gone too deeply beyond the epidermis, which explained the sting. The deeper the cut, the less it ultimately hurt. A dab of alcohol would fix it up fine.

Did Manuel's compulsion go so far as to make him track back the previous handlers of the crown to further clear it of the negative energies he claimed it took on with touch? Russell Jones in London had had his hands on it, according to his secretary.

El Bravo had been booked solid at the corrida, and during the summer most matadors slept and fought; they had little time to do anything else.

Ava had said Cristo wanted Bravo's favor.

The details of the murder and motives were being gathered by Soto's team, and they would track the culprit. She made a mental note to give Jones's name to Soto in case it may aid the murder investigation.

But would that lead them to the party who had bought and sold the votive crown to El Bravo? That person had to have placed it in Diego's hands for delivery. She teased the idea of a dirty cop who may have looted Crockett's site also having access to the crown. If it had originated in London, it had to have been a special order, not another artifact a looter happened upon and was trying to get rid of quickly.

The rapper/flamenco group moved up the street, seeking a new audience to scatter coins in the box they'd set out before the spray-painted sign Nouveau Flamenco—We're Hungry.

Annja headed back to the hotel. The door to her room stood open an inch.

You've got to be kidding me. Apparently, there was not a single hotel in this city she could stay without attracting bad news.

She approached cautiously, and in a moment of instinct, hand held down at her side, she willed the sword into her grip. The leather-wrapped hilt filled her curled palm. The plain but strong blade stretched out along the wall. Sliding the blade tip along the door, she pried it open with a flick of her wrist.

A female silhouette stood in front of the patio window sheers, her back to Annja. A twist of dark hair was secured at the back of her head. No ponytail today. Red ruffles edged her sleeves at the elbows. Black leather pants replaced her usual festive skirt. Fitted black leather biker boots sported buckles from knee to ankle. At her side, she wielded a long blade, not so long as Annja's, but close in size to the *estoque* the matador used.

Annja pulled the door shut, making sure the lock clicked.

Ava turned around and smiled a tight grin. She

dragged the tip of her blade down the thigh of her snug leather pants. "I was hoping you'd have your sword. That'll make this a fair fight."

"Really? You want to give your mark a fighting chance?"

She shrugged minutely.

"Why me?"

"You've been asking a lot of questions. That one was plain stupid. Do you really expect an answer?"

No. She knew why her. Someone in this city had it out for her. Probably more than a someone. Manuel Bravo and César Soto were tops on that list. Ava was inextricably tied to both. But how often did assassins allow their marks to fight in their defense?

No sense in arguing the point. Annja raised the battle sword before her, clasping it in both hands. "El Bravo just tried to kill me, but since he failed, my first guess is he sent you to clean up what he couldn't accomplish."

"I do nothing to please that man."

"Then I got nothing."

"You'll never have the answers you want," Ava said. "And yet, you already have the answers you need. Don't you?"

"Manuel Bravo—"

"The matador will pay for his crime."

"Killing Diego Montera?"

"Exactly."

"Do you have proof?" Annja asked. "It could have been any matador."

Ava stepped a few paces forward, wielding the blade as if ready to stab. Her hair was styled back with a dark curl spilling down her forehead. The top half of her looked ready to dance; the bottom half was forged to kick ass.

She spun the blade with her fingers, catching it smartly and on aim with Annja's heart. Her switchblade smirk crimped. "Promise I'll make it easy on you."

"Is that so? You going to sever my aorta by coming in over my head?"

"Wasn't me. But you know that already." Ava stepped toward her, feinting to the left. Annja stepped right, expecting the double cross, and was rewarded with a clang of blade to sword.

"You'll never match me with that little blade," she said, ducking under the attack and running through it to place herself before the patio doors so they could stand off in the largest open space in the room.

Ava spun, viciously slashing the blade.

Thrusting with a fencing move, Annja worked Ava back toward the door. She suspected if they got too loud the neighbors might become suspicious. Then again, the city was alive and vibrant. Nobody was in their hotel room right now. Below the window, the flamenco group beat the ground with their rapid footwork and the tunes blared.

The dancer moved with agile grace, dashing to the left. She jumped, slashing her blade randomly, and

Annja stumbled backward, losing her balance. She landed on the floor on her side and rolled to her knees.

"I don't get it," Annja said, rising and coming en garde.

Ava sneered and flicked a loose strand of hair from her face.

"Manuel is the only one crazed enough to want to get rid of me, so I assume he sent you. But I thought you and he stood on opposite sides?"

"You've guessed this one wrong, Creed. I do not work for the matador."

"I think you do, and you just don't know it."

The suggestion gave Ava pause. She was thinking about it, but without dropping her guard. Annja had no intention of killing her; she wanted to incapacitate the crazy chick with the blade and then call the police—

"Wait." She dodged Ava's blade. "Don't tell me you're working for César Soto?"

No change in the assassin's expression. Intent on killing her, Ava grunted as she stabbed. Annja blocked the move with the edge of her sword. While she did have the advantage of a longer blade, and a longer reach, she had the disadvantage that the blade was heavy and her best swings were performed with both hands.

"Soto sent you after me," she decided. "Because I was getting too deep. Into what?"

The only conclusion she'd come close to making was that Manuel Bravo could have possibly murdered Diego for the votive crown. And if Soto was protecting Bravo, then he'd have reason to get her out of the picture. He'd already escorted her from the city once.

"So it's César Soto behind the antiquities ring, and you're his muscle."

Ava smirked. "I never for one moment thought you were stupid, even though I suspect that was a wild guess. A wrong guess. Soto isn't involved in illegal antiquities trade."

"You know that for certain?"

"The man you're looking for is right under your thumb. And then there is the woman."

They shuffled through the open patio door. Annja slammed the heel of her palm against Ava's chest as her opponent's back hit the iron railing. Ava's hand, gripping the blade, swayed out above her head.

Annja dropped her sword into the otherwhere and used both hands to clutch the woman by the shoulders. Below, a few onlookers noticed the commotion above. She flung Ava away from the railing and shoved her back inside the room.

Before Ava could turn to face her, she'd called the sword back to her grip, stalking inside after her.

"A woman? Other than you?" she asked.

"She works closely with the man at the museum. I couldn't believe César didn't know it. I was the one who suggested he look into her background."

"Are you and César dating? To be close enough to share these conversations?"

Blood drooled down her chin as Ava snarled and

pushed herself up, collapsing with a yelp. It looked as if her arm was hurt, maybe broken. Annja kicked the blade out of her hand. It clattered across the tiled floor, the blade wedging under the bathroom door.

Spearing the tip of her battle sword against Ava's throat, Annja slammed down her groping free hand with the sole of her boot.

"Do it!" Ava cried.

"And spoil your dancing career?" Annja stepped back.

"If you don't end this," Ava hissed, "the matador dies at tomorrow's corrida."

Much as Annja didn't condone murder for murder's sake, she felt an empty disinterest regarding whether or not the matador lived or died. He needed to pay for Diego's death. Yet she could get to the authorities before Ava could limp out after him. That is, if she could locate an authority not in collusion with Bravo and Ava Vital.

"He's killed too many," Ava said. "He has to be stopped."

"Are you talking about animals or humans?"

"He believes he is some kind of god who has the power over life and death."

That was all Annja needed to hear regarding who had killed Diego. "Who is the woman associated with the stolen artifacts?"

"On the police force. César already knows about her. He wants you out of the way so he can catch her. That's why I'm here. Keeping you out of the way."

"I think you'd better stick with dancing and leave the assassination gigs to the professionals. It's been swell," Annja said. Bending, she delivered a fist to Ava's jaw, slamming her skull backward, her head hitting the wall as she collapsed. Annja released her sword into the otherwhere.

Annja collected the dancer's weapon, and not sure what to do with it, but not wanting to leave it in Ava's hands, she tested the bend of the blade. It gave. It was too short to break over her knee, so, gripping the blade tip and the hilt, she wedged it into the bed frame and succeeded in breaking off the hilt.

She grabbed her backpack and shoved the laptop inside, then swung it over her arm. She walked out of the room, leaving behind the failed assassin.

The police didn't want her sticking her nose into their business? Fine. But they needn't send an assassin after her. Soto could have asked nicely.

Annja smirked. Okay, so her habit of following things through to the end tended to put her in situations she would be wise to avoid.

She'd be seeing James Harlow in the morning.

CÉSAR SOTO SAT DOWN before Hannibal Drake, hastily introduced himself and apologized for the early hour. He judged from the man's calm demeanor he'd been in this kind of situation before and would know exactly how much he could say and was willing to say.

Fine by him. He only needed the man to identify one

person. He opened a manila file and sorted through three photos, wondering why he'd even pulled two of them. Ava had suggested a name that had startled him, yet when he'd run the background check, he'd been shocked that things on her history hadn't shown up during her application to the force. Like a stint at the University of Madrid on an archaeological team.

He turned the photo around and slid it across the table toward Drake. "Have you seen this person before, Señor Drake?"

The man gave it a meager glance and nodded. "Yes."

"In the vicinity of the warehouse located directly across from your business office on the Campo del Sur?"

Another nod. "Yes."

"Have you spoken directly to the person in this picture?"

"I don't recall if I have or have not."

He did recall, and he had, César guessed. But it didn't matter. He'd only needed positive identification.

"I understand."

"Am I being charged today? I wasn't given opportunity to call my lawyer."

The suspicion that Hannibal Drake had received items from the person in the picture was just that: a suspicion. Soto had seen the man's name many times in cases involving illegal antiquities trade. He knew Drake bought and sold artifacts, but had no proof the items were stolen or obtained legally. And he hadn't enough man-hours on the force to research and get such proof.

He was no fool. Of course the man was dirty.

"No, you are not being charged with a crime today, Señor Drake. You are free to go. I thank you for your cooperation."

Hannibal nodded and stood to shake César's hand. The man had a good, firm handshake. Trying too hard, actually.

César wiped his hand across his thigh as the man left the interrogation room.

22

Back at the hostel she'd originally been staying at, Annja was pleased to find it had cleared out, except for an elderly British couple who, after they'd introduced themselves, offered to share their tea. She politely refused, claiming exhaustion from touring the city.

Yesterday had been a long day. Being almost run down in the morning, then the fire at the warehouse, followed by a swim in the ocean. Manuel Bravo had tried to kill her, and then Ava Vital.

"That woman is a tough one to figure."

Opening her laptop, Annja ran a search for Ava Vital. The first time she'd found her she had only been snooping about the Gato Negra.

On a hunch, she typed in César Soto's name, and the search line that featured thumbnails of larger photos flashed a familiar face. It was a professional portrait of Soto showing him in full police gear and a bio listing his eight years of service. No mention of his failed shot at the corrida circuit. Nor were there any links associating him with Ava Vital.

Ava had alluded the two of them were close enough for her to learn information Annja suspected only officers on the force should have.

She typed in Manuel Bravo's name and kept Ava's name in the search. Bravo's darkly handsome face appeared in a row of thumbnails. She scanned the pictures. Most featured him in the corrida in a classic bullfighter's pose or caping the bull in a flurry of magenta and yellow. Only a few were of him in casual wear, signing autographs, and one looked like a snapshot taken in his villa, probably for a lifestyle magazine, as he posed out on the patio under the paper lanterns with a cigar and Scotch.

Annja paused on one that didn't fit with the rest. Manuel looked at the cameraman as if he were surprised to have his picture taken. And a hand was in the fore of the thumbnail.

She clicked the thumbnail and sat back when the whole photo came up. Manuel had his arm around a woman's hips as he led her toward a local restaurant. And hers was the hand up to block the photographer from getting a good shot. Her hand successfully blocked her face, but Annja didn't need to see the face. The tattoo revealed on the woman's wrist—a single wing—told her all she needed to know.

"The matador's nemesis," she murmured. "But apparently, not always."

A click on the image took her to the original site. The gossip section of the local paper, *Diario de Cádiz*.

The caption declared El Bravo's fiery love affair with a local dancer was fraught with fighting and public screaming matches.

Annja sat back against the pillow on the narrow bed. Ava seemed to want the guy dead. And if the caption was true, perhaps she perceived a good reason if they had been at each other's throats during their relationship.

"Which was when?" She clicked through the article to find the byline was dated six months earlier.

If the matador had confided his extreme obsession over people touching his artifacts and his methods for exacting revenge, he may have confessed murder to Ava. And now the dancer felt he must pay for those crimes after Diego Montera's death.

Made sense. The dancer wasn't at all concerned with the stolen artifacts linked to the case, which also made sense if she were merely seeking vengeance.

But if Manuel was receiving stolen goods, Annja needed to get to the core of the operation before some crazed ex-lover took him out.

Her cell phone buzzed and James Harlow's name appeared. Tilting a look at the buzzing phone, Annja wondered how the professor was involved. Ava had said a female was working with someone at the museum.

The morning she'd found Montera in his room, she'd later run into Harlow in the plaza before the museum and they had stopped into the tapas bar to eat. He'd seemed calm and not like a man who had just committed murder.

"Hello?" she said, answering.

"Still in town?"

Why was he so eager to see her leave town? He and César Soto should get together.

Were they together? Harlow had made it clear he felt the Cádiz police were helpful and couldn't possibly be dirty. So if someone from the police department really had been out to Crockett's site, either Harlow was way off the mark or he was protecting someone.

A female on the force?

"There's a fight this evening," she answered. "El Bravo's one-hundredth corrida. I had hoped to catch it."

"I see. No luck with the problem?"

"Actually, I did find a warehouse by the shore that I suspect was trafficking in stolen goods."

Harlow cleared his throat. "You don't say?"

"It was blazing by the time I left."

"On fire? How?"

"Don't know. I think someone followed us there and decided to destroy the evidence. You ever visit those kinds of warehouses, James?"

"Why would I? What they represent is reprehensible."

"You can find a lot of quality items in them."

"Are you accusing me of something, Annja?"

"No." Not yet. "Did you contact the police department about getting the Baal statue returned when it's let out of evidence?"

"I will. I marvel over your concern for such a small problem, Annja. Haven't you big adventures to pursue? The bull statue hardly seems worth your effort."

Had she mentioned her phone call to LePlante to him? Yes, but she hadn't mentioned the possibility there could be a ruby in the belly of the bull. Could Harlow know about that?

"I don't know where you get all your energy. You know…" She heard the distinctive tap of a fingernail against a crystal watch face.

"What?"

"I do know a name that may be connected to the stolen artifacts. Hell, he could be in collusion with Jonathan Crockett. The man likes to lie low, but I'm aware he receives stolen goods and resells it to elite clients from a fancy office by the shore."

"Who is that?"

"His name is Hannibal Drake. I believe his office is off Campo del Sur."

"That could be the area next to the warehouse that burned last night. How come you never mentioned Hannibal Drake before?"

"It only now occurred to me. Yes, I think you should investigate that man. Though, really, Annja, this is a police matter."

As he'd reminded her many times over. Sounded

like a man who wanted her out of town, along with the Cádiz police. And to keep foisting the blame on others?

"Thanks, James. I'm going to rest before the fights. I'll leave town first thing. I appreciate the invitation to inspect the Hercules coins. The hands-on time I got with them will really be valuable for my article."

"No problem. Have a good flight."

She hung up and dug in her backpack for her camera. It wasn't there.

She tracked through her whereabouts over the past few days and remembered she'd last used it at the museum.

That gave her an excuse to stop by again, and for reasons she couldn't quite finger, she wanted to look into James Harlow's eyes and measure his sincerity face-to-face.

GARIN PULLED THE JEEP to the curb a block from the police station. The second Jeep he'd rented since the first one was in the drink. Hannibal Drake slid onto the passenger seat and nodded his thanks. Garin drove toward the bridge connecting Cádiz to the mainland and headed for the Jerez de la Frontera airport.

Drake knew when to stick around and when to count his losses. He owned offices across the world. If the heat became unbearable, he could move at the snap of his fingers.

"Any idea why they tagged you?"

Hannibal tugged a pack of cigarettes from his pocket

but didn't open the pack. Instead, he compressed the cellophane, crinkling it repeatedly. "James Harlow is my suspicion. That bastard has been my nemesis since I moved into town. He's a professor at the museum. He likes to put on a front that he's aboveboard and untouchable. Wouldn't touch a hot bit of pottery if his life depended on it. Damned liar. He's taken more bits and bobs than I could ever hope to. Bastard."

"So you're going to run?" Garin left out the last part of the sentence—*with your tail between your legs.*

"You know me."

"Staying off police radar is paramount. You're doing a swell job of it, man."

"Yes, well, I'm sitting beside you right now and not some bruiser in the market for a boyfriend, so I'll take swell. They asked me about an Annja Creed. Do you know that name? Some actress?"

"A television host. I know her."

"I don't think I like her, either."

The woman had stuck her nose in too deep. "I'll talk to her."

"You know her that well, eh? You're getting too close to things that might burn you, my friend."

Garin frowned. That had been a definite threat. But well deserved, if indeed Annja's fumbling had resulted in one of his friends being picked up by the police.

"My apologies," he offered, hating that any apology was necessary.

"It's all right." Drake looked out the window. The

skyline hugged the bridge connecting Cádiz to the mainland. "My therapist tells me karma always bites the right ass."

THE MUSEUM WAS QUIET and cool in the early-afternoon hours. Most people were out for siesta, Annja knew, having learned the employees' schedules during the few days she'd spent looking over the coins. Harlow usually slipped out for a sherry and tapas around this time, so she expected to find the camera and go.

Harlow had a large office in the museum basement, stacked with textbooks and the requisite skulls, damaged artifacts, collections of keys, coins, and bones in various states of decay and damage. Crates containing recent acquisitions sat unopened, awaiting his perusal. Annja would have loved a moment to go through them all, like Christmas in the summertime.

She located the camera and picked it up from the top of a small stack of notebooks, which set them askew across Harlow's desk. Straightening them, Annja uncovered a small bronze bull beneath a white handkerchief.

"I just can't seem to be rid of you."

Bull statue in hand, she turned to face James Harlow.

23

Not at all intimidated by a man wearing a plaid blazer with leather elbows patches, Annja held up the bronze bull. "Tell me how this went from the dirt where I dug it up three days ago, to the hotel room of a dead man, to a police evidence locker, to your desktop?"

"I thought that was your expertise. Figuring things out? Isn't that what archaeologists do with the evidence presented them?" He clanged his cane against the side of the desk, which made Annja flinch. "You are too nosy for your own good, Creed. Why did you have to persist?"

"You've always known the origins of this little piece. How it was designed by Philip III as a wedding gift for Louis XIII and that it possibly hides a treasure inside. The moment I mentioned this statue had been uncovered at the site, you started making plans to obtain it, didn't you?"

"Does it matter? I have it now. Obviously it was not let out of the evidence room without an official signed release, so I've done nothing wrong. That little beauty now belongs to the Cádiz museum."

"This is evidence from a murder investigation. I can't believe the police would release it. And I don't suspect you'll tell me the truth since you've been lying to me all this time."

Harlow moved quickly with his cane, slapping it on top of her hand painfully. "Hand it over."

"And then what?"

"You get yourself out of Cádiz."

"And you are going to what? Break this thing open? Destroy it?" Continue trafficking in the very artifacts he claimed to want to protect? "I don't think so. This has to be reported to César Soto."

"Thought you'd say that." He reached inside the ugly blazer and pulled out a pistol. Annja thought it looked like a four-shot Derringer. Old, but probably well cared for and very usable.

"You're going to kill me?"

"You'd be surprised the people I know who can take care of cleaning up a crime scene."

"They didn't do a very good job out at Crockett's site."

"That was unfortunate. But it did net me the bronze bull."

"In a roundabout way. So the police really did kill Simon Klosky."

"Just one particular officer."

"A woman, I've been told."

"There you go, treading on police territory again, Annja. Bad form."

The bull still in hand, she carefully tilted it, aware the pistol followed her movement. "Is this thing really worth two dead men?"

"I didn't have anything to do with the delivery boy's death. Sounds like he was sent on two jobs at one time. Unfortunately for me, he did not make the morning delivery."

"So when I ran into you outside the museum that morning, you weren't late because you'd slept in—it was because you'd missed an appointment with Diego Montera?"

"I wasn't given his name. Just a meeting place. Annja, you know the world isn't fair, and artifacts are bought and sold every day without care for provenance. I'm trying to keep my head in the game. Show me a museum that doesn't purchase trafficked goods and I'll mark that one in the record books."

"There are plenty of museums that operate on the up-and-up." Usually underhanded dealings could be traced to a specific employee of questionable ethics. "Your explanation is a poor excuse for what you've done. And what is one small statue to the museum's collection?"

"It once belonged to this very museum. You uncovered that yourself."

"Right. But stealing it back?" She shook her head ruefully.

"Who said it was for the museum?"

"You did."

"Yes, well, I fancy bull items. Couldn't resist this one."

"Don't give me that. You want what's inside."

"Don't you want to crack that puppy open like a Christmas cracker? It's a huge ruby, Annja. It could be worth millions."

"Millions that belong to the country of France, since this item can be traced to Louis XIII."

"Posh. Finders keepers, I like to say."

"You are not the man I thought you to be."

Harlow set back his shoulders, the gun held more casually now, but Annja would not let down her guard. She could draw up the sword and finish this conversation with one sweep of the blade, but getting a confession was more important right now.

"No one ever is who they claim to be," he said. "We all wear a mask. Even you, Annja. After finding the dead body, you let Jonathan Crockett leave."

"Because I had no reason to suspect Crockett. I reported Simon's death as soon as I returned to Cádiz. The professor isn't guilty of a crime." At least not recently, that she could be sure of. "Why do you insist on implicating him? And for that matter, you tossed out Hannibal Drake's name into the matter."

"Someone had to go down." He gestured with the gun toward the bull she held.

"Does that pistol even work?"

"Let's have a look-see." He aimed for her head.

At times like this, Annja wished she could keep her mouth closed.

She had time to call the sword to fruition, but before she could the pistol Harlow held flipped out of his grasp and blood sprayed from his damaged fingers.

What the...? Annja didn't move a muscle.

Shot by an unseen party out in the hallway, Harlow dropped his cane and gripped his hand, swearing, as he stumbled against a stack of crated acquisitions.

Cautious not to make a wrong move, Annja waited for the shooter to show himself. With her luck, the next shot could be aimed at her.

When she saw the brim of César Soto's cowboy hat move into view, she fought the urge to go at him sword to pistol. The sight of him didn't make her feel any safer.

"Fancy meeting you here, Officer Soto," she tried carefully. "Did you hear our conversation?"

"I did." Soto held his pistol aimed on Harlow, who dropped to his knees, groaning. "You have a way of putting yourself in the most interesting situations, Señorita Creed."

"It's the curiosity seeker in me." She held the bronze bull up and made a show of carefully placing it on the desk. "The statue that was once in police evidence. Of course, you are aware it was removed, I'm sure."

Soto's eyebrows rose. "No, I was not. We have a dirty cop in our department who likes to go shopping in the evidence room. I'll take that back into Cádiz police custody." He tapped a button on the radio hooked at his collar and asked for backup to bring in a suspect. "Not you," he said to Annja after he signed off. "But if you'll step back for a moment and allow me to do my job, I'd appreciate the cooperation."

"Drop the damn thing. Crack it open!" Harlow insisted. A gesture of his hand sent blood spattering across Annja's pant leg. "Annja, this is your one chance to see what's inside." The man's eyelids fluttered; he was obviously getting woozy from blood loss. "Just… do it. I need to know the truth. Please?"

Finding the treasure was always the ultimate goal. Annja vacillated for a moment. "Sorry, James. I'm not keen on destroying evidence or historical artifacts."

"But it was *meant* to be cracked open. You saw LePlante's sketch."

"If so, the sketch, along with this artifact, will make for a fascinating display in a museum."

"You're no archaeologist," Harlow hissed. "We seek the truth, the answers beneath the outer crust."

"There are ways to learn the truth without damaging the object," Annja said. "You know that."

"So much for adventure," he muttered.

Officer Soto cuffed Harlow and delivered him to the backup officer who arrived three minutes later. After getting the details from her and taking down a few notes about the layout of Harlow's office, Soto walked Annja out of the museum, where a crowd had begun to gather because three police cars with flashing lights were parked out front.

"There's something inside that little bronze bull?" he asked.

"Supposedly a ruby of immense size and value. It was designed as a gift to Louis XIII of France on his wedding day."

"And you don't want to crack it open?"

She caught a rare grin on his face and chuckled along with him. "There are X-ray scanning methods that can reveal what's inside. Won't have to crack a thing to find out. I'm surprised, Officer Soto. You'd destroy it?"

He shrugged. "No, I would not, but I would be interested in learning if there is actual treasure inside."

"If you'll allow it, I'd like to have the bull sent to the Harwell Science and Innovation Campus in Oxfordshire for an X-ray. An ordinary X-ray machine won't work and it's the only place that has the equipment to do it right now. Then we can both find out the secrets of what's in the belly of the bull."

"I think that can be arranged. Now, I probably can't ask you to leave town again," he said, tugging down his cowboy hat against the afternoon sun. "But I sure would appreciate it if you would."

"You really believe I contributed to hampering your investigation?"

He shrugged minutely. "I won't say, one way or the other. I like you fine, Señorita Creed. But I'd like you a lot better in another country."

"Fair enough. I have plans to attend El Bravo's fight

this afternoon, then I promise I'll get on a plane soon after."

"Sounds like a deal." He offered his hand and she shook it. "I guess I owe you my thanks. If Harlow hadn't explained the details to you in there I might still be searching."

"You said there was a dirty cop on the force. Would that be a woman?"

"I'm not sure I even want to know how you come by your information, but yes, the officer is female. Maria Alonzo. We arrested her less than an hour ago and she gave us Harlow."

Annja recalled the officer who'd first taken down her report at the station. "Is she the one who killed Simon Klosky?"

"Yes."

"And chased me last night out of the burning warehouse?"

Soto winced. He hadn't known that detail. "Seems we've got more chatting to do before you head to the fight."

"I'm all yours, Officer. You have any idea where Ava Vital is right now?"

"Why? What does a dancer have to do with Harlow's arrest?"

"Nothing at all. But she's got a death wish for El Bravo."

Soto tilted back his head to eye her directly.

"She told me," Annja added, "and then she tried to kill me."

The officer shook his head in disbelief and whistled. He chuckled, but didn't say a word.

"She also alluded the two of you may have a relationship—"

He put up a palm between them. "I can have you escorted out of the city again. No fight, not even a chance to pack your bags."

"All right. I'll forget she ever mentioned it. But I think she's going to go after El Bravo at the fight. Do you trust my suspicion?"

"If I didn't know either of you better, I'd say no. But I do know you both, so yes. Let's go for a ride, señorita."

MANUEL BRAVO CROSSED himself and kissed his knuckles, then bowed before the altar in his sanctuary. Today was the day. One hundred kills this year. He knew what had to be done. Things had not gone as he wished, but he believed all things happened for a reason.

It was a punishment for his evil ways. Had to be.

He did not regret. He learned. He lived. He experienced. He tried to make his life, and the lives of others, as good as they could be.

He had failed himself.

With a heavy sigh, he stood before the altar and gazed at the gleaming gold crown that had been tainted by her touch.

"I will do what must be done. *A la lucha!*"

24

Annja received a police escort to the stadium in Jerez, arriving after the third bull had been dragged from the ring by a team of mules. César Soto accompanied her in, and while she wasn't under arrest, she got the feeling he didn't want her to stray too far from his side. Fair enough.

She spied Garin Braden in his summer linen suit. The seat next to him was empty. He puffed away at a cigar, a bottle of beer in his other hand.

"I'm going to talk to a friend. Just over there," she said to Soto.

"Fine. I'll take a look around."

They both had their eye out for Ava Vital.

Shuffling by those patrons seated on cushions—fanning themselves against the oppressive heat, even at six in the evening—she arrived at the empty seat. "Mind if I sit?"

Garin looked up at her, shook his head in disbelief, then splayed a hand toward the seat. She sat and eyed the matadors, who were currently caping the fourth bull, while El Bravo watched from the *barrera*.

"Thought you'd be in New York City by now," Garin commented around the stub of his cigar. "Or did you take my threat as a joke?"

"No. Didn't take it as a threat, either. I had some loose ends to tie up."

"Not at this corrida, you don't."

"No, not here. Back at the city museum. I found the man responsible for looting Crockett's dig and his associate, who may be connected with the warehouse by the sea. And now I wanted to take in the matador's last fight."

"It's not his last—" Garin swiveled to stare at her. "What do you have planned?"

"Nothing. Not yet. I'm here to watch the fight. I promise. The professor at the museum was arrested for trafficking in stolen antiquities."

Garin didn't even smirk. She had expected a triumphant "see, I told you so" smile.

"Still doesn't explain Diego Montera's death," she continued.

"Don't want to hear it, Annja. Just shut up and watch or find another seat."

She could abide by those terms. With Officer Soto's position marked to her left, Annja observed as the fourth and fifth bulls charged out into the ring and El Bravo dispatched both within the fifteen-minute time limit. One bull remained. If he were successful, it would be the matador's sixth kill of the day and the one hundredth of the season.

Garin lit up another cigar. Twilight overtook the day and a cool breeze sifted down among the *contrabarrera* where they sat. "You talk to Roux?" he asked.

"Is there a reason I should?"

"Just trying to make conversation."

Which meant he didn't want to talk about anything she'd learned here in Cádiz. Annja would put this visit down as something she should never again bring up with Garin. Soto had mentioned an arrest of a dealer who worked along the shore. She could guess that perhaps Garin had done his *shopping* there. It was the only reason he would be offended by her involvement in solving the antiquities theft.

Fair enough. They both had things they didn't wish to discuss with the other, and best keep it that way.

The final bull was released and it charged into the ring with explosive aggression, kicking out its back hooves and stirring up the dust. After that display it settled immediately and looked around, eyeing, it seemed, everyone in the first row behind the *barrera* and then the two matadors who approached it with the bright magenta-and-yellow capes.

Out of the ring, a flash of red caught Annja's eye. Standing below and to her left, a woman with black hair pulled tightly back in a bun with two curls on her forehead wandered along the exit aisle. Ava Vital, in full flamenco dress. The dancer winked at her, then walked along the front row. She greeted an older man in a black fedora with a kiss to either of his cheeks and sat next to him.

Annja exchanged glances with César Soto. He nodded once and tugged down his cowboy hat, maintaining his post five rows behind Ava on the aisle. Had Ava seen him? Couldn't have. If they were seeing each other in any way beyond mere friendship, Annja wondered what was going through César's mind right now. Perhaps it had been an assumption on her part to put the twosome together. They obviously shared secrets, though, so she intended to keep an eye on both of them.

"You know the dancer?" Garin asked.

"Yes. Shared a beer and a sword fight with her. She's the one who wants El Bravo dead."

"The sniper?" He observed her through the wispy cigar smoke. "Wonder if that's the one Manuel had such a fiery relationship with."

"She is. I found an article about them online. But they're no longer dating?"

"No, he got rid of her months ago. Very domineering, as I understand, and not faithful. She wants him dead? Not a surprise, considering their tempestuous relationship. Do you think she's carrying?"

"Who can know what she's got hidden in those ruffles? I don't know the man she's sitting next to. Do you?"

"Can't get a look at his face, but he doesn't seem familiar."

"I can't imagine she'd risk taking a shot at El Bravo before a stadium full of people." And especially with her miserable aim. "I should move closer."

Garin gripped her arm, staying her. "Bravo has stepped out before the bull. She won't make a move now. Too risky with all these witnesses."

"She could put a bullet through his brain and be gone before anyone can identify the direction of the shooter."

"Annja." He pressed a warning palm on her thigh.

She nodded. "Fine, but I won't be able to concentrate on the fight."

"You watch whatever draws your attention." He turned and leaned forward, elbows on his knees.

Only half-confident César Soto would get to Ava before she could make a move—because if the two were involved, and he had a bone to pick against El Bravo, what would stop him from allowing Ava to make the shot?—Annja had to force her attention to the ring.

El Bravo, wearing a sky-blue suit of lights, stirred the audience to their feet with rousing cheers as he performed an exquisite veronica that swept the bull along his body. The matador, strong and straight, arced his arm over the bull's back, guiding it almost, yet making it appear to be as soft as a caress. It was a beautiful moment, and Annja found herself with the crowd standing and cheering.

Bravo walked skillfully before the bull, assessing its next move. It was still frisky, not having been stabbed by the picador. In fact, when the mounted picador appeared at the gate, the matador waved him off. The crowd gasped in unison. Highly unusual not to pic the bull. Instead, El Bravo gestured toward his second in command. Cristo stepped out from the *barrera* and handed Bravo two barbed darts frilled with red paper.

The crowd leaned in as the matador raised the spikes above his head, one in each hand, defying the bull to rush him while his body was at its most vulnerable. The bull did. El Bravo lunged, seeming to rise from the ground without effort, and landed the banderillas dead center of the massive hump behind the bull's neck. Cheers erupted as the bull made a circle around the matador, testing the pain it had been delivered, but determined to charge the cape again.

This bull was still strong, not having been properly weakened by the lance.

"Is this common?" Annja asked Garin.

"Never seen it done before. He's putting on a show. But it's dangerous."

Another set of banderillas was placed with equal bravery, and Annja heard Garin remark at Bravo's masterful skill.

Her attention dropped to the first row where Ava watched, the dancer's back straight and chin level. She didn't react with the crowd, maintaining a stoic posture. Where did she keep her weapon?

Annja glanced to where César stood—he wasn't there.

Never had she felt so at odds. Clearly, she had no

authority. She must trust Soto had everything under control.

El Bravo caped the bull using grand sweeping veronicas that elicited enthusiastic olés from the audience. As he'd explained to Annja when he'd been teaching her, he slowly revealed his body to the bull. First his feet, then his knees, then with a big gesture that splayed the cape in a circle about his body, all of him. Toying with his opponent, but also tiring the animal that continued to charge the cape. Blood soaked the bull's back where the darts clung. The *morillo* had swollen, and she sensed in this heat, the animal was suffering.

When Bravo returned to the barrier to claim the smaller muleta cape and *estoque,* the crowd was startlingly still. The bull stood, both front hooves planted firmly in the sand, shoulders squared. The matador had placed him correctly for the faena, which would end in the kill.

Manuel turned to the crowd, lifting his *montera* hat high to salute them. He turned the entire circle, acknowledging all. Stillness hung in the air like a humid cloud. El Bravo twisted around, and when he stopped, Annja felt as if he looked directly at her.

He *was* looking directly at her.

She glanced at Garin. He tilted his head, as if to say, yes, he is.

The matador bowed grandly toward Annja, tucking his hat against his stomach, and then kissed his fingers and blew the acknowledgment toward her.

"Hell," Garin muttered. "He's dedicated the kill to you."

"That is so wrong. I don't want—"

"Quiet, Annja."

She decided an acknowledging nod was necessary. The crowd erupted in applause at sight of her acceptance. She certainly hoped none of them thought she was Bravo's girlfriend. A glance toward where Ava sat found her posture stiff. She wasn't applauding.

What was El Bravo up to?

The bull hadn't moved. Its tongue lolling, it had been exhausted from the fight. Yet, it held its head up, which indicated there may be fight left in it.

Bravo lifted the muleta cape and stepped forward, approaching the bull. He bowed to the animal. Placing the cape between his knees to hold it, he then took the *estoque* and, gripping the ponytail he'd secured at the back of his head, neatly sliced it off.

Garin hissed and said, "No."

Before she could figure out what that meant, Annja found herself crying out with the rest of the crowd.

Cape again in hand, the matador stepped forward, arm raised with the *estoque* aimed downward—yet he didn't leap to deliver the coup de grâce.

The bull lifted its head.

A woman behind Annja screamed. Others cried out and men groaned.

The bull charged. A horn gored the matador's chest, right through the heart. Manuel's sword hand swung backward. The blade dropped to the ground. The horn emerged through his back. El Bravo's body was lifted as if it was a rag doll and joggled on the bull's horn, which turned bloody as the matador's life spilled from the wound.

The bull hadn't expected such a heavy load, and falling to its knees, its exhausted head dropped. The horn was still impaled in Bravo's chest.

The matador didn't struggle because he was dead.

The other matadors rushed to assist their maestro. One picced the bull on the back with the picador's lance, and another lunged to place the coup de grâce at the base of the bull's brain, forgoing the cut to sever the aorta.

The bull dropped to its side. Pulled from the horn, the matador tumbled to the bloodied ground. In one great, heartbroken howl, the crowd cried out in shock.

Unsure what had just occurred—why had Manuel seemingly walked right into the horn?—Annja had the sense to look for Ava. The dancer was no longer seated.

César Soto stood at the end of the row where Ava had been, his attention on the exit and not the ring. He was watching the woman in the red flamenco dress leave.

Ava Vital paused before she was out of Annja's sight and turned to look directly at her. She winked, then nodded once and left the stadium.

Soto exchanged glances with her. He shrugged and stepped aside as some from the patrons rushed up to the barrier wall to get a closer look at the tragedy. It

was out of his hands. He'd come to stop a potential assassin, not witness a suicide.

Garin stood, as did Annja. The five-hundred-year-
old warrior buttoned his linen suit coat and cocked his
head to the side as if to stretch out a kink. He stepped
around her and, without a word, walked out of the stadium.

She didn't go after him. His hero had just committed suicide. And Annja knew the guilt that had haunted
El Bravo glittered back at his villa over the sanctuary
altar. Two Visigothic crowns, bought for the price of
human lives.

25

The following morning Garin Braden didn't offer Annja a ride to the airport. She did see him drive by the hostel in the rental Jeep, but if he had noticed her walking toward the bus station, he gave no clue.

She lugged the backpack over a shoulder and pulled out her cell phone to verify she had received an electronic boarding pass. The night she'd been escorted to the airport, she had exchanged her ticket to fly out to London this afternoon. She had about two hours to make Jerez de la Frontera.

A patrol car stopped beside her, and César Soto nodded through the open window. "Señorita Creed. Need a ride?"

"Yes, to the airport."

"That's what I was hoping you'd say. Hop in."

She tossed her backpack in the backseat and slid into the passenger seat. Soto headed toward La Pepa Bridge.

"How's James Harlow?" she asked.

Soto signaled, checked his rearview mirror and made a turn. "He posted bail."

"What? But I thought…"

"We were unable to make any charges stick. It's impossible to determine if Señor Harlow had a hand in accepting stolen goods. And we don't have the man-hours to go through the records at the museum."

"I can't believe that. You had enough man-hours to track the guy and arrest him in the first place. I thought Maria Alonzo—"

"We managed to connect her weapon to the bullet in Simon Klosky's back. But even though she's pinned Harlow as a partner in crime, there's no evidence. Only hearsay."

"But Harlow was behind the robbery at Jonathan Crockett's dig site. He said as much to me. You were outside the door when he confessed."

"Impossible to prove, and he has an alibi. Namely, you." He waited for her to respond, but Annja knew that was the truth.

"And Ava Vital?"

"The only crime she may have committed was wanting the matador dead."

"Attempted murder. Don't forget that."

"Right. But she didn't get her man. And wanting someone dead is very different than actually making them dead."

"If I were you, I'd tread carefully around that woman."

"I'll take that suggestion to heart. The case is closed, Señorita Creed. The torero who received stolen goods is dead."

"At least one votive crown in his sanctuary was stolen from the Cluny museum about six months ago. I'm sure they'll appreciate its return."

"I'll make a note of that. After it's been run through evidence, I'm sure it'll find its way home. We've already contacted that place in Oxfordshire to have the bronze bull scanned. I've given them your number as an additional contact."

"Thank you. I'm sorry about Manuel's death. You two were once friends."

"Never friends. Our families had a blood debt that had gone on too long. I should have ended it years ago."

"He was supporting you, but you didn't need the money."

"You'd be surprised at the medical bills I still owe for that accident over a decade ago on the Bravo ranch. Blood debts run deep, señorita. It isn't something you can understand."

"Probably not."

"El Bravo will be lauded as a hero tomorrow and buried the next day. The bull that took his life has been donated to St. Mary's children's home in the old city as Manuel would have wished. He will be missed. That's all I wish to say about it."

She nodded. "Thanks for telling me that. I can now leave the country knowing the police have a handle on at least one illegal antiquities operation. Or do they? If you can't pin it on Harlow, and I suspect Maria Alonzo was only a liaison, do you have the suspect?"

"The warehouse that burned by the ocean is connected to one other shop in town. I've already got men on it. We do what we can, Señorita Creed. Stolen artifacts aren't high on the list when we've got to protect our citizens first and foremost."

She wouldn't mention that they'd neglected to protect Diego and Simon Klosky.

Twenty minutes later, Soto drove her up to the curb at the Jerez airport.

"Thanks," she said and got out to retrieve her backpack. She slapped the open passenger door and waved him off.

"I think I'll stick around to watch you fly out," Soto called.

She deserved that one.

BROOKLYN WAS HER HOME, and Annja was glad to be back. She jogged down the running path in Prospect Park and noted a crew of three men trimming an oak tree set back about fifty yards. Chain saw in hand, or man swung from a branch high up in the tree usi only a rope. He had no safety harness and wasn't se cured with belts.

She waved as she ran by, and one of the men whis tled at her.

Her cell phone rang. She paused, still walking in a circle to keep her blood rushing, and answered.

A lab technician from Diamond Light Source, th synchrotron facility at the Harwell Science and Inn vation Campus in Oxfordshire, let her know the results on the scan of the bull statue. "I can send you a pdf of the scan if you like."

"Yes, I'd like that." She gave him her email address. "What did you find?"

"Nothing."

"Seriously? There's nothing inside the bronze bull?" She stopped, her free hand on her hip. A pair of joggers ran around her, and she stepped onto the grass beneath the cool shade of a weeping willow.

"I suspect you've been talking to Rockford Le-Plante," the technician said.

That he assumed the correct answer so easily made Annja feel the dupe. Kicking herself for not taking the time to check LePlante's credentials, she asked, "Not a reliable source?"

"Far from it. The man collects conspiracies. Every year it seems he's off on a new adventure to find another legendary village, jewel or lost civilization. The ruby in the bull's belly was an urban legend, Miss Creed. Sorry to disappoint you."

"Not as sorry as I am to have been duped. But thank you for your time and expense. I appreciate the information."

"Thank you. We've been able to pass this little bull statue, as worthless as it may be, along to the British Museum, where they will decide if provenance proves it belongs to France. It can be traced to the Anne of Austria dowry, though, so chin up, eh?"

"Thanks again. Goodbye."

She opened the file of the scan, and even though the cell phone screen was small, it was very clear there was nothing inside the bull's belly.

"And two men, possibly more, died because of it." She shook her head and tucked her phone away and started up a fast walk. She didn't feel energetic enough for the jog now.

She couldn't win them all.

* * * * *

TAKE 'EM FREE
2 action-packed novels plus a mystery bonus

NO RISK
NO OBLIGATION TO BUY

GE11B